A Caroline Rhodes Mystery

A DEADLY LITTLE CHRISTMAS

MARY WELK

#22439869

*Kleworks Publishing Co.
Chicago*

East Baton Rouge Parish Library
Baton Rouge, Louisiana

A DEADLY LITTLE CHRISTMAS
Published by Klework Publishing Co.
First Printing 1998

All rights reserved.
Copyright © 1998 by Mary V. Welk
No part of this book may be reproduced in any form,
except for the inclusion of brief quotations in a review or article,
without written permission from the publisher.
For information, address: Kleworks Publishing Co.,
6127 N. Ozark Ave., Chicago, IL. 60631

The author gratefully acknowledges
Mary Engelbreit
for permission to use her name
and a description of her artwork in this book.

ISBN 0-9665157-0-6
Library of Congress Catalog Card Number: 98-91554

Printed in the USA by
Morris Publishing
3212 East Highway 30, Kearney, NE 68847
1-800-650-7888

In loving memory of my father,
Dr. Lawrence Anthony Thoennes

♦

Many thanks
to all who believed in me

*Voice of the dead whom we loved, our Lawrence
the best of the brave*

*The Defense of Lucknow
Alfred Lord Tennyson*

PROLOGUE

December 14

For an artificial Christmas tree, this one wasn't half bad. At least that's what Martha Schoen said and she ought to know. Martha Schoen was an authority on Christmas trees, much as she was an authority on everything else.

"I chaired St. Mark's Beautification Committee for thirty-two years!" the silver haired matron sputtered when Gail Garvy rebuffed her offer to supervise the trimming of the seven foot balsam. "No one's more qualified for the job than I!"

With a snort of contempt, Martha snatched the decorations from the girl and sailed across the room, her progress punctuated by a running commentary on the stupidity of modern youth. Only when she spied May Eberle did she pause for breath, and then it was merely to refocus her outrage on the tiny woman standing slumped against the room's west window. Frail in stature and spirit, May's very existence offended the tough-minded Mrs. Schoen. Weaklings had no place in Martha's world. She was a firm believer in survival of the fittest, and May was far from fit in any sense of the word. When she wasn't whimpering over some perceived slight or whining about life in general, the aged spinster spent her waking hours wrapped in a cocoon of silence, her body held rigidly still, her face an inscrutable mask as she stared blankly off into space.

Right now May's attention was riveted on a glazed section of the windowpane. Frost fairies had traced icy tendrils across the surface of the glass, but Martha doubted the artistry of winter had captured the other woman's fancy. More likely than not, senility had just punched another giant hole in the swiss cheese brain of little Miss Eberle. Much as she disliked May, Martha knew her duty when she saw it.

"Snap out of it, Eberle! You're daydreaming again."

May Eberle winced. The choir had begun its final hymn. Six men in black suits lifted her casket to their shoulders and processed solemnly down the aisle. In their pews, the congregation wept.

"Did you hear me, May? Stop all that nonsense and come lend a hand with these ornaments."

The choir faltered, its sweet harmony disintegrating into cacophonous gibberish that grated on May's ears. She forced herself to concentrate, but the fantasy continued to fade. First her casket disappeared, then the mourners vanished. When she could no longer smell the incense on the altar, May turned from the window in surrender. It was useless; the cemetery would have to wait.

"I'm coming, Martha." May glared across the room at her nemesis. Today had been ruined, but tomorrow she'd take revenge. Tomorrow she would plan Martha's funeral. How different it would be from her own!

"Be careful now," Martha commanded when May sidled up to her. "I spent all morning making this." She handed the other woman a string of popcorn and cranberries and pointed to the tree. "Drape it on the branches, but don't break it."

May momentarily forgot her hatred for Martha Schoen as her bony fingers caressed the garland. A wave of memories flooded over her.

"My sister April and I used to string cranberries at Christmas," she whispered. Her brow puckered in a frown. "But Papa was so particular. If even one berry didn't meet his approval, he'd make us take the whole string apart and start over."

"Humph!" Martha dismissed Papa Eberle with a wave of her plump hand. "I'd *never* put up with such behavior from a man." She tucked a dented tin Santa deep in the tree where it wouldn't be noticed.

Satisfied with the result, she favored May with a tight smile before continuing smugly, "Of course, one should do things right the first time, shouldn't one? Sloppiness is a most wicked habit. It springs from sloth, and you know what the Bible says about that!"

May Eberle's head shot up. She stared at Martha but it was Papa who scowled back at her, Papa whose mouth twisted in condemnation. May clamped her hands to her ears to shut out the sound of her father's wrath.

"Watch what you're doing! You'll crush the garland!" Martha screamed as shredded popcorn fluttered to the floor.

May buried her wrinkled face in the berries, terrified at the extent of Papa's rage. She prayed he wouldn't hit her. Papa had hit April and now April was dead.

"Oh, give me that!" Martha lunged at May, but the frightened woman pulled away. The garland tore in two and cranberries cascaded down May's legs.

"Now look what you've done!" Martha cried out. She fell to her knees and scrabbled at the berries. Horrified, May retreated a step. Thick drops of blood rolled past her feet and she cringed when Papa plucked some from the carpet and hurled them at her.

"You stupid woman!" Martha pitched another handful of berries at May. "You destroy everything you touch!"

"For God's sake, woman, turn it off!"

The sudden intrusion of another angry voice so startled Martha that she pitched forward and sprawled unbecomingly on the carpet. Overcome with fury and embarrassment, she twisted round to lash out at the newcomer.

"Who do you think...Oh!"

Martha blanched at the sight of Thomas Adrian's clenched hand quivering inches above her head. Adrian's face was contorted, his olive skin suffused with an unhealthy reddish glow that extended from collar to hairline. The cords on his neck bulged like twisted wire ropes, and his breathing was shallow and ragged.

"Nobody gives a damn about you and your berries!" Adrian snarled. "You're not as important as you think." He whirled on May who shrank against the tree. "*I'm* the one they're after! It's *me* they're out to get!"

Martha scrambled to her feet and retreated to safety behind a worn leather recliner.

"You're mad," she gasped. "Absolutely mad!"

"Shut up, you old souse!" Adrian's eyes glittered darkly and flecks of spittle dampened his lips and chin. High on his left cheek a muscle twitched.

"You tell 'er, Tommy boy."

Will Chapell strolled into the room, his fists tightly balled in the side pockets of his grease stained jeans. A wicked grin creased his craggy features as he took in the scene near the Christmas tree.

"Havin' a little argument, are we?" No one answered as Chapell approached, his gaze sliding over the group, then settling on Thomas Adrian. Having chosen his victim, Chapell edged nearer and clapped the other man on the back. "Now, now, Tommy. Mustn't let these old biddies get under yer skin. If they're causin' trouble, just shoot 'em 'tween the eyes and be done with it."

"Stay away from me!" Adrian growled, spinning out of Chapell's grasp. He despised the big blond oaf with his work-worn hands and hillbilly accent.

"Oooh, Tommy! Aren't we touchy today," Chapell sneered.

"That's just about enough."

Gail Garvy appeared in the doorway, arms akimbo and eyes blazing. Anger gave her the voice of a drill sergeant as she bore down on the group.

"Keep it up and there'll be no Christmas party today, tomorrow, or any other day this year." Gail's gaze wandered down to the mess on the floor, then up to the frightened face of Martha Schoen. For a brief moment she almost pitied the woman. "We'll clean this up later, Mrs. Schoen. For now, let's just get back to work."

Ignoring an eruption of complaints from the suddenly loquacious quartet, she herded them towards the tree, then bullied them into decorating it. Chapell and Adrian traded jibes despite Gail's threats while May Eberle cowered in the background eyeing both men anxiously. Only Martha Schoen seemed relaxed as she poured all her energy into preparing the big balsam. When the last ornament was in place she claimed the privilege of fixing the angel on the top branch.

"It's done!" she exclaimed after backing ponderously down the step ladder. A perfectionist to the end, she checked the angel's position from all sides of the tree before nodding in satisfaction. "Nice and straight, just as it should be."

"Ain't a bad lookin' tree, if ya'll like institutional trees," Chapell drawled.

"Bea-u-ti-ful! Bea-u-ti-ful! The tree is just bea-u-ti-ful!"

Curled in a fetal position on the corner sofa, Richard Canty awakened from his nap and clapped his hands in delight. Martha pursed her lips and frowned down at the pale little man with the bald head and watery eyes. She'd forgotten he was there in the room, almost forgotten he'd existed.

"*Do* something about him, Garvy. He's...he's...*sick*!"

"Ain't she the perceptive one," Chapell crowed. He grinned at Martha, then whispered, "Angel's crooked, Mrs. Mayor."

Martha threw him a whithering look. "Mind your own..."

"Institutional tree! Institutional tea! You can pay a hefty fee to sit in here with tree and tea! I'm a poet and don't I know it!" Richard Canty rocked back and forth, his high pitched voice harsh with adolescent excitement.

"Shut him up with this, Tommy," Chapell said. He plucked a peppermint cane from the tree and tossed it to Adrian. "Unless you'd rather eat it yourself."

Adrian stared at the striped candy in his hand before dropping it to the carpet and crushing it beneath his shoe. He grinned triumphantly at Chapell.

"You think I'm some kind of fool? You can't poison me that easily."

Chapell appeared ready to retort but Gail held up a restraining hand.

"Enough! We need to light the tree before everyone arrives for the party. How about doing the honors, Mr. Chapell?"

"Got a match, Garvy?" Chapell's eyes slid towards May and Martha. "I'll bet the little ladies would enjoy warmin' their britches by a bonfire."

Martha gasped, her fleshy jowls quivering in disapproval, but May's expression remained benign. She hadn't heard the crude reply; she was absorbed in planning Richard Canty's funeral. Gail disregarded the remark also. She was tired of Chapell's word games just as she was tired of Martha's bossiness, May's tears, and Adrian's paranoia. Canty didn't count; the man was brain dead. The only one worth bothering with was the bronze-skinned ex-soldier standing quietly at attention near the fireplace. The elusive James Belding, the man with nothing to say. Unfortunately for Gail, even the silent James was fast becoming a bore.

"Could we get on with it?" Martha demanded. "Just light the tree, Garvy."

"Light the tree," May Eberle echoed dreamily.

"Light the tree and serve the tea!" sang Richard Canty.

"It's traditional to gather around it first," Gail insisted. "Then we can..."

"Traditions are well and good," interrupted Martha, "but *someone* must light the tree!"

"Let Mr. Belding do it."

Of course, thought Gail. What better way to draw the recluse into the group. She turned with a pleased little smile and walked over to

Belding. "How about it?" she said, coaxing the man forward. "Will you light our tree?"

James Belding, lost in a world where Christmas no longer existed, chanced a look at the present and saw in the eyes of his jailer the pain of empathy.

'This one knows,' his first self said.

James raised his index finger, then slowly the second, third, and fourth fingers uncurled. "Four to go," he whispered.

Gail inclined her head and nodded.

'She only thinks she knows!' warned his second self.

James Belding groaned. Resigned to captivity, he obeyed the order given him and followed Gail across the room. She pointed to the electric cord dangling from the tree trunk. He reached for it as she signaled the others to come closer.

"Si-i-lent night..." Gail sang.

Belding gripped the cord with trembling fingers.

"Ho-o-ly night..." caroled Martha Schoen.

He sank to one knee, then he forced himself to concentrate on what was required of him.

"All is calm..." May Eberle added sotto voce.

'Fool!' hissed his second self. 'They've got you now!'

"All is bright..." they sang in unison.

'I know!' cried his first self.

"Thy will be done!" James shouted. He plunged the plug into the outlet.

The explosion was immediate and devastating. By the time Caroline Rhodes reached the doorway, Recreation Room 2, Psychiatric Ward One, St. Anne's Hospital, no longer existed. Neither did its inhabitants.

One

December 19

Caroline Rhodes stood on the nursing dorm steps and plotted murder. The methods she considered were primitive -- boiling oil, the guillotine, a quiver of arrows through the heart -- but effective nonetheless.

"And exactly what he deserves!" she growled. He'd been bursting with confidence at noon, cocksure of his ability to predict the future.

"Take my word for it, Rhineburg! You can put away those shovels until after Christmas. We're in for a spell of blue skies and sunshine clear through the holidays!"

Then at two o'clock a breeze had ruffled the treetops along Wilhelm Avenue. A gray haze crept catlike into the western sky and an hour later shadows slunk across the fields outside of town. Still, the voice on the radio jeered at the doubters.

"OK, you worrywarts. Lay off the lines! I told you no snow and I meant it. Relax!"

By four o'clock the weakening sun had disappeared behind a barricade of clouds. Gusts rattled the windows of City Hall and weather vanes spun crazily on farmhouse roofs. Rhineburg held its breath and waited for the next report.

"There's really no need for concern, folks." His bravado had vanished, but the forecaster was sticking to his guns. "It's too warm for snow, although we just might see a shower or two tonight. We could use it though," he added cheerfully. "Let Mother Nature clean up our roads!"

"So much for weathermen!" Caroline grumbled. Good old Mother Nature was cleaning up all right, but not with any gentle rainfall. Ambushed by shifting winds, Rhineburg had surrendered to a squall so intense that last week's blizzard paled by comparison. By eight o'clock four inches of sleet and snow whitened the dirty mounds heaped along the highway. Drifts rippled across the roads and the temperature was plunging. Tomorrow the landscape would resemble that of Antarctica.

Caroline grimaced at the thought. She could cope with a normal winter, but like the ghost voters of Chicago, the snow had come early and often this year. It was only the third week of December and already the hospital's snow gauge measured a two foot accumulation. Rhineburg's youngsters were delighted; Caroline's generation was not.

"No use putting this off any longer." She tugged the hood of her parka lower over her forehead and trudged down the unplowed driveway, the wind buffeting her till she felt like a punch drunk boxer. It squealed through the treetops overhead and spit showers of ice crystals into her face and down her neck. She jerked at her scarf, already stiff with frozen snow, and pulled it up over her nose. The smell of wet wool only annoyed her more.

"Damnation!" Caroline longed for the protection of her ancient Buick, but the twelve-year-old car lacked the punch for tackling the storm. It was a fair weather friend, tending to balk at the slightest hint of cold. Right now it sat cringing in the hospital parking lot, a worn blanket protecting its battery from the frigid midwest temperatures. Caroline knew it was either walk or stay home, and she had no intention of doing the latter. She'd promised Martin she'd show up at Bruck Hall for the university's holiday bash, and come hell, high water, or twelve inches of snow, she was determined to keep her word.

"If Hannibal could cross the Alps in winter, I can surely make it to Bruck Hall in a little blizzard!"

Of course Hannibal had elephants to carry him. Caroline had to rely on her own two feet, not exactly the best mode of transportation tonight. A dog sled would have come in handy, or at least a pair of snowshoes. Ice lurked beneath the drifts and her boots crunched on it as she struggled against the wind towards Circle Road. Irked that the walk hadn't been shoveled, she kicked at the remnants of a snowman littering the pavement and immediately regretted the impulse. Her right foot skidded forward, her left one flew back. Like a drunk on a Friday night binge, she staggered the length of the frozen path until she lurched to a halt at the corner.

"This is ridiculous!" she snarled as a blast of wind pommeled her with sleet. "I could be home in my warm bed, a stiff drink in one hand and a good book in the other, but no! Here I am, tramping through the god-awful snow to some god-awful party with a bunch of god-awful people I don't even know. And all because of my damned son!"

Caroline immediately regretted referring to her first-born in those terms. The storm wasn't Martin's fault. Neither was the invitation to the faculty party. Martin was a Ph.D. candidate vying for a teaching post at Bruck U. His inclusion on the guest list was fortuitous; hers was a different matter altogether. The invitation had arrived only yesterday, and the apologetic note accompanying it was couched in such effusive language that Caroline's suspicions were quickly aroused. Could her sudden popularity be related to the bombing at St. Anne's Hospital? Had some committee selected her as the evening's entertainment, her role that of survivor eager to tell all? Well, she had no intention of playing the part. As far as she was concerned, she was going to a Christmas party, not some TV talk show.

Caroline pushed that problem out of her mind and considered a more immediate one. Across the road lay Bruck Green, a wooded oval separating the hospital from the campus of Bruck University. At the south end of the campus stood Bruck Hall. The building should have been visible from the corner, but tonight it was camouflaged by the storm.

'Great!' she thought disgustedly. She'd intended to cut across the Green. In better weather that would have meant a five minute trip to the Hall, but attempting it now would be suicidal. Blinded by the blizzard, she'd probably collide with one of the massive oaks straddling the Green's cobbled walks. If she fell into a snow bank she'd have one hell of a time extricating herself from its suffocating softness.

Giving up her initial plan, Caroline turned to examine the street girdling the Green. The parkway was oval in shape, but for reasons she'd still not fathomed, the town fathers had christened the tarmac Circle Road. At the moment the Circle, as it was called by the locals, was awash in mounds of snow. If Caroline zig-zagged between drifts she could follow the curve of the road all the way to Bruck Hall. Not a bad idea as long as she didn't encounter a snowplow along the way.

The only other route lay to Caroline's left. South of the road a sidewalk meandered past look-alike bungalows reserved for faculty housing. The walk curled in and out of cul-de-sacs before finally reaching the campus, making it the longest of the three approaches to the Hall.

Caroline hunched her shoulders against the biting wind and considered her choices. The snow lay as deep on the walk as on the street, but the former offered one advantage. Victorian-style gas lamps sprouted from the pavement at ten yard intervals. To a native Chicagoan like herself, even this modest lighting provided a sense of security not found on a darkened road. People weren't mugged under street lights. Muggings were reserved for shadows -- alley shadows, park shadows, gangway shadows -- but certainly not for street lights.

'But this isn't Chicago,' Caroline mused. 'This is quiet little Rhineburg, home to wealthy farmers and poor professors. Sedate as sedate can be!'

"Also," she said aloud, "home to a mad bomber!"

She shivered, more from the memory of recent events than from the cold, and hurried across the street. Psychopaths who blew up hospital wards probably didn't stoop to mugging middle aged women struggling through snow storms. Still, she'd feel better once she was safe in Bruck Hall. If only the pavement wasn't knee deep in drifts!

"Doesn't anyone here believe in shovels?" Caroline muttered. In Chicago people would have been out long before the snow reached this level, cleaning sidewalks and parking spots, waving to neighbors and wondering aloud just where the hell the city plows were. She missed her old home. She missed Chicago and the people there. Rhineburg was so very -- different.

Lost in memories, Caroline barely noticed the shift in the weather. The wind was dying and with it the snow. It was the absolute silence that finally drew her attention. She paused beneath a street lamp, puzzled, then pulled back the hood of her parka and gazed up at the sky. A single star glimmered in the darkness. Off to the east the moon crept out from behind a bank of clouds. The storm had blown over and Caroline heaved a sigh of relief.

Walking became easier without the wind battling her every step. Caroline quickened her pace and soon reached the final stretch of sidewalk leading to the campus. The houses along here glittered with Christmas lights and jolly plastic Santas glowed greetings from several of the porches. A common theme united the block: each lawn featured a plywood reindeer studded with miniature white lights, a larger red bulb blinking merrily on its umber nose. The animals struck different poses beside oversized alphabet letters outlined in strings of red, blue, and green colored lights.

Caroline passed three homes before the significance of the display registered in her mind. A smile softened her features as she slid to a halt before a slightly tipsy reindeer leaning against a four foot tall letter 'P'. The deer's nose flashed on and off like an errant stoplight above his crooked grin. His left lid drooped in a wink while his right brow arched over a noticeably bloodshot eye. One slender foreleg crossed the other, and his body tilted toward the letter in a most unreindeer-like manner.

Caroline gazed back down the path. The 'H' and 'A' were barely in view, but the 'P' next door was visible. She walked on to the next house where a bright blue 'Y' decorated the lawn. The head of a very sleepy reindeer lolled between the branches of the 'Y', a bottle of champagne cradled in its antlers.

Caroline chuckled. Whoever'd thought up this one must be quite a joker. A line of inebriated reindeer toasting the New Year was an unusual sight to behold and almost made up for the long cold trek to Bruck Hall.

"Almost! Only almost!" she reminded herself as, chilled to the bone, she plunged on. She did a quick count: twelve letters, twelve houses. She slid past a 'Y', an 'E', then an 'A', regained her balance near the letter 'R', and slowed to a more decorous pace as she approached the Hall's spacious lawn.

Bruck Hall was impressive at any time with its pink stone walls rising to twin towers fore and aft, but the storm had worked a kind of magic on the building. It shimmered in icy elegance like a spun sugar castle, moonlight bouncing off the frost-scored mullioned windows and the icicled gargoyles perched above them. Caroline's spirits rose when she saw it, then lifted even higher as the great oak doors beneath the portico swung open and other snowmen-and-women scurried inside. She fairly skipped down the cleared path and, on reaching the Hall, took the staircase two steps at a time.

Grasping the bronze handle, Caroline was about to push on the heavy door when it was unexpectedly flung open from inside. Off balance, she pitched headlong into the brightly lit lobby of Bruck Hall. The only thing that saved her from a face-to-face encounter with the floor was a pair of strong hands that grabbed her by the shoulders and yanked her unceremoniously to her feet.

"Mother! I thought you'd never get here!"From a foot above her head, Martin Rhodes frowned down at Caroline. "Where in the world have you been?"

"I took the scenic route, my dear," Caroline snarled testily. She shrugged off her parka and shook the dampness from her short ash brown hair. "In case you hadn't noticed, our latest blizzard has fouled up the streets again!"

"Hey! Watch it!"

Martin ducked as a shower of melting snow spattered his immaculate white shirt. Dancing out of the way, he collided with his wife Nikki.

"Don't mind your son," chuckled Nikki, her jet-black eyes sparkling with mirth. She sidestepped around Martin and reaching for Caroline's parka, tossed it to her husband and pointed to the coat rack near the door. "He's just in a hurry to show you off to his friends," she added with a wink.

Caroline relented.

"I meant to be on time, but that old rattletrap of mine wasn't up to the storm." She slid off her boots and wiggled her frozen toes. Collapsing on a cushioned bench set against the wall, she called to Martin. "There's a pair of shoes in the inner pocket of my coat. Bring them here, will you? I tell you, Nikki, this has been quite a day so far!"

Her daughter-in-law clucked sympathetically. "Bad day in ER?"

"No more than usual," Caroline replied. "It's these constant interruptions by the police that are so irritating. They ask the same questions over and over again. I'm really getting fed up with it all."

"Why are they badgering you?" Martin asked in annoyance. "They must realize you've told them all you know about the bombing."

"Of course they do!" Caroline retorted. She drew a deep breath to calm herself. "Forgive me if I'm grouchy tonight, but every time I turn around there's another officer from a different agency asking to speak to me. Today it was the ATF. I've already told my story to the FBI, the Rhineburg police, the State Police, and even to some bigwig from JCAHO."

"JCAHO? What's that?"

"That, my dear boy, is the Joint Commission on Accreditation of Healthcare Organizations. JCAHO accredits hospitals and they have what's called a Sentinel Event Policy that covers unexpected occurrences involving death or serious injury. JCAHO sends in an investigator to determine what happened and if the hospital could have prevented it. God only knows what *they'll* come up with! Probably a recommendation to ban all Christmas trees on the wards!"

Nikki rolled her eyes. "So which agency is in charge of the investigation? I know it can't be our own police."

"You guess is as good as mine. Seems like everyone has their finger in the pie, but I'd bet on the FBI." Caroline rose. "We'd better go in to the party. Your friends will be wondering where you are."

"Especially Professor Carl Atwater," exclaimed Martin. His rugged face registered a mix of pride and amusement. "My boss wants to talk to you about the bombing. As official town historian, these murders are grist to his mill. He's hoping for some inside information!"

Caroline's left eyebrow shot up, but before she could reply they were interrupted by the very man they were discussing.

"Well, Mr. Rhodes! Don't tell me this lovely young woman is your mother!"

If Caroline hadn't known better, she'd have sworn it was Santa himself come to greet them. Carl Atwater was a massive man with a shock of white hair and a snowy beard and mustache. Twinkling blue eyes peered out of a face so plump and wind burned that one was immediately reminded of sleigh bells. He had no waist, being as round on the top as on the bottom, and his red and black plaid shirt only served to accentuate his three hundred plus pounds. Sturdy leather suspenders supported his black corduroy pants and his stubby legs were encased in knee-high laced hiking boots. His voice was husky yet pleasant. Caroline imagined him using the full power of his lungs; few would dare sleep in his class!

"And you must be Professor Atwater." Caroline ignored the man's compliment. With her damp hair and frozen feet she felt about as lovely as the Ugly Duckling. As for the 'young' part, she was long past forty and felt no need to hide it. "Martin's told me so much about you. You're Chairman of the History Department at Bruck University, right?"

"Due to a lack of contenders, that honor was bestowed on me many years ago. Since then, I've simply outlived my rivals."

Caroline smiled. "I'll bet your ability has something to do with it too."

"I consider myself a fairly good teacher," Atwater replied with a shrug. "But as far as the chairmanship goes, that's more a matter of tenure and politics."

Caroline was pleasantly surprised at the Professor's candor. Maybe the man was the paragon of virtue her son claimed him to be.

"So," Atwater continued as they started down the hall together. "I hear you've moved to Rhineburg permanently. Thinking of buying a house soon?"

Caroline glanced at her son. His face was a study in innocence.

"Actually, I haven't yet made up my mind to stay. I've taken the position of nursing dorm housemother only on a temporary basis."

"Oh really? And here I was under the impression you enjoyed working with young people. Of course, it does have its drawbacks," the Professor conceded with a shrug.

Caroline considered her answer. She had no real complaints. Still, keeping track of forty students was no picnic, especially when it came to curfew. There wasn't a trick in the book they didn't try.

"It's certainly not a dull job," she said. "But I'm not sure I'd want to make it a lifelong occupation!"

"I suppose not. You're a nurse also, aren't you?"

Caroline nodded. "I'm in the float pool at St. Anne's. I work in ER most of the time, but I go wherever they need some extra help."

"Yes, I believe Marty told me you were on the psychiatric ward the day of the explosion."

So the perfect Professor had at least one flaw: curiosity.

"I was there all right, but I really don't want to spoil your party with talk of bombs and blood. It was quite an unnerving experience." Caroline turned to Nikki. "Speaking of experiences, I had an interesting one on my way to Bruck Hall. Tell me about those crazy decorations down the street. Who's behind the inebriated reindeer on all the lawns?"

"Aren't they hilarious?" Nikki laughed. "They were Dr. Pauly's idea. He convinced everyone on the block to put one up."

"You should have seen the crowds the first night they were lit," crowed Martin. "Half the student body was out on the street!"

"Now, children, behave yourselves!" Atwater jested. "You know our esteemed President highly disapproves of said decorations. They're quite out of character with the dignity of this fine institution!"

"I'm glad to hear you agree with me, Professor."

Martin and Nikki froze like a couple of horrified statues. They stared at Caroline who in turn stared at Professor Atwater. The Professor didn't seem the least bit disturbed as he turned to greet the newcomer.

"Ah! President Hurst. Welcome to our little circle. May I introduce my teaching assistant, Martin Rhodes, and his lovely wife Nikki. And this is Martin's mother, Mrs. Caroline Rhodes. We were just discussing Dr. Pauly's reindeer."

"So I heard. For once you concur with me!"

Opposite of Atwater in size and stature, Hurst puffed up his scrawny chest and glared at them through horn rimmed glasses.

"You misunderstand," Professor Atwater said smoothly. "I wasn't agreeing with you, just stating your point of view."

The two men exchanged artificial smiles. With the atmosphere getting chillier by the minute, Caroline decided a change of subject was definitely in order.

"You have a beautiful campus here, President Hurst. I always enjoyed visiting when Martin was an undergraduate."

For a moment she thought he would ignore her, but then Hurst's hooded eyes swiveled round to meet her own. Dark pools of granite, they radiated none of the warmth of his words.

"We try to maintain a gracious setting, Mrs. Rhodes. It's difficult since we rely heavily on our alumni for financial support." He turned to Martin. "You graduated from Bruck, Mr. Rhodes?"

"Y-yes, sir!" Martin stammered. "I'm doing my postgraduate work under Professor Atwater. I hope to teach history on the college level after I earn my PhD."

"Really?" Hurst's head bobbed in the direction of the chairman before his gaze returned to Martin. "Well, good luck, young man. I'm sure you'll do Bruck proud some day."

He favored the women with a tight smile, then excused himself. Atwater watched him head towards the faculty lounge.

"Observe a master at work, Martin. If you hope to rise in the academic world, remember one thing: flattery will get you everywhere!"

Caroline noted the contempt in the Professor's voice. At the same time she saw Nikki surreptitiously tug on her husband's coat sleeve. Martin glanced down and the girl shook her head ever so slightly.

It didn't take a genius to understand Nikki's gesture, but her mother-in-law was taking no chances.

"I don't know about the rest of you, but right about now I could do with a good stiff drink! Isn't there a bar set up somewhere, Martin?"

"How rude of me!" the Professor apologized. He bowed to his guest and extended a chubby arm. "If you will do me the honor, madam?

Caroline latched on to his elbow like a fish to bait.

"Lead on, McDuff!" she replied jauntily.

Bruck's faculty lounge was overflowing with revelers when the foursome made their entrance. Atwater cut a path through the crowd, his goal an unoccupied settee near the buffet table.

"This should do nicely!" he shouted above the din. "Close to the food and the fireplace!"

Caroline nodded while taking in the scene with some surprise. She'd expected the room to be utilitarian in nature, furnished in chrome and vinyl with steel shelving for bookcases and sensible stain free carpeting on the floor. Instead, the motif was down home cozy. Tartan plaid easy chairs stood scattered in groupings near an enormous stone fireplace at the far end of the lounge. Matching sofas flanked the door on the opposite side. The plank flooring gleamed like burnished gold except where an occasional throw rug concealed the shine. Smack in the center of the room stood a massive oak table, its surface hidden by an ivory tablecloth on which rested a smorgasbord of delights already being sampled by Professor Atwater. He gestured for Caroline to join him, but her attention had strayed to the decorations.

"How beautiful!" she murmured.

What had captured her admiration was more than just a casual arrangement of holiday objects. Someone had lent a professional touch to the job and the room showed it. Massive pots of crimson and pink poinsettias crowded the windowsills bracketing the far corner of the lounge. To the left of the windows a four foot wreath embellished with scarlet and silver streamers graced the chimney piece of the fireplace. Tall vanilla scented candles marched across the stone mantel above a balsam garland. Smaller candles flickered next to ceramic bowls of holly scattered about the shelves of four floor-to-ceiling oak bookcases.

The piece de resistance occupied the corner just left of the fireplace. There, a grouping of three pines, the smallest perhaps five feet tall, the largest almost touching the ceiling, sparkled with miniature red lights and silver glass balls. Nestled in the center of the trees was a magnificently carved candle in peppermint shades of pink, deep rose, and white. Pots of scarlet poinsettias surrounded its wrought-iron stand.

"Very nice!" Caroline exclaimed.

"Credit Mrs. Pauly," Atwater replied between mouthfuls. "This room is off limits for a week while she's transforming it from drab to magnificent. Well worth it, though. Our faculty party is the high point of the social season at Bruck."

"I can understand that," Caroline reflected. "I imagine life in a small town offers few opportunities for this kind of gathering."

The Professor shot an incredulous look at Martin who merely shrugged his shoulders.

"Actually," Atwater retorted, "You'd be amazed at the number of 'opportunities' we poor Rhineburgers have for celebrating. We may be short on opera and ballet, but we manage to amuse ourselves in various backward ways!"

Caroline blushed. "I didn't mean it that way!"

Nikki rushed to her rescue.

"How about some nice hot cider, mom? Marty!" She poked her husband sharply in the ribs. "Go get us something to drink, OK?"

Martin took the hint and turned to his boss. "Cider or beer?"

"Beer of course, unless that cider is well spiked!" Atwater picked up another canape and followed his protege towards the bar.

"What a gaffe!" Caroline muttered in disgust. "I must have sounded totally condescending."

"Don't worry about it," Nikki reassured her with a broad grin. "Most urban refugees consider Rhineburg a bit provincial at first."

Caroline smiled ruefully. She knew Nikki had adapted easily to life in the boonies, but could she ever do the same?

"Tell me," she said, changing the subject. "What's up with

President Hurst and Professor Atwater? They react to each other like charter members of the Mutual *Un*-admiration Society."

"So you noticed! Well..." Nikki glanced at the people nearest them before drawing Caroline over to a deserted corner. "You have to be careful what you say around here. At Bruck the walls not only have ears but hearing aids as well!"

Caroline laughed. Still, she got the message. She lowered her voice to match Nikki's.

"Did something happen recently?"

"Oh, no! Those two have been arguing for years. In fact, they began soon after Hurst arrived at Bruck."

"When was that?"

"Nineteen eighty-five."

Caroline's eyes widened. "Now I'd call that a long-standing feud! What started it?"

"Jealousy on Hurst's part. Professor Atwater is practically an institution in Rhineburg. He went to college on the GI Bill after World War II, then came here to teach. He says he started at Bruck and he'll finish at Bruck, no date of retirement specified."

Caroline watched the subject of their conversation wend his way through the clots of people blocking the path to the bar.

"Martin's boss could afford to shed a few pounds, but on the whole he looks pretty good for a man in his seventies."

"Don't ever allude to his age, mom. The Professor goes bananas over the term 'senior citizen'. Those are two words he never applies to himself!"

"Young at heart, huh? OK, I'll forego any mention of white hair in his presence. Now, tell me more about Hurst's jealousy."

"Well, the Professor is a born historian. He's written several books about rural America and they've all sold well."

"I've read two of them," Caroline said. "He delves into a particular town's past and the stories he digs up are fascinating!"

"Marty's doing research on Atwater's next project, a book about company-owned coal mining towns. All in all, the Professor has earned a pile of money, plus a reputation for educating folks who normally don't take to history. The university simply adores using his name to attract new students. It looks so impressive on those glossy brochures they hand out on open house days!"

"So Bruck needs the Professor more than he needs Bruck."

Nikki nodded. "And that's why our dear President despises him so. Hurst hates to share the limelight. It bugs him that Professor Atwater draws more attention from the press than he does."

It was Caroline's turn to look incredulous.

"Come on, Nikki! There has to be more to it than that! Professional jealousy I can understand, but President Hurst is an important man in his own right. Why, he runs the entire university!"

"And quite poorly, if you ask me," Nikki countered darkly. "Look around this room, mom. The faculty is almost evenly divided between supporters of the President and those who'd like to see Professor Atwater elevated to that role."

Caroline's eyebrows rose a fraction. "Is the Professor gunning for the job?"

Nikki tucked a silky strand of coal-black hair behind her ear as she shrugged off the question.

"He says he doesn't want it, but he's been outspoken concerning the curriculum changes Hurst is making. The President is decimating the liberal arts program. He's slashed classes across the board, especially in history."

"Well, I can see how that would upset the Professor," Caroline remarked dryly. "There's nothing so irritating as losing a piece of one's own turf."

"The Professor's not like that!" Nikki retorted. "He just doesn't think the liberal arts program should suffer because the Emperor -- that's what everyone calls him -- wants a football stadium."

"Hold on, Nikki!" Caroline was totally confused. "Since when has Bruck had a football team?"

"We don't now, but we will if Hurst has his way. He says that emphasizing sports will attract more kids to the school, as if that's what college is all about!"

Caroline saw a glimmer of sense in the plan. Bruck relied on its graduates for a portion of its funding, and it was well known that alumni cherished their sports teams. Look at the dough Notre Dame raked in from its Knute Rockne devotees. There wasn't a college in the country that didn't wish Ronald Reagan had made them famous with that "Win one for the gipper" line!

"The Emperor's in thick with Mayor Schoen," Nikki continued. "He wants the town to refurbish the old high school stadium so he can field a team there."

"Rhineburg doesn't have that kind of money, does it?"

"A lot of folks live and die by their sports teams. If Hurst can convince them of the need for a decent stadium, they'll hold bake sales from here to eternity to pay for it! He's already pledged reduced tuition for any kid from Rhineburg who attends Bruck and hinted at other concessions as well. And Mayor Schoen's all for it since the quarry would supply new stone for the stadium walls."

Caroline knew there was a quarry outside of town. She'd never seen it but it probably employed a lot of locals. A contract to repair the stadium would benefit both the workers and the town's treasury.

"Hurst claims Bruck can pay part of the cost by cutting what he calls 'nonessential classes'. He's pink-slipping teachers who haven't earned tenure, but only in certain departments. The business school is actually growing because everybody and their uncle wants to major in business!"

"So the professors in the school of business are backing Hurst."

Nikki nodded. "And those in the liberal arts are supporting the Professor. The problem is, their numbers are shrinking every semester."

"And I suppose some teachers are simply sitting on the fence waiting to see which way the wind blows."

"Yeah. They're no help at all," Nikki replied glumly. "I think the Emperor is going to win this battle."

"If he does, Martin stands little chance of being hired at Bruck, Nikki."

"I know that." Nikki smiled weakly at her mother-in-law. "We love Rhineburg, but we may have to move on once Marty finishes school. I doubt there'll be any job openings here."

Caroline heard the pain in Nikki's voice. She put an arm around the girl and hugged her.

"Things will work out for you two. Martin's a bright young man and he'll get a job somewhere, believe me!"

"Sure he will," Nikki responded. "I really shouldn't have laid all this on you. Please don't worry about it, OK?"

"Hey! Aren't moms supposed to worry about their kids? Some day you'll do the same thing with your children."

That brought a grin to Nikki's face.

Caroline was exhausted. In the two hours since her arrival at the party she'd been bombarded with questions about the explosion at St. Anne's. Word had spread concerning her presence on the ill-fated ward and folks assumed she had an inside track on the investigation. She'd sidestepped all questions by replying, "I'm sorry, but the police have asked me not to discuss the case." It was a trite answer but it seemed to satisfy most of the crowd. In fact, it lent an aura of mystery to Professor Atwater's guest. Faculty members exchanged knowing looks and Martin reported overhearing his mother labeled a 'prime witness'. Caroline found it amusing; still, she gave it little thought.

She worked instead on stifling her yawns. The walk to the Hall had been arduous and the thought of bed grew more attractive by the minute. Noting the time, Caroline decided she'd done her motherly duty. She said as much to Martin, but phrased it more acceptably.

"I think I've met everyone who's here, Marty. It's been a great party, but if you don't mind, I'm going to call it a night."

Distracted by loud laughter in one corner of the lounge, Martin made no protest. "Hmm? Oh! Sure, mom. If you want a lift home..."

Caroline shook her head.

"Don't worry about me. The fresh air will do me good. Have a wonderful time with your friends and say 'bye' to Nikki for me."

She squeezed his arm affectionately and made a beeline for the door. It was noticeably quieter outside the lounge. As she padded down the carpeted hallway, Caroline noticed the quality of the paintings lining the walls. One particular landscape made her pause in admiration. The artist had captured the ephemeral beauty of a Maine sunset viewed off the ocean. The wispy pinks and oranges splashed above the craggy coastline served as a backdrop for the lazy flight of two sea birds. A double-masted schooner rocked in the tide, its deck deserted, its sails furled. Two chunky lobster boats floated nearby. The intimate quality of the ships at rest contrasted sharply with the remoteness of the bouldered shore stretching back to wooded cliffs. They provided not so much an intrusion on nature as a compliment to it.

The water-color reminded Caroline of a happier time. She had walked those stony bluffs and sailed on a schooner much like the one pictured. She hadn't been alone then, hadn't even considered what alone could really mean. Now, gazing at the painting, the pain of loss engulfed her. Life was transient, fleeting. Only the rocks and hills endured the whims of nature and survived.

The picture opened a floodgate of memories, not all of them pleasant. 'Don't do this!' Caroline warned herself. 'He's gone and it's over.' The past was dead, despite its effort to reclaim her soul. She'd made it through the evening poise intact and now was not the time to fall apart, even if no one was watching.

"Damn it to hell!"

Caroline jumped, her reverie shattered by the angry expletive. The corridor remained empty, but from a room opposite her came a voice raised in indignation.

"It had nothing to do with us! Some maniac planted it!"

Caroline heard a low murmur but couldn't make out any words. Curiosity dispelled all former thoughts and she tiptoed quietly across the hall. A soldier's portrait hanging near the doorway provided a convenient excuse for her presence outside the room. She feigned an interest in the picture as she strained to hear the conversation.

"That's a pile of crap and you know it, Gary! And don't tell me to be quiet! I don't care if the entire university hears me!"

The second voice broke in, once more indistinguishable except as a rumble of sound. Caroline knew she was eavesdropping, still she couldn't resist leaning just a little closer to the door.

"Listen to me!" the first voice shouted. The man must have moved farther into the room because his words suddenly faded and Caroline caught only bits and pieces of a sentence.

"too much at stake...protect your interests...go off halfcocked.."

She was about to give in to her baser instincts and put her ear to the door when the knob suddenly turned. Startled, Caroline bolted down the hall, colliding with the coat rack just as the door was flung open.

"I'm warning you, Gary! Be careful what you say and who you say it to!"

Caroline struggled to appear nonchalant as she clung to the swaying rack. She glanced back over her shoulder in time to see a heavyset man emerge from the room and stride rapidly towards the lounge. His face was turned away from her but she recognized him immediately. Having met him but once, Caroline knew it was impossible to mistake Charles Paine for anyone else. That broad streak of silver in an otherwise totally red head of hair was a dead giveaway for the Administrator of St. Anne's Hospital.

'Now what's Charles Paine doing here?' she mused. 'And why

is he so angry? Or so frightened?'

Intrigued by the peculiar argument she'd overheard, Caroline searched distractedly for her parka. The two men -- she assumed Paine had been talking to another man; he'd called him 'Gary' -- must have been discussing the bombing. Paine's reference to a maniac made that clear at least. But what did he mean by 'too much at stake'? Was he worried about the hospital's reputation? Or was there a more personal reason for the confrontation?

Caroline finally found her coat buried beneath two others. She shrugged it on and stepped out into the night still contemplating the Administrator's words.

"Chilly out here, isn't it?"

For the second time that evening, Caroline was startled into losing her balance. This time it was Professor Atwater who saved her from tumbling down the stairs.

"I didn't mean to frighten you!" he said gruffly. "I was waiting for you to come out."

Caroline extracted herself from the Professor's arms while mumbling her thanks.

"You didn't frighten me," she said in embarrassment. "I simply wasn't expecting to see you here. Why aren't you inside with the others?"

Atwater shrugged.

"I never was good at these affairs. Too many people trying to impress each other with their academic achievements. All very boring really."

"Come now, Professor. Isn't that a bit snobbish?"

Atwater shrugged a second time as they descended the steps.

"That may by your opinion now, but attend a few more of these faculty shindigs and then let's see how snobbish you think I am!"

"To be truthful, some of the conversations in there were slightly esoteric. Comparing Shakespeare's sonnets to modern rap music..."

"That had to be Andrew Littlewort," the Professor chuckled. "Dr. Littlewort loves to shock people with daring pronouncements on literature. His theories are so off the wall that arguing with him only dignifies his silliness. The best thing to do is simply avoid the man."

"I take it that's what you do."

"All the time!" Atwater grinned.

They turned onto the sidewalk bordering Circle Road. Caroline gazed in astonishment at the clean pavement stretching all the way to the hospital.

"What happened to all the snow? This sidewalk was buried in drifts when I arrived at Bruck Hall!"

The Professor nodded in satisfaction.

"Considering the severity of the storm, I'd say the troops did well tonight."

"The troops? Who exactly are the troops?"

"The troops, milady, are Bruck's answer to crime in the streets. Law and order the Rhineburg way!"

Caroline's eyes narrowed as she studied Atwater. He sounded perfectly serious, but he had to be joking.

"You're related to Professor Littlewort, aren't you? I should be avoiding you too, right?"

"No, no!" Atwater laughed. He took Caroline by the arm, swung her around toward the west, and pointed to a small stone building across Bruck Green. "You see before you the home of the Archangels. Miracles are born there on a daily basis!"

Caroline's right eyebrow rose. Other than that, she managed to contain herself. Too many beers or too long in the boonies, she decided. Still, he was Martin's boss; she'd have to be tactful.

"How delightful! Some day you'll have to tell me all about your ...your angels! But...it *is* cold out here..." She hunched her shoulders to emphasize the point. "And it's been a *very* long day. So..."

"Nonsense!" boomed Atwater. "The night is still young! You

don't work tomorrow -- Marty told me so! -- and we have lots to talk about." He propelled her toward a line of parked cars. "Let's head out to the Blue Cat Lounge and get to know each other."

Caroline silently cursed Martin. Why hadn't he picked someone more normal to work for? Someone like an axe-murderer with a penchant for chopping up recalcitrant students?

"Really, Professor..."

They came to an abrupt halt beside a fire-engine-red Jeep four-by-four. Caroline melted as she looked from the Jeep to Atwater, then back at the Jeep.

"I should have guessed," she said, a smile tugging at her lips. "You really go for the Santa Claus bit, don't you?"

The Professor stroked his snowy beard.

"I always say, if you've got it, flaunt it! Ho, ho, ho!"

Caroline had been on edge all evening, but standing there in the crisp night air, seeing the man so obviously pleased with the image he and his Jeep Cherokee created, she couldn't help but dissolve into laughter. Once begun, she couldn't stop.

"You're perfect!" she gasped between giggles. "White beard, pink cheeks, and a shiny red nose!"

"You might even say it glows!" Atwater rejoined. He waggled his eyebrows at Caroline who cracked up totally. Her laughter proved infectious; before long, she and the Professor were leaning against each other, choking back tears as they held their aching sides.

"Oh my!" Caroline gulped. She wiped her eyes with the back of one hand. "You really are something else, Professor!"

"You aren't too bad yourself, Mrs. Rhodes. But why don't we drop the formalities? I'll be Carl and you can be Caroline, OK?"

Caroline hesitated, then nodded with a shy smile. Aware that some self-imposed barrier had just come crashing down around her, she took a deep breath before straightening her disheveled clothing. The Professor opened the door of the Cherokee and waited. His grin was inviting yet undemanding and Caroline sensed he wouldn't hold it against her if she turned him down. At that moment, though, she couldn't think of anything more enjoyable than a drive through the country with this jolly companion. Without another word she climbed into the car.

"Tell me about your angels."

They had circled Bruck Green and everywhere Caroline looked the pavement was scraped bare. Considering the state of affairs earlier in the evening, the transformation was nothing short of magical.

"Angels? Oh! You mean the Bruck boys!"

"I'm not sure *who* I mean," Caroline replied. "It's just that you mentioned angels and miracles and I wondered..."

"If I was putting you on? Of course not." Carl turned onto the highway leading north. He gestured at the property around them. "All this was wilderness when Joseph Bruck arrived in America. He came from Germany looking for good farm land and he found it in Rhineburg. By the time old Joe died, he was the wealthiest man in the county."

"Until I moved here, I thought all farmers lived from hand to mouth. You know what I mean; a constant struggle to survive."

"Some do," Atwater replied. "The young ones who can't afford enough acres to realize a decent profit, and the older ones who over invested back in the '80's. But the early settlers got their land cheap, so if they were good farmers and good managers, they prospered.

"Joseph Bruck *really* prospered. Much of this area was forest back then. He and his brothers cleared the timber and sold it to buy more land. Once their farms were in place, they branched out into all sorts of endeavors and succeeded in everything they put their hand to. Joseph was a natural born leader. He guided the family enterprises and made money for all of them.

"He made his greatest killing when the railroad came through Rhineburg. It was his land they laid the tracks on and even today there are people who claim old Joe cut a deal with the company that resulted in the solidification of the family fortune."

"A regular land baron, hmm?"

"Don't let the Bruck boys hear you say that!" Atwater laughed. "They're a trifle sensitive about their family history."

"So a later generation named the university for Rhineburg's founding father."

"Actually, the college was Joe's idea. I told you Bruck was an intelligent man. He knew the growth of the country was dependent upon an educated populace governing it. Joseph envisioned a center of learning in Rhineburg, something patterned after the great universities of Europe, so before he died, he made provisions for part of his land to be set aside for such a school. His will stipulated that his money stay in the family only if they agreed to build it."

"That had to be expensive! How'd the Brucks manage it?"

"Oh, they made various deals with other powerful people in the county. They also drummed up support among the common folk. You know, it's amazing what families can do if the incentives are great enough! The Bruck family had absolutely no intention of losing their inheritance. And while the present Bruck U. can't compare to the University of Heidelberg, it's still a decent enough college."

"So where do the 'Bruck boys', as you call them, fit in?"

"Joseph was determined to safeguard his dream," the Professor explained. "His instructions called for a Bruck to preside over the Board of Trustees as long as the institution existed. He also demanded that university security be managed in perpetuum by his descendants."

"Interesting concept!" Caroline commented.

"You must remember, Joseph was still very German in his way of thinking. Education was high on his list of priorities, but so was law and order! The Bruck brothers who currently head security are quite adept at keeping the more rambunctious students in line. They have unique penalties for infractions of the rules."

"How unique?" Caroline asked suspiciously.

"Let's just say they believe in the value of physical labor!"

Caroline's face registered astonishment. "You mean all that snow was shoveled by students?"

Carl grinned. "We have the cleanest campus in the world. Of course we have regular grounds keepers, but don't be shocked if you notice students manning snow plows or cleaning up litter on the Green. That's the way it works at Bruck U.!"

"I'm surprised the students don't object. You'd never get away with such a policy at a Chicago college."

"It's all spelled out in the university handbook. You either agree to it or you don't enroll at Bruck. Mainly, the kids just try to stay out of trouble."

They rode the rest of the way in silence, the Professor intent on the icy road and Caroline contemplating the customs of small towns. She was beginning to think that life in Rhineburg might not be so bad after all.

"We're here," Carl suddenly said. He steered the Jeep into a clearing left of the road and pulled up in front of a long low slung wooden building. "The Blue Cat Lounge."

Caroline stared open-mouthed at the old roadhouse. It had the seedy appearance of a business hanging on by the skin of its teeth. Two grimy windows flanked the entrance and a crooked neon cat flashed blue above the door. There was no sign; evidently the cat said it all.

"Are you sure it's open?" Caroline was having second thoughts as she looked around the clearing for other cars.

"Sure it is." Atwater pointed off to the left. "There's a parking lot behind those trees. It's probably packed since Andy Parker's band is playing tonight." He locked the Jeep, then guided Caroline toward the entrance. "Hope you like jazz," he said as they entered the lounge.

It was indeed packed inside. Tables for two were surrounded by four or five people each. Every single bar stool was taken and bodies jammed nooks and crannies the length of the room. Despite the number of people, the lounge was relatively quiet. Occasional laughter interrupted the scrape of beer bottles sliding down the bar, but on the whole it was a subdued crowd that filled the Blue Cat. As Caroline's eyes adjusted to the dim lighting, she saw why.

At the end of the room a raised plywood platform supported three musicians preparing for a set. A tall willowy youth in faded denims cradled a tenor sax to his chest, his eyes closed, his fingers roaming the stops as he silently rehearsed a piece. Another boy, this one even younger looking than the first, stood hunched over a keyboard at center stage. The third fellow, older and stockier than the others, huddled behind a drum set adjusting the snare. Together the three men presented a study in concentrated energy waiting to explode.

The Professor gestured to Caroline who followed him over to a reserved table near the bar. They were barely seated when an expectant hush descended on the room. Caroline looked over to the stage. Blue light bulbs dangling from overhead wires illuminated it just enough to cast shadows on the platform edges. It was an oddly reverent setting and the audience seemed to sense it. They waited silently until, without a word of introduction, the pianist swept his fingers across the keyboard executing a complicated series of chords in a crescendo of sound. He paused for a fraction of a second, then the sax filled the silence with a muted wail before the drummer dragged his brushes across the snare head. The wild fury of the prologue gave way to a dreamlike passage that dipped and rose in soulful strains. It transformed the atmosphere of the lounge into one of haunting intimacy where the audience was enticed to feel rather than hear the message of the music. Oblivious to Carl's presence, Caroline closed her eyes and let the melodies sweep over and into her. With sensuous fingers the sounds caressed her mind. Old memories were chased away, new ones created in her imagination. Time and reason became irrelevant. Pleasure existed solely in succumbing to the mood of the music.

Without warning, it was over. Caroline opened her eyes to find the Professor staring at her and she ducked her head in unexpected embarrassment. The crowd came to her rescue as people stood to cheer the band. She turned in her chair, craning her neck to see the musicians wave their thanks before they moved off stage. When she finally turned back to Carl, the blush had mercifully left her cheeks.

"I can't believe it's over already," she commented.

"They played a good long set," Carl replied. "You felt it, didn't you?"

"They're very good," hedged Caroline. For some unexplainable reason she was reluctant to share the emotions laid bare by the music.

The Professor was watching her closely. "I've heard the band before, but I don't think I've ever enjoyed them as I did tonight."

Caroline perceived a double meaning to his words. She smiled to hide her uneasiness, but it was a tight little smile conveying none of her thoughts. Carl must have sensed her discomfort though; he quickly turned his attention to the hired help.

Four hot chocolates and a lot of small talk later, the Professor finally got down to business.

"Martin's told me quite a bit about you, Caroline. He says you're a student of human nature."

Caroline's eyebrows rose. "I'm interested in people, Carl, but I don't pretend to understand them."

"According to your son, you're very perceptive."

"Marty credits me with talents beyond my abilities. Lately," she added moodily, "I've had difficulty comprehending my own motives. I no longer speculate on those of others."

Carl stroked his beard thoughtfully. "I presumed you were over it, but I guess I was wrong. You still haven't reached the stage of acceptance, have you?"

Caroline almost bolted from her chair. "I've no idea what you're talking about, Professor Atwater," she said nervously. She knew she had to get away before she started babbling. "It's very late. I'd like to go home now."

"A moment ago it was 'Carl'! I must have struck a raw nerve to turn you against me so quickly." Atwater leaned over the table and touched her hand. "I may be an old man, Caroline, but I'm not a fool. I can see when someone's hurting."

Caroline pulled her hand away. Her stomach churned and she could feel her heart pounding in her chest. Fear tore at her, still she refused to let the Professor see it in her eyes. What had Martin told this man? He must know about Ed, but was he also aware of her illness? She'd told no one at St. Anne's, not even when she'd applied for her job. She was no fool either. They'd never have hired her if they'd suspected the truth. She struggled to hide her agitation.

"I'm perfectly fine, Professor. Just a little too tired for an introspective conversation."

Carl sighed. "Perhaps my timing is a bit off. I thought after five days you'd be handling this better."

Agitation gave way to confusion. 'What's he talking about?' Caroline wondered. 'It's been months, not days, since Ed's death!'

"But you see," Carl continued, "after what Martin said, I really thought you could help me figure out who's behind this bombing. I'm convinced it was no random act of violence. With your knowledge of the hospital..." He limped to a halt when he saw the look of astonishment on Caroline's face. "Now I've really upset you, haven't I?"

Caroline pressed her fingertips to her forehead. She'd leaped to all the wrong conclusions. Instead of prying into her secrets, Carl had only been prattling on about the damned bombing. She certainly didn't want to recall that hellish day, still the subject was less threatening than a recital of her own personal history. She had to pull herself together, apologize somehow.

"Forgive me...Carl." She lifted her eyes to meet his. How in the world could she explain her coldness? Her downright bitchy behavior? "I didn't mean to be rude. It's just that I'm trying to straighten out my own life right now. Things have been...well...difficult lately. I've been going through a lot of changes and I'm a little on edge at times."

Carl nodded in empathy. "Life can be tough. I know about your husband's death. Martin took it hard and we had some long talks after the funeral."

Caroline wasn't surprised. Obviously Martin confided in his mentor. The question was, how much had he confided?

"It seems like you've adjusted to living here in Rhineburg. That must mean the depression has eased up, right? You're getting back on track again."

Caroline frowned. Apparently Carl did know the whole story.

"It could happen to anyone," the Professor said quietly. When she didn't answer, he went on. "If it would help to talk about it, I'm a pretty good listener. And I know how to keep a confidence."

Caroline hesitated. The man was a relative stranger, yet Martin trusted him. It couldn't hurt to tell him just a small part of the story.

"I didn't cope well with widowhood," she finally said. "Ed and I grew up in the same neighborhood. We dated in high school and were married right after graduation. We were very young, but so much in love." She paused as memories of those early days engulfed her. "I thought we'd live happily ever after, just like lovers do in the movies. It sounds silly, I know, but everything just seemed to work out for us. Ed applied to the Fire Department and after he started working there, I returned to school. I got my nursing degree when Martin was seven."

She told Carl about the house they'd bought in Chicago and how her daughters, Krista and Kerry, had been born there. She related stories of vacations in Kentucky and birthday parties at the Foster Avenue beach. She talked for so long that when she finally paused for breath she discovered they were the last patrons left in the lounge.

"Oh my!" she exclaimed. "They're closing up, aren't they?"

Waiters were whisking empty glasses and full ashtrays off the tables around them. It was a broad enough hint, but the Professor showed no inclination to leave.

"Don't worry." He signaled for refills, then smiled sheepishly. "When you've put money into a place, you can stay as long as you like."

"You own the Blue Cat?" Caroline asked in surprise.

"Part owner. Jazz is my hobby. Fortunately, my bank account is sufficient to support both me and this," Carl said, gesturing to the room at large. "But my life story can wait. Why don't you tell me about Ed's accident?"

Caroline had been avoiding the subject. It was easier recalling the good days than the bad.

"Ed was a jogger," she said slowly. "He preferred running at night when the streets were free of heavy traffic. The evening of the accident I decided to do a little work in the garden while he was gone. I saw him rounding the corner on his way back and he waved to me. He slowed his pace and that's when this car came weaving down the street behind him. Ed never even saw it coming. It hit him and just kept on going." Caroline paused, a puzzled expression on her face. "To this day I don't know what make or color that car was. I only saw Ed go flying across the street, and then it was over."

"I hadn't realized you were there when it happened."

Caroline nodded and took a deep breath. "I went through the motions of a wake and funeral, but it was more like a bad dream I thought I'd wake up from. I couldn't believe Ed was really gone. After Martin and Nikki and my daughters left, I sat around in that big empty house with nothing to do but think of my husband."

She glossed over the details of her plunge into despair. She'd eaten little, slept less, and gradually withdrew completely into herself. Her sense of loss was so great that even her children meant nothing to her. She'd shut them out, refusing to answer their calls and letters. She preferred the dark solitude of her memories to the comfort of her family.

"I guess I was afraid of being alone," she told Carl ruefully. "I just self-destructed and finally the kids stepped in. They had me admitted to a psychiatric hospital for treatment of my depression."

Carl pursed his lips but said nothing. Caroline hadn't intended to relate this much. She was a private person, not used to revealing her innermost thoughts. For some reason, though, she felt compelled to tell him the rest of the story.

"I could have accepted death. But to be locked away, handed over to a keeper..." She shook her head. How could she explain what it felt like being enrolled in the ranks of the emotionally lost? "Fear can be a powerful incentive to recovery. I forced myself back into life."

"That couldn't have been easy."

A whisper of a smile crossed Caroline's lips. "It's amazing what you can do when the adrenalin starts flowing. I was like a trapped animal fighting the cage. I *had* to get out of that hospital!"

She didn't mention how she'd done it. She'd suppressed all thoughts except those of escape, and concentrated solely on appeasing her doctors. Her nursing experience had taught her the rules and she'd played the game to perfection. The first step had been simply to get out of bed. She'd put on make-up and forced herself to eat the bland meals set before her, always remembering to compliment the staff when they'd come to pick up the empty trays. She'd begun walking the halls, smiling and nodding to the nurses she'd met. When the doctors made their rounds, she'd hidden her trembling hands in her pockets and answered their questions with contrived eloquence. And she'd watched them nod in satisfaction, fooling them all until the day came when they could find no reason to keep her any longer.

"Martin told me some of this," the Professor responded. "I must say I was surprised at the rapidity of your recovery. In my experience, emotions take longer to heal."

Caroline avoided Carl's eyes. It had been easy to delude her children; they'd wanted to believe the doctors. But the Professor would be more difficult to hoodwink.

"I can't say I was totally over the depression when I left the hospital," she admitted. "But I'm winning the battle now. Moving to Rhineburg was the best thing I could have done. I've put the past behind me and I'm getting on with my life."

At least she hoped she was.

"Hmm. I've heard that said before and I've always wondered if it's possible to do. 'Putting the past behind' can be an excuse for not dealing with one's problems."

"I don't think that's the case with me!" Caroline said archly, although she'd wrestled with that same thought several times since leaving Chicago. "The temporary job as housemother is ideal at the moment, and the float pool provides a way for me to ease back into nursing." She smiled to take the sting out of her words. "Ed didn't leave me a wealthy woman, Carl. I still have to work for a living."

The Professor nodded. "Life presents us with hard choices. Sometimes it's difficult to make the right ones."

Caroline recalled the Mary Engelbreit card a friend had sent. A banner at the top of the card proclaimed 'Don't Look Back'. Beneath it a little girl carrying a suitcase strode purposefully down one of two forks in a path. A signpost pointing her way read 'Your Life' while the other fork was labeled 'No Longer An Option'. Caroline had framed the card. It hung on a wall in her apartment, a daily reminder of what she herself must do. She thought of it now as she replied,

"Often the choices are quite limited. For now, I think I'm where I ought to be. As for the future, who knows?"

Atwater had gone off to talk with one of the waiters. It gave Caroline a chance to compose herself after their discussion. She still didn't know why she'd been so frank with the Professor concerning her illness. True, she hadn't told him everything, but it was more than her entire family knew. In fact, only her two best friends were privy to the complete truth of her situation. Perhaps she'd confided in Carl because they were no longer around. Maybe her present loneliness had less to do with missing Ed and more to do with missing companionship in general. The thought was disturbing.

"Feeling better?"

Caroline looked up to see Professor Atwater maneuvering his massive body onto the too small chair across from her. He plunked two bottles of beer down on the table.

"Sorry, but hot chocolate does very little for me. Care for one?"

Caroline shook her head. "It's late, Carl. We should be going."

"Soon," Carl replied. "But first we have to discuss the bombing at St. Anne's."

Caroline leaned back in her chair. She felt totally betrayed.

"So that's what all this is about," she said bitterly. "You kidnap me off the street, then you soften me up with music and...hot chocolate, of all things! You pretend to be sympathetic, worming your way into my confidence, then bingo! 'Would you please tell me what it's like to see seven people blown to bits, Mrs. Rhodes?'. Well, listen to me, Carl Atwater! I have no intention of satisfying your morbid curiosity! If you want information about the bombing, go ask the police!"

She got up and strode angrily to the door.

"It's cold out there. Sure you wouldn't like your coat?"

Caroline whipped around, glowered at Carl, and grabbed her parka from the chair. She shoved her arms into the sleeves of the coat as she headed once more for the exit.

"It's a mighty long walk back to the dormitory. You could try hitchhiking, but the road is pretty deserted at this time of night."

"I'll get a ride from one of the waiters," Caroline snapped.

Carl shook his head. "They're long gone, Caroline. I told them I'd lock up the place."

Caroline looked around and sure enough the room was deserted except for them. Furious, she stalked back to the table and sat down.

"I can understand why you think I'm driven by curiosity," the Professor remarked. "Everyone else at the part was pumping you for information."

"So you noticed!"

Atwater ignored the sarcasm. "I notice a lot of things, and that's precisely why I have to talk with you about the explosion. There's something very wrong going on in Rhineburg!"

"It doesn't take a genius to see that, Professor! I'd hardly call blowing up a hospital a socially acceptable act!"

Carl wrinkled his nose. "I'm not talking about the bombing itself. I mean the way the police are investigating this case!"

"It seems to me they're being very thorough. They've practically invaded St. Anne's! You can't turn a corner without running into some officer or another."

"I know what you mean. It's the same way at the university."

Caroline frowned. "What are they doing over there?"

"Looking for a killer, of course! They seem to think one of our students may be responsible for the bomb."

Despite her initial aversion to the subject, Caroline found this latest piece of news intriguing. She couldn't help but speculate on it.

"I suppose the science majors have come under scrutiny. It is possible one of them has the ability to build a bomb."

"That's ridiculous!" Carl snorted. "Our students are interested in only one thing: a college education. We don't attract bombers to Bruck!"

It was Caroline's turn to sound contemptuous. "Ah, ha!! Aren't *you* the elitist!" She leaned over the table, her tone suddenly more serious. "What are you trying to say, Carl? Is Bruck so removed from the outside world that it's immune to the problems of society? Troubled kids pop up everywhere today. Why shouldn't one land in your lap?"

Atwater raised one hand. "I'm not denying reality, Caroline, but you don't know our students. Think about what I told you earlier tonight. These kids have to agree to shovel snow and pick up garbage if they misbehave. If we had a truly troubled kid here, he'd rebel at that rule long before he got to the bomber stage! The faculty met two days ago and not one single teacher could name a student capable of committing this crime."

Caroline relented. "I agree it's unlikely, Carl, simply because I don't see the motive. But it's not impossible. The police have to examine every lead they get. I'm sure they're investigating people in Rhineburg too."

"Oh, sure," Carl agreed. "But they'll get nowhere fast with that approach!"

"Why not?"

"Rhineburgers don't talk about each other. It's a very close community where people don't easily open up about their neighbors."

"That's a laugh!" Caroline exclaimed. "I've overheard all the gossip going on in the hospital. It seems to me Rhineburg has a well oiled grapevine in place!"

"The operative word is 'overheard', Caroline. I'll bet no one has confided in *you* yet!"

Caroline shrugged. "No, but I'm a newcomer to St. Anne's.".

"Exactly!" Carl said triumphantly. "And those FBI agents are even worse than newcomers; they don't belong to this town at all! I tell you, Caroline, they'll have to pull teeth to get Rhineburgers to talk to them. The cops are going to need some help if they want to solve this case. They're going to need us!"

Flash bulbs started popping in Caroline's brain. She was finally beginning to see the light.

"I can't believe what I'm hearing!" she protested. "You want to play detective! Martin's fed you some line about me being perceptive and you think I'll be your Watson. Well, no thank you, Sherlock! You're not dragging me into this!"

"Come on, Caroline. Think how perfect it would be. I'm the insider who can plug into that grapevine, and you're the outsider with a direct link to the hospital. Not only can you go anywhere you want in that building, but you're also a reliable witness to the bombing!"

Caroline was furious. "Who the hell do you think you are asking this of me? I came to Rhineburg to start a new life, to put a lot of unhappiness behind me. And I'm here only a few months when I get mixed up in one of the bloodiest affairs in the history of this town! Do you think it was a picnic on the ward that day? Do you imagine I enjoyed seeing seven bodies lying there with Christmas tree branches sticking out of their chests like firry arrows?"

"Of course not! And I didn't mean to imply that! But you were there, Caroline, and that means you're involved, like it or not. You have a stake in the outcome of this case. You must want to see the killer put behind bars!"

"Listen to me, Carl!" Caroline's voice shook with emotion. "I told the police everything I know about that day. I have no intention of getting any more involved than that. I've had enough grief to last me a lifetime and all I want now is a little peace!"

Atwater said nothing, but his eyes narrowed as he watched Caroline twist the silver band on her left ring finger. She appeared mesmerized, her eyes locked on her hands and the symbol of her past. When she spoke again, the words came out in a strangled whisper.

"I can't help you, don't you understand? I just can't!"

Carl pushed back his chair and stood up. He shook his head slowly, his face devoid of any warmth.

"History is a compilation of man's misery," he said quietly. "No one ever born on this earth has escaped sorrow or suffering. Why should you be any different from the rest of us, Caroline?"

He picked up his coat and walked out, leaving her there staring numbly at her wedding ring.

Two

December 20

Caroline awoke to the clamor of the telephone. Eyes still heavy with sleep, she groped for the receiver and cradled it between her ear and the pillow.

"Hullo?"

"Mother? Is that you?" Martin was his usual brisk self.

"No, it's the cleaning lady," Caroline mumbled. "Your mother is sleeping, but I'll tell her you called."

She started to hang up but Martin hollered into the receiver.

"Wait a minute! I thought mom did her own housework!"

Caroline yawned and rolled onto her back.

"Martin!" She forced her eyes open, then glanced at the alarm clock. "It's nine fifteen on my day off. Give me a break, will you?"

"Sorry," Martin apologized. "But I was worried about you."

"Why, dear?" Caroline asked patiently.

"Well, the Professor's in a stinking mood this morning. When I asked him what the problem was, he just looked sad and said, 'Your mother'. Then he told me to go home 'cause he was taking the day off. Mom, the Professor never skips work!"

Caroline closed her eyes again. "Marty, nothing's wrong with me or Professor Atwater. We both like an occasional day off, that's all."

"Oh! I get it!" Martin exclaimed. "You're spending the day together!"

"In your dreams, my boy. In your dreams! Good-bye, Martin."

"Hold on, mom!"

But Caroline dropped the receiver on the bedside table and

pulled the blanket over her head. Unfortunately, she was now wide awake. After ten minutes of tossing and turning, she accepted the inevitable and climbed out of bed.

She'd had a rotten night. An old recurrent nightmare jolted her awake at two a.m. She'd sat up in bed, sweaty and trembling, waiting for her childhood bogey man to recede into the shadows of her subconscious. The ancient monster had modernized itself with the addition of a white beard and mustache. It pursued her exactly as it had when she was seven, but now, instead of the throaty growl she'd feared as a child, it shrieked the word 'History!' over and over again. When her heart finally stopped its wild beating, she'd leaned back against the pillows and chided herself for succumbing to such silliness.

"I wish I had never met you, Carl Atwater!" she'd moaned. Expelling the Professor from her thoughts, she'd snuggled down under the comforter and awaited sleep. It didn't come until dawn and then it was disturbed by further dark dreams.

Four hours of fitful sleep did nothing to improve Caroline's mood of the night before. She padded to the kitchen, poured a glass of orange juice, and swallowed two aspirin. Her head was pounding and every inch of her body ached. Aggravated now not only with Carl but also Martin, she turned the shower on full blast and stood under it. The steam slowly cleared her head while the water massaged her muscles.

By the time she toweled off and pulled on jeans and a shirt, the heat and aspirin were taking effect. She made a bowl of oatmeal, mixed in some peach jam, and drank another glass of juice. The breakfast completed what the shower had begun. Caroline felt almost human again as she cleared the table.

Once the breakfast dishes were out of the way, she considered cleaning the apartment. Lord knew it needed it but Caroline really wasn't in the mood for work. 'The hell with it!' she concluded and opted instead for a shopping spree. A drive into Rhineburg would hopefully distract her from further thoughts of the men in her life. And, she reminded herself, Christmas was only a few days away. That gave her an excuse to do some serious spending.

The crisp December air was invigorating and Caroline perked up as she walked to the hospital parking garage. It was a perfect winter day with the sun shining high in a cloudless sky. Her spirits rose considerably higher when the old Buick started on the first try. It was a good omen, she decided, and she pulled away from the hospital humming a Christmas carol.

Driving past the university, she slowed to a crawl and gazed out the window at the pristine beauty of the campus. Most of the students were already gone for the holidays so the new snow lay undisturbed on the rolling lawns. It billowed against the walls of the five buildings bordering Circle Road and spilled over into a deserted parking lot nestled next to the library.

The structures themselves glowed brightly in the sunlight, their rosy hue the result of nature rather than man. They'd been constructed of pink rhyolite from the stone quarry outside of Rhineburg. The stone was unique in color and many of the older homes in town, along with City Hall, the court house, and the police station, were built of the same material. It was hard to take a pink police station seriously, but the early Rhineburgers were practical men. They used what was at hand and dared outsiders to laugh.

Unlike the buildings, which were somber unadorned rectangles, the grounds of Bruck U. belied the pragmatism of its founders. Here the farmers' natural love of the land prevailed. Ancient oaks stood tall where they'd been planted, their twisted arms now crystallized with ice. Hyacinth, wild rose, and honeysuckle bushes lined the paths crisscrossing the campus and Bruck Green. They too reflected the fury of last night's storm with their spindly branches bowing low under the weight of the snow. Nearer to the buildings, flower beds curved in formal patterns beneath three foot drifts. Caroline had seen them in October when russet and gold chrysanthemums filled their borders. She wondered how they'd look in spring as the daffodils emerged.

Dressed in winter white, the campus exuded a picture postcard prettiness. Caroline drove on down Circle Road, the Green to her left, the university to her right, admiring the peacefulness of the landscape. She switched on the radio and fiddled with the dial until she found a station playing carols. Humming to the music, she left the university grounds and made a sharp right onto the highway leading into town.

The intersection was slick and the Buick's tires spun wickedly before grabbing the pavement. Caroline eased up on the accelerator as the car jumped forward. Gripping the steering wheel more firmly, she considered the need to buy new tires.

"Not today!" she resolved aloud. Today was reserved for Christmas shopping. Caroline drew up a mental gift list as the Buick skimmed along the highway towards Rhineburg. Snow covered fields stretched endlessly on both sides of the road, but she took no notice as she concentrated on the perfect present for each of her children. Her mind barely registered the stand of stubby pines ahead to the right beyond which the road turned and dipped into a shaded hollow of trees and scrub brush. She automatically guided the Buick into the curve, unaware that the sun hadn't touched this section of shadowed pavement. A layer of black ice covered its surface and the Buick's tires proved no match for the challenge. Despite the rotation of the wheels, the car plunged straight ahead. Thoughts of Christmas evaporated as Caroline tightened her grip on the wheel and steered frantically to the right. The car continued to resist her directions, skidding across the yellow center line of the highway. Caroline slammed on the brake.

'Wrong!' her brain screamed. The Buick veered sideways across the road as a fraction too late Caroline released the pedal. Spinning the wheel to the left, she pumped the brake in an attempt to go with the slide. The pedal depressed twice, then flattened uselessly to the floor. Horrified, Caroline clung helplessly to the wheel while the car fishtailed towards the far embankment, its tires spinning unchecked.

The forested slope was a blur of brown and white rushing straight at her. Caroline threw up her hands in an instinctive gesture of self-protection as the Buick plowed head on into a wall of brush. The car lurched skyward, hung motionless for the briefest of moments, then slammed violently back to earth. It pitched forward and sank into the snow, its front bumper crumpling against a jagged tree stump.

Thrown against the steering wheel in the sudden stop, Caroline felt rather than heard herself cry out in pain before passing into unconsciousness.

Someone was playing basketball inside her head. It was Marty, she decided, dribbling that damned ball again.

"Cut it out, Martin," Caroline mumbled. "You're giving me a headache."

"It's alright, Mrs. Rhodes. Just hold still now."

She felt a sharp jab in her left arm. She tried turning that way but something tightened around her forehead and neck. Caroline was flat on her back and she couldn't budge an inch.

"What are you doing?" she cried out in alarm. A large fuzzy form loomed over her. It bent close to her face, murmuring soft noises.

"What's happening? Who are you?" She strained to focus her eyes on the semi-human shape.

"Take it easy, Cari. They're only trying to help you."

The voice was vaguely familiar. Was it Ed? He'd always called her Cari, never Caroline. 'But Ed's gone,' she reasoned disjointedly. 'Maybe I'm dead too. But then I wouldn't be hurting like this, would I?'

Caroline blinked once, then again to clear her misted vision. Shapes slowly sharpened in detail and she was able to make out a hand holding something above her. She concentrated on the hand, forcing her mind into clarity. Fingers. Yes, she could make out fingers. Long ones with short nails. Squeezing something clear and shiny. Rectangular with black lettering. Long tubing extending from one end. A wave of nausea swept over her and she closed her eyes.

"I'm going to be sick," she said through clenched teeth.

"You'll be all right, Cari. Just take a deep breath."

That voice again. Definitely not Ed's. She really should know whose it was but she couldn't place it.

"This oxygen should help, Mrs. Rhodes. Hang on now. We'll have you at St. Anne's in no time flat!"

St. Anne's? Well, why not? It was where she worked, wasn't it? Martin better hurry or she'd be late for her shift.

"OK, Bob. We're ready to roll."

Bob? She didn't know any Bob! Oh, dear! Mother had always told her never take a ride from a stranger. She certainly wouldn't approve of this! Caroline focused on the hand again. "Are you a stranger?" she asked it.

Through a fog of pain she heard male laughter. 'How impolite!' she thought as she closed her eyes and drifted into sleep.

Caroline woke as she was lifted from the ambulance. Her head throbbed but her vision was no longer blurred.

"How you feelin', Mrs. Rhodes?" A tall slim man smiled down on her.

"You're a paramedic," she said slowly as she searched his face for confirmation.

"Absolutely right! You're coming around OK now. Pretty soon you'll remember everything."

Hands reached out and Caroline felt the stretcher sway as she was wheeled through a door marked Emergency Department. The motion made her stomach queasy but she was beginning to think more clearly. She realized she was strapped to a backboard, a plastic brace supporting her neck. Tape secured her head to the board and intravenous fluids dripped into her left arm.

"Caroline! What have you been up to?"

Caroline smiled up at the sandy haired young man bending over her. Paul Wakely was one of the newer ER docs. He'd done his residency in Chicago, but preferred rural Rhineburg to the city. Paul was not only capable but kind; Caroline felt secure in his hands.

"I went for a spin, Paul," she answered wryly. It was coming back to her: the car refusing to take the curve, the headlong plunge into the snowbank. "I think I have a concussion."

Paul laughed and patted her hand reassuringly. "I'd say that's a good diagnosis. The paramedics told me you were out of it for a while."

"I must have bumped my head."

"Well, you know the routine, Caroline. First an X-ray, then a scan of the brain to make sure you're not bleeding." He probed the back of her neck with his fingers. "Any pain or numbness?"

"I feel like death warmed over, Paul. Every inch of me hurts."

"You can't be in too bad shape if you're able to joke about it!"

Paul motioned to the paramedics and they transferred Caroline, backboard and all, to an ER cart. A nurse began the triage process.

"This ought to get you a few days off," the woman joked. "The next time you want a break, pretend you have the flu!"

Caroline relaxed as she traded barbs with her coworker. Triage went quickly and before she knew it she was being wheeled off to X-ray and the CT scan room. When she finally arrived back in ER, Martin and Nikki were waiting for her.

"Mother!" Martin said anxiously. "Are you OK?"

'Not really,' Caroline thought, but she replied instead, "I'm fine, Marty. Just a bit shaken up."

"More than a bit," Nikki remarked, "judging by that lump on your head."

"Thank God for Professor Atwater. You might have been trapped in that car for hours if he hadn't found you."

"Carl Atwater was there?" Caroline frowned at Martin. She tried to recall the Professor's presence at the accident site, but her mind drew a blank.

"He arrived right after it happened," Marty continued. "He told us there was steam pouring out from under the Buick's hood. You must have blown the radiator."

"I blew a little more than that, I'll bet!" The Buick had been old; it was probably old and crumpled now.

"Don't worry about the car, mom. Marty called the garage and they're going to tow it in."

Caroline smiled her thanks at her daughter-in-law. Nikki was the practical one in that marriage. Having the car towed was probably her idea.

"Good news, Caroline!" Doctor Wakely covered the distance from the desk to Caroline's side in long easy strides. He grinned down at her as he began to unfasten the hard neck brace. "Nothing's broken, and the scan's clean. You're going to be sore for a couple of days, and I'll have to stitch up that cut..."

"What cut?" Caroline asked in alarm.

Paul laughed and touched the side of her head. "Nothing that'll mar your natural beauty! Still, it'll require about six sutures. And you'll be staying in the hospital overnight."

Caroline began to protest but Paul raised his hand.

"Forget it, lady. You're ours now for twenty-four hours. You've had a good concussion. Loss of consciousness, remember? Can't release you until we're sure all your working parts are working right. Now you two," he motioned to Martin and Nikki. "Get out of here while I do a little sewing."

Martin fled willingly. Nikki threw a smile Caroline's way and followed her husband to the waiting room.

"Nice young couple," Paul remarked, pulling the curtain closed around the little cubicle. "They're worried about you, though."

His manner was too nonchalant for Caroline's liking. She watched him closely, her head aching but her mind firmly back on track.

"Why should they worry? They heard you say I'm fine."

Paul nodded. He fumbled with the suture set, then struggled to tear off the metal ring securing the top of the lidocaine bottle.

"Damn things!" he muttered. "Can't they make them any easier to open?"

"Let me do it." Caroline reached for the bottle and pulled on the tab. The lid flipped off easily. "You need a nurse, Paul. You're all thumbs today."

Paul's only answer was a grunt. He turned away and drew the lidocaine up into a syringe.

"Spit it out, doc. What's on your mind?"

Paul looked over at Caroline and placed the syringe back on the tray. His face was sober, his tone of voice even more so.

"They would have kept their mouths shut, but they were shook up. Scared for you. I'm sure it didn't have anything to do with the accident, Caroline, but I have to ask you since they brought it up." He hesitated, then said, "Was it a suicide attempt, Caroline?"

Caroline was so shocked she couldn't speak. Just what did her children think of her? she wondered dismally.

"Martin told me about your recent hospitalization. I didn't write anything on your chart. This is strictly between you, me, and these four walls. I need to know the truth, Caroline."

She pulled herself together and met his steady gaze. "It was not a suicide attempt, Paul. I slid on a patch of ice, then panicked and hit the brake. The car went into a skid. If I wanted to kill myself, I'd do it a lot less painfully," she added angrily. "Pills, probably. Not as messy as body parts all over the highway!"

Paul raised a hand. "I believe you, OK? It's my job to ask. I'd be a lousy doctor if I didn't."

"I know." Caroline closed her eyes. "It just make me uneasy to think Martin could imagine I'd do such a thing."

Paul started to work on the laceration. Suddenly he chuckled.

"Strange, isn't it? Parents worry about their kids, and kids worry about their parents. A never-ending circle of concern."

Caroline smiled sadly as he continued.

"I meant it when I told you this conversation was confidential. I hope you won't feel uncomfortable next time we work together."

"Thank you, Paul. I realize depression is nothing to be ashamed of, but it's not the kind of illness employers want to hear about."

"Well, they won't hear about it from me, Caroline. That about does it." He tied off the last stitch. "Kathy will put a dressing on it and as soon as we hear from the admitting office, we'll get you up to your room. Want something for the headache?"

Caroline nodded. Paul pulled back the curtain and walked off leaving her alone to fight back tears of anger and humiliation. How could Martin have betrayed her so? Would it all never end?

"Cari?"

She turned her head to see Carl standing there, concern written across his face. It struck her that Carl's voice was the one she'd heard when the paramedics had been working on her.

"You were there, weren't you? At the accident."

"I drove up just as you hit the snowbank. You scared the life out of me, Cari. I thought you were dead when I first reached the car."

"Martin says you saved my life."

"Martin is overly dramatic." Carl took her hand and patted it. She looked away but left her hand in his.

"I didn't do it on purpose."

Atwater frowned. "Do what on purpose, Cari?"

"Try to kill myself. I'm sure Martin told you something to that effect."

Carl grasped her hand more tightly.

"Look at me, Caroline Rhodes!" he demanded. "Your son said no such thing. And if he had, I would have told him he was a fool."

"You would? You really mean that?"

"Of course I do!" Carl shook his head in annoyance. "It doesn't take a genius to see that someone tampered with your car, Caroline. Somebody wants you dead, but I certainly don't think it's you!"

It was eight-thirty and visiting hours were over. Tucked up in a private room in the east wing of St. Anne's, Caroline was exhausted but relatively pain-free. The muscle relaxants had worked magic on her sore neck and shoulders. Unfortunately, they'd done nothing for her mental distress.

Martin and Nikki had left, but not before Caroline had a chance to confront them about their conversation with Paul Wakely. Unable to hide the betrayal she felt, she'd tackled the subject as soon as they were alone in the room.

"Evidently you two think I'm some kind of nut case," she said bitterly. "Why did you tell Doctor Wakely about my depression? Did I lose my right to privacy when I moved to Rhineburg?"

Martin's face was red with embarrassment. He'd spoken to the Professor and now knew the brakes had failed. "I'm sorry, mom, but we were worried sick when we heard what happened to you. I was afraid you might have gone and done something silly."

"Like try to kill myself? Martin, Martin! You should know me better than that."

"Why, mom?" Nikki inquired softly. "What makes you think Marty knows what's going on inside your head?"

"Leave it alone, Nik," her husband pleaded. "We don't need to discuss that now."

Nikki's dark eyes flashed. "Yes, we do," she insisted. "Your mother may be angry, but then so are you. Why not tell her the truth?" She turned to face Caroline. "It's about time you heard it."

Caroline was flabbergasted. Why in the hell were Martin and Nikki so upset? They weren't the victims here. She was!

"What are you talking about? I've done nothing to hurt Marty!"

"You've done nothing to make him feel better either!" Nikki retorted. "You've worried him all these months, and you don't even seem to notice he's doing it! Don't you think of anyone but yourself?"

Caroline was startled by Nikki's passionate attack. Gentleness was the girl's middle name; something had to be terribly wrong for her to react this way.

"I don't understand," she said, shaking her head. She turned to her son. "What's going on, Martin? Tell me, please!"

Martin leaned forward and took his mother's hand. He had difficulty meeting her steady gaze, but Nikki's eyes were boring into his back, willing him to be honest. "It's true that Nik and I have been concerned about...your state of mind. Krista and Kerry are worried too, mom! We just don't know what you're thinking any more!" He took a deep breath before continuing. "How can I explain it to you? We all miss dad a lot. He was our best friend besides being our father. When he died, we wanted to tell you how we felt about him, but you were so wrapped up in your own grief..." His voice trailed off.

Caroline tightened her fingers around Martin's. His face was etched with pain when he spoke of Ed. Why hadn't she noticed it before?

'Because I didn't want to,' she thought bitterly. 'I was too busy thinking about myself.'

"I'm sorry, Martin. I never meant to hurt you and your sisters."

"Of course not!"

"I guess I was totally absorbed by my own loss." She dropped Marty's hand and picked absently at the blanket, searching for the right words to explain her behavior. He had a right to some answers, but was she ready to bare her soul to him? Had she healed enough to do that?

"Your father's wake was like some grotesque circus where I was the star performer," she said slowly. "Everyone was so curious about Ed's accident and I resented having to tell the story over and over again! Then there were you two and the girls." She shook her head. "You must have asked me a hundred times if I was all right, and I thought I had to say 'yes' so you all wouldn't worry. But I wasn't all right. I wanted to scream at all those people in the funeral parlor! I wanted to tell them, 'Get out of here! Leave me alone so I can say good-bye to my husband!'" Caroline looked up at Martin. If only she could make him understand. "I never got that chance, Martin. Before I knew it, the funeral was over and Ed was in his grave."

She saw the tears in her son's eyes, but she had to go on.

"Martin, I was furious with your father for leaving me that way, and I couldn't express it to any of you. Instead, I began harboring enough self-pity to last me a life time. It wasn't until I was hospitalized that I realized how engrossed I'd become in my own sorrow. I thought I'd gotten beyond that kind of selfishness, but it seems I'm still thinking only of myself. All I can say is, I'm sorry. I'm truly very sorry."

Martin leaned over the bed and without a word, he gathered her into his arms. For several minutes they clung to each other, their sorrow binding them as one. Caroline recovered first. She reached up and wiped a tear from her son's cheek.

"You're a good man, Martin. There's a whole lot of your father in you." She turned and smiled at Nikki. "And you're a better daughter-in-law than I deserve, Nikki. Thanks for having the courage to tell me the truth."

"We both love you, mom," Nikki assured her solemnly. "We want you to be happy again."

Caroline nodded. If wanting could make it so, she should be feeling glorious. She was trying so hard to get on with her life, to put the past behind. Unfortunately, in doing so, she'd cut off the very people she loved the most: her family.

"I haven't coped very well the past few months, Marty. Deep inside of me, I know that and it scares me to death. I'm afraid of sinking back into that awful depression.I'm afraid to talk about your dad in case it starts all over again."

"That won't happen, mom, if you let us share what you're feeling. We need to be open and honest about our sorrow, talk it out so we can get past this together."

She knew Martin was right. Now, after hours of conversation, Caroline was alone again with her memories. They were less threatening than before; still, she wasn't totally at peace. Guilt tugged at her and she moodily considered its source. She'd driven a wedge in the family by denying her children the right to grieve with her. Could she undo the harm her selfishness had caused? Could she find a way to make things right again?

She was still brooding over her failures when Atwater appeared at the door, poinsettia in hand.

"Up to some company?" the professor queried.

Caroline smiled wanly. How could she refuse the man who'd saved her life?

"Of course. That's a beautiful plant."

"Thought you'd like it. Martin told me you're a Christmas nut. You even play carols in June, right?"

"Is there anything about me that Martin hasn't told you?"

Caroline spoke lightly but there was a trace of annoyance in her voice.

"Now, Cari! Privacy is well and good, but it's knowing the little things about people -- what gives them pleasure, what causes pain -- that allows friendships to grow. Take Mrs. Ferguson for example," Carl said. He placed the poinsettia on the bedside table and settled down on a vinyl chair that sagged dangerously beneath his three hundred plus pounds. "Your nurse is a connoisseur of confections. I know that because I've seen her in the Fudge Shoppe agonizing over the unlimited choices there. Well, she was about to throw me out of here -- it is after visiting hours! -- but when I presented her with a box of chocolate, she suddenly decided my visit would do you a world of good.

Those chocolates were meant for you," he added. "I'll bring you another box tomorrow."

"Save your money," Caroline answered. "I'll be out of here tommorow."

"Then you're feeling better?"

"Occasional aches and pains, but I can't complain. At least I'm still in one piece!"

"Thank God for that!" Carl exclaimed. "When I saw your car fly up that embankment, I thought you were a goner for sure."

"So you actually witnessed the entire accident."

Carl nodded. "I was driving home from a funeral and suddenly your Buick came careening across the road. I braked so quickly that I nearly ended up in a snow drift myself."

"I'm sorry," Caroline said automatically.

Carl waved it off and continued. "I keep a cellular phone in my Jeep. The paramedics were there within minutes. By the way, I stopped by the garage to check on your car. You'll be needing a new one."

"I suspected that. Do you know what caused the brakes to fail? I slid entering the highway, but I assumed it was the tires, not the brakes."

"There was really nothing you could have done to prevent what happened, Cari. Somebody tampered with your car."

"Wait a minute!" Caroline sat up straighter in bed. "You said something to that effect back in ER. What do you mean, somebody tampered with it? I don't know enough about mechanics to even guess how that could be done!"

"It's not all that difficult to do. Someone simply cut the hoses to your wheel cylinders."

Caroline was mystified. She had no idea what wheel cylinders even were. "You'll have to explain better than that," she said. "I told you, I know next to nothing about cars."

Carl drew a pad of paper from his pocket and began scribbling.

When he finished, he handed it to Caroline.

"This is a diagram of your brake system. You've got a master cylinder under your hood, a reservoir holding brake fluid. The fluid passes down a tube to the metering valve, then flows on through two other tubes to the wheel cylinders stationed behind your back tires. The tubes are made of aluminum but they're connected to the wheel cylinder with flexible rubber hoses. If there's damage to the system, the fluid will leak out. You'll lose some each time you put on the brakes until it's finally all gone. No more brake fluid, no more brakes. Caroline, anyone could have reached around the tires and slashed those hoses."

"Anyone who knew what they were doing!" Caroline retorted. "Until now, I didn't have a clue those hoses even existed."

"But you're a woman," Carl said with a shrug. "You're not expected to understand cars. Most men, though, have tinkered with an automobile at some time in their life. I'm sure Martin knows all about brake systems."

Caroline doubted it. Her husband had been the mechanical one in the family. Somehow the gene was lost on their son.

"I'm not sure I like your sexist attitude, Carl, but it's comforting to know it wasn't a fellow female who tried to kill me! I wonder who did, though. And why?"

"Do you really want the answers to those questions, Cari?"

Carl leaned forward in his chair and stared at her. Caroline saw the challenge in his eyes.

"What's that supposed to mean?" she snapped. "Why wouldn't I want them?"

"Because you couldn't do what you did last night. You couldn't just say, 'Gee whiz! That's awful, but if I don't think about it, it'll all go away!'."

Carl's words were like a hard slap in the face. Caroline sunk back against her pillows, furious with herself and him. Perhaps she deserved that blow, but did it have to come so soon after the one delivered by Martin?

"You don't think too highly of me, do you?"

"On the contrary, Caroline. I've been led to believe you're quite a woman. You've survived a lot of pain in the past year. But survival alone isn't good enough. You have to come fully back to life. You have to start caring again."

"I care!" Caroline retorted. "About my children, my patients..."

"But not about yourself. At least, not yet."

"I don't know what you mean," she said impatiently. "If there's one thing I've been guilty of lately, it's caring too much about myself."

"Humbug!" Carl exclaimed. "You've been preoccupied with your problems, Cari. That's not the same as caring about yourself." He shook his head in exasperation. "You're a stubborn woman, Caroline Rhodes. Still, I refuse to give up on you, so I'm going to say some things you probably won't like to hear. Let's start with that line you fed me last night about moving here to start a new life. That was a bunch of bull, wasn't it?"

Caroline raised one eyebrow and answered sarcastically, "Why don't you tell me, Professor? After all, you seem to be the one with all the answers."

Carl ignored the taunt. "You came to Rhineburg because Nikki and Martin told you to. They gave you some song and dance about your family not wanting you to live alone, about how worried everyone was, and how they'd move back to Chicago if you decided to stay there. Marty practically read me the letter, Cari. I told him to leave you be, but he's as bullheaded as you."

"I wasn't exactly the Rock of Gibraltar back then, Carl. I was acting...irrational, and I see now that they had a right to be concerned."

"Concern is one thing. Blackmail is another!"

"It wasn't blackmail," Caroline insisted. "I didn't want Martin to give up everything he had here. And it was a good idea to get out of that house. It was much too big for one person."

"Bah! You loved that old place and you know it." Carl stood up and started pacing the room. "You were on a guilt trip, Caroline. You were ashamed of your depression, desperate to fool everyone into thinking you were just fine. Moving to Rhineburg was your way of proving you still loved your kids. It was the ultimate motherly self-sacrifice."

Caroline slammed her fist into the bed covers. "Who the hell do you think you are?" she cried. "And what gives you the right to judge me?"

"I'm not judging you, Cari," Carl said sadly. "I'm trying to open your eyes. Your husband died suddenly and before you even knew what was happening, your whole world changed completely. You weren't prepared to live alone, to give up that one special person you'd shared so much with."

They stared at each other in silence. It seemed like an eternity before Caroline began to speak again.

"Ed made me laugh." She collapsed against the pillows, all the fight gone out of her. "I don't know if you can understand..."

"I hear what you're saying, Cari. I was married once too."

Startled, Caroline tried to make amends. "I'm so sorry, Carl. I didn't know."

Carl waved off her apology. "How could you? I don't talk about it any more, but I do understand what you mean. When you have a special relationship with a person, it's hard to let go of it." He sat down on the edge of the bed. "Cari, we all have a right to grieve a loss, but there comes a time when we have to accept that the pain, in some degree, will always be with us."

"I think I have accepted it, Carl. I've tried to get on with living as best as I can."

Carl shook his head. "Take my word for it: what you've been doing is surviving, not living. You've isolated that one big pain of losing Ed and you've told yourself, 'That's enough! That's all I can take!' Why haven't you noticed how troubled Martin is over his father's death? Why was it you refused to help me last night? You've decided you'll never risk being hurt again. You'll stay uninvolved, untouched by the pain of life. Of course you'll miss out on its pleasures, too, but never mind that! At least you'll survive!"

"You make it sound so awful," Caroline whispered. She turned her head away from him. "I feel like a total disaster. I've failed Martin and my daughters just like I failed Ed."

Carl cocked his head to one side. "Now we're finally getting to the truth. What's really holding you back is the knowledge you're just not Superwoman."

"Carl!"

"Don't 'Carl!' me!" the Professor exclaimed. "Come clean, Cari. You're punishing yourself because you couldn't save your husband. Here you were, the mother, the nurse, always there to solve other people's problems, and you couldn't solve your own."

"Stop it!"

"Not until you admit the truth." He took her hand and held it tightly until she faced him. "You were right there when Ed was run down, but you couldn't prevent it, or save him. That had to be hard for you, Cari. You're a natural-born 'fixer', always around to clean up somebody else's mess. Ed's death was one mess you couldn't fix, not for yourself or your children."

"I'm a nurse, Carl," Caroline murmured. "I should have been able to *do* something."

"Stop trying to make amends for being human, Caroline. Only God can save some people."

Caroline frowned at him. Every instinct told her he was right. Ed had died instantly from massive brain damage. The medical examiner's report was explicit in detailing the wounds he'd received and it was obvious he'd never had a chance.

"You're beating up on yourself for no good reason," continued

Carl. "Talk things out with your kids. Let them know what you've been going through these past few months, then listen to what they've been experiencing. You're very lucky to have a family, Caroline. Don't lose them, OK?"

He stood up and gathered his coat. "I'd better get out of here before Mrs. Ferguson finishes those chocolates. She'll be after me to buy her another box!"

Caroline smiled. She raised her hand in salute, unsure she could say anything without bursting into tears. When the Professor reached the door, though, she called out to him.

"I don't know how to thank you, Carl Atwater. It seems you've saved my life twice today."

Atwater stroked his beard self-consciously. "I just want to be a friend, Cari. It would be a shame to see an intelligent woman like yourself tied to a ghost for the rest of her days."

"I promise you, I won't be, Carl."

The Professor nodded. "I'll hold you to that promise. And you remember: life starts today. Give it a chance, Cari."

He turned and walked out of the room. Caroline watched him go, her vision blurred by salty tears.

Three

December 21

At seven a.m. Caroline was cleared for discharge by a reluctant young resident. Adamantly refusing any further excursions into the realm of diagnostic medicine, she slipped into her clothes, thanked the nursing staff, and fled the halls of the hospital. Her headache was gone and outside of a few stiff muscles, she felt fairly normal again.

She took the underground tunnel connecting the hospital to the nursing dorm and within minutes was passing through the building's green brick lobby. As a concession to her bruised body, Caroline chose the ancient grillwork elevator over the stairs and ascended at a snail's pace to the third floor where her apartment took up the far end of the south wing.

The building had originally been a rectangular three story structure erected in the late 1930's. Classrooms and offices occupied the ground floor and dorm rooms lay east and west of the central staircase on the upper two levels. The west wing of the third floor had been heavily damaged in a fire in the '70's. Faced with declining enrollment in its diploma program and tight economic conditions, St. Anne's had chosen to forego repairs to the building. The hospital had instead sealed off the ravaged area and converted the remaining wing to storage space.

There were still enough rooms available for the dwindling number of students because a south wing had been added in 1952. The school was bursting at the seams with future nurses in those postwar glory days and a spanking new auditorium and up-to-date chemistry lab were considered modern necessities. As in the older building, these filled the first floor while additional dorm rooms were located in the two stories above. The wing was named for the Stromberg family who had donated the majority of the building's funding, and its living area was the exclusive domain of the senior students. With larger rooms, a lounge, kitchen, and laundromat, Stromberg was the wing freshmen dreamed of and juniors lusted after.

It was in Stromberg that Caroline lived. Her apartment at the end of the top floor was 'L' shaped and consisted of two rooms on one side of the corridor joined with a room across the hall. The resultant suite was comfortable and spacious enough for a single person. From her doorway she could look the length of the hallway and easily catch seniors slipping in after curfew. The fact that she seldom did this made her a much appreciated housemother in the eyes of the upperclassmen.

Stromberg was deserted, as was the entire dorm due to the holiday break. Caroline walked through the silent halls planning the day ahead. Once inside her apartment, she headed for the telephone and dialed Martin's home number. Nikki answered on the second ring.

"Hi, Nikki. It's mom. I'm back home -- yes, I'm fine. I wanted you to know that all is well and, if you have it handy, I need Carl Atwater's home phone number."

Within a minute Nikki was back on the line with the information. Caroline reassured her again on the subject of her health, then hung up and called Carl.

"Hi there! It's Caroline Rhodes. Did I wake you?"

"Nope!" Carl responded cheerfully. "I normally rise at five so I can do a little writing before school. By evening my brain is too crammed with trivia for serious work."

Caroline laughed. "I thought trivia was imperative to a historian. It fills in the blanks between important dates."

"That's a low blow, Cari!" Carl feigned an injured tone.. "Now what did I do to deserve that?"

"You gave my chocolates to Mrs. Ferguson. Actually, I'm just kidding, Carl. I called to say I've been thinking about our conversation last night, and..." Caroline hesitated, suddenly embarrassed by the admission she'd intended to make.

"And what, Cari?"

"And I need a car!" she blurted out. "A new one, I mean!"

She heard strangled laughter on the other end of the line and held the phone away from her ear, cursing herself for her cowardice. Why was it so difficult to admit she was indebted to this man?

"Are you done?" she asked in irritation. Carl's chortling was like a knife stabbing at her ego.

"You know what, Cari? You really are something else!"

"What do you mean by that?" Caroline snapped. The chuckling noises had deepened into belly laughs. "It's not all that funny, Carl," she said darkly. "If you're waiting for me to say you'd make a great psychiatrist..."

"Never that!" Carl scoffed. "It satisfies me simply to see you taking my advice. You needn't thank me," he added self-righteously.

"Thank you," Caroline muttered.

"What was that you said? You're speaking so quietly I didn't catch the message."

"Will you help me buy a car, or won't you?" Caroline asked through clenched teeth.

"Sure! It would be fun to check out the new models. We could do it today as soon as you're released from the hospital."

"I've already been discharged. Give me thirty minutes to shower and change, then I'll meet you in front of the dorm."

"Sounds good to me. Oh, and Cari?" The professor allowed himself one last burst of laughter. "Congratulations!"

Once again, words failed her. She hung up without answering.

"A Jeep? Are you sure you want a Jeep?"

Caroline nodded firmly. "I like yours a lot, but I'm sure you're not ready to part with it. Just take me to wherever you bought it and I'll pick one out."

Carl shook his head in disbelief as he pulled out of the nursing dorm driveway. "Don't you think you'd better drive one before you decide to buy a Jeep?'

"Why? It seems to be the perfect car for these country roads. I've made up my mind, Carl, so don't argue with me. Anyway, we have more important things to talk about than Jeeps." She settled back in her seat. "I want to find out who cut my brake lines."

Carl's eyebrows practically shot up off his forehead. "Are you sure?" he asked in surprise. "Yesterday..."

"Was yesterday, Carl. Today I need to know what's going on."

"OK! I was just checking to make sure you meant it."

"I figure it was done the night of the faculty party. The car was braking perfectly that afternoon and then I parked it in the hospital garage. It's dark enough in there to hide any trespasser. Still, there's enough illumination from the overhead lights to see under a car."

Carl nodded, his eyes never leaving the road. "It wouldn't take long to slash the hoses. All our man had to do was get past the guard."

"That wouldn't be difficult. He sits in an office near the entrance where he can watch who's coming and going. But every half hour he patrols the garage in his pickup truck. Our friend could have slipped in then, or he might have entered by the door near the ER parking lot. People use that shortcut all the time."

"Who knows you park there?" Carl asked.

"Anyone with half a brain!" Caroline said scornfully. "There's no other place for employee cars. But you're assuming whoever did it was after me specifically. Couldn't it have been a random act of vandalism?"

"I doubt it. I've lived in this town for a long time, Cari. The Rhineburg version of vandalism is a few high school kids climbing to the top of the water tower to spray paint their team's logo. A beer brawl out at the Decatur Inn is our idea of rampant crime."

Caroline frowned. "I guess you're right. Vandals usually throw eggs at cars, or break their windows. They don't try to kill people by cutting their brake lines!"

"And if it had been vandalism, you'd think other people would have been affected too. Why stop at one car when you have a whole parking lot to work on?"

Caroline sighed. "It makes sense, but Carl, why did he pick on me? I don't have any enemies in Rhineburg. At least I don't think I do."

"Perhaps you represent a threat to someone."

"Me? A threat?" Caroline almost laughed, the implication was so ludicrous, but she sobered when she glanced at the Professor. His mouth was set in a grim line, his eyes devoid of humor. "What are you thinking, Carl?" she demanded.

"Consider this," he responded. "You're present on the psych ward the day of the bombing. Afterwards, you're interviewed by a variety of police types, all of them asking the same question: did you see or hear anything unusual that might point to a suspect? You insist you didn't, but you can't be sure. Perhaps you spotted some small inconsistency, something so insignificant that you've discarded it from memory. You're answering the police truthfully; still, the killer knows better. He's worried you might remember so he decides to get rid of you. What better way than an accident? It's winter after all, and you're unfamiliar with the roads around here. You go into an uncontrolled slide on the ice, hit a tree, and bingo! One less problem to contend with."

"You think it's one and the same person behind both acts." Caroline was shocked more than she wanted to admit. Vandalism she could handle; a deliberate attempt at murder was something else entirely.

"I do," Carl said emphatically. "Look at the way you evaded questions at the faculty party. Your excused yourself by saying the cops had asked you not to discuss the case. Each time you repeated it, you aroused more curiosity. People concluded you were a major witness."

"Martin told me he'd heard a comment to that effect. Actually, I made that line up. I just didn't want to talk about the explosion."

Carl nodded. "I understand that, but still, it added an aura of mystery to you. That phrase may have reached the wrong ears. It's possible you made someone very nervous."

"Are you suggesting the bomber was right there at the party? That he's a faculty member?" The thought upset Caroline. What if he was someone Martin knew? What if her son and Nikki were in danger?

"I would hate to think so, but nothing is impossible. Of course, if you've been using that line around the hospital, it could be someone from St. Anne's. Any way you look at it, this was an inside job."

"Not according to Charles Paine!" Caroline retorted.

Carl wrinkled his nose. "Your Mr. Paine is a fool. He keeps spouting that nonsense about a 'mad bomber' being responsible for the explosion. As if some nut would just walk into town, plant a bomb in a Christmas tree, and walk out again!"

"Better that than having to explain why anybody would hate the hospital enough to blow it up!" A memory pushed forward in Caroline's mind, then slipped away as quickly as it had come. Annoyed, she tried unsuccessfully to force it to the surface.

"Why waste a bomb on a hick town like Rhineburg," Carl continued, "when you can create a big splash blowing up Cook County? No; psychos gravitate to cities like Chicago where they can get the publicity they crave. Whoever did this is no stranger to Rhineburg."

Caroline looked at him quizzically. "How so?" she asked. "Minutes ago you implied Rhineburg is immune to crime."

"Nothing of this proportion has ever occurred here," Carl said. He slowed the Jeep as they passed a sign welcoming them to Rhineburg. "The bombing sent shock waves through this place. People depend on St. Anne's both for health care and for jobs. You don't bite the hand that feeds you, Cari. Beside that, several of the victims were from Rhineburg. The whole town's in mourning."

"Can you say that with absolute certainty?"

"Yes I can! If you'd lived here as long as I have, you'd realize that Rhineburgers are not like..."

"Chicagoans? Thanks a lot, Carl. For your information, I can't recall a hospital back home ever being bombed. We aren't the gangsters you hicks picture us to be."

"I'm sorry, Cari. I didn't mean it like that. It's just that these people are my friends. Somebody has to defend them!"

"I understand," Caroline admitted. "And I apologize for calling you a hick, but you're not thinking straight. You're leading with your heart instead of your head."

Carl refused to answer. After a minute, Caroline sighed. "Ok, Professor, but if our killer isn't a local, then what do you mean by 'no stranger to Rhineburg'? Who else fits the profile?"

"Someone like you," Carl answered calmly.

"Me?! What the hell do you mean by that?"

"Now don't get your dander up, Caroline. I wasn't implying you bombed St. Anne's. I said, someone like you. Someone who knows the town, the campus, and the hospital well enough to get around on his own. Not a long time resident of Rhineburg, but a person with a reasonable knowledge of the place."

"You're really jumping to conclusions, Carl. You hesitate to blame a Rhineburger, but a casual visitor will do nicely!"

Carl shook his head adamantly. "I'm not looking at this crime through rose-colored glasses. I'm convinced there was a purpose behind the bombing, and it wasn't to harm the hospital. I'm equally sure you're an important link in a chain of deadly events."

Caroline disliked being compared to the bomber yet she saw the sense in Carl's analogy. The killer, like herself, might be a newcomer to Rhineburg, or even a relative of someone living in the town. Either way, he had to be familiar with the hospital in general and the psych ward in particular. How else would he have known about the tree? She was about to voice that thought when Carl suddenly pulled over to the curb.

"Here we are," he announced as he switched off the ignition. "Stromberg and Morgan, Purveyors of Fine Automobiles. The sign is pretty fancy, but you'll find the owner a regular down-to-earth guy."

Caroline frowned at the wording on the plate glass window. Her discussion with Carl had pushed all other thoughts aside. She was no longer in a mood to enjoy shopping for a Jeep, but she pulled herself together and climbed out of the car. As long as they were at the dealership, she might as well get it over with.

"Hey there, Professor! How you doin'?"

A tall blond haired man in an open necked blue denim shirt rose from behind a desk and hurried towards them, his hand outstretched. Atwater grasped it firmly.

"Still breathing, James. And business? You're doing well I presume?"

The younger man flashed a grin, his dark blue eyes sparkling mischievously. "Couldn't be better. I sold that red Jag you were so fond of."

"You didn't!" Carl gazed ruefully out a window towards the lot next to the dealership. "You knew I wanted that car!"

James punched him playfully in the stomach. "You couldn't fit in that car and you know it. The Jeep suits you just fine."

Carl shook his head and turned to Caroline. "Cari, this is Mr. James Morgan, car salesman extraordinaire--but certainly no gentleman! Jim, may I introduce Caroline Rhodes, a prospective buyer and a true lady."

"At your service, madam!" James executed a neat bow. A lock of curly hair tumbled over his forehead and he brushed it back with a muscular forearm. "I heard about your accident, Mrs. Rhodes. Glad to see you're OK, but I heard your car's pretty banged up."

"It's a goner," Caroline responded with a smile. She took an immediate liking to the genial salesman with his easy going manner and cheerful grin. "I want to buy a Jeep," she said as James led her to a chair. "Something similar to the Professor's."

She outlined her wishes while James jotted down options and prices. They discussed horsepower, multi-port injection systems, and gas mileage while Carl sat by fuming.

"I can't believe this!" he finally exploded. "You haven't even looked at a car, much less test driven one! How can you buy an automobile that way?"

"I told you," Caroline said sweetly, "I know what I want. I'm sure Mr. Morgan can offer me a suitable deal on a Jeep. By the way, Jim, it doesn't have to be new. I'll settle for a late model used car."

"Oh, really?" James' blue eyes sparkled. "I may have just the thing you're looking for. Come on out back with me." He led them through a side door, turned behind the building, and crossed to a brick garage at the back of the lot. "This just arrived this morning," he said, pointing to a forest green Jeep Cherokee parked in the service bay. "Mayor Schoen brought it in. It belonged to his wife."

Caroline circled the Jeep, examining it for dents and scratches.

"It appears to be in good shape."

"The Mayor takes excellent care of his cars. Brings them in for service right on schedule." James slapped the hood. "This baby is a beaut. Only two years old and fully loaded with options. A reasonable price to boot." He mentioned a number and Caroline's eyebrows rose.

"That's pretty expensive for a used car!"

James shrugged. "Not for one of this caliber. Martha Schoen enjoyed her comfort. When she bought this honey, she ordered every possible luxury installed in it. This Jeep will last you a lifetime. It'll get you wherever you want to go, and you'll go there in style!"

Caroline glanced at Carl who nodded his approval. She circled the Jeep again, then made up her mind. "Let's go in and sign the papers."

Twenty minutes later, they were shaking hands over the deal.

"It's been a pleasure working with you, Mrs. Rhodes. Some of our customers," he grinned at the Professor, "just can't make up their minds when it comes to cars. I only wish my dad was here to meet you."

"So where is your father?" Carl inquired grumpily. "Doesn't he know better than to leave the place in your hands?"

"He's off on a buying trip. I think he's picking up a new Santa suit for you also. The old one's a bit tight, wouldn't you say?"

Carl shook his head in mock sorrow. "What have I done to deserve such treatment? I gave this boy an 'A' in history, Cari, and look how he repays me!"

"That was over twenty years ago, Mrs. Rhodes," Jim said with a smile. "The Professor still won't let me forget it."

Caroline was surprised. Morgan must have been in his early forties, yet he looked much younger than that.

"I want my mechanic to go over the Jeep," he continued. "I'll give you a ring tomorrow to set up a delivery time."

"The sooner, the better, Mr. Morgan. I have lots of Christmas shopping to do!"

"By the way," Carl broke in. "Who bought that Jaguar?"

"Some new doctor from St. Anne's. He didn't even haggle over the price like you would have done. Just walked in, pointed to the car, and said, 'I'll take it'. And," James added gleefully, "he paid for it in cash!"

They stopped for lunch in Rhineburg at a restaurant specializing in German cuisine and home town atmosphere. Carl recommended the potato pancakes and Caroline concurred. She recalled how her mother used to grate potatoes by hand for the family's favorite Lenten dish.

"It was hard work," she told the Professor. Then one year, right after they came out on the market, my brother and I gave her a blender for Christmas. After that, we had potato pancakes twice a week."

Carl took a sip of beer. "You'll love the way they serve them here. Lots of sour cream, and a side dish of hot homemade applesauce. I get hungry just thinking about it!"

"Do you eat here often?"

"Too often, can't you tell?" Carl wiped foam from his mustache with a red checked napkin. "I'll bet James has been coming here also. He's beginning to develop a paunch."

That was like the pot calling the kettle black, thought Caroline. The Professor's girth was three times the size of Jim Morgan's, but she politely refrained from mentioning it. Instead, she inquired into the age of the jovial salesman.

"Jim turned forty-two in March. He looks younger, but then all the Morgans age gracefully. His dad could pass for fifty, although he's closer to retirement than you'd think. And his grandmother -- well, you wouldn't believe she's ninety. She celebrated her birthday last month and she's healthier than both of us combined. Alexsa Stromberg Morgan. Now there's someone you should meet!"

"There must be good genes in that family." Caroline suddenly frowned. "Did you say Stromberg Morgan? That was the name of the dealership, and the dormitory wing I live in is called Stromberg also."

Carl nodded. "Alexsa Stromberg's marriage to Thomas Morgan consolidated not only two of the oldest families in the county, but also most of the wealth in Rhineburg. The Brucks run a close second, but I'd say the Stromberg-Morgan fortune edges out theirs by a million or so."

"Amazing. I'd never guess that kind of wealth existed out here."

"Old money, earned long ago and invested wisely. But that's another story. Let's get back to our present dilemma."

"Right," Caroline replied soberly. "If we're going to solve this mystery, we'd better put our heads together and come up with a plan. I think you're right about the bomber being no stranger to Rhineburg. He had to be aware of what was going on at the hospital or he'd never have sent that tree."

Carl was so pleased with Caroline's decision to help him that he missed the implication of her last words. "You're really going to join forces with me?" he asked.

"It appears I have no other choice," she answered wryly. "I've never been the target of a murderer before, and I don't exactly like the feeling. One thing, though," she added. "Not a word of this to Martin and Nikki. They'd throw a fit if they knew what we were up to."

"Mum's the word," Carl agreed. "I'm not above conspiracy if the cause is worth it. Martin would quit the department if he thought I was putting you in any danger. He's very good at research, so I can't afford to lose him."

The waitress arrived with their lunch and they dug into the food with gusto. Carl was right. The pancakes were delicious and the applesauce laced with cinnamon complimented them perfectly. Maybe it was the clear country air, or the stimulation of a thousand brain cells pondering a mystery, that gave Caroline such a hearty appetite. Whatever the cause, she downed her stack of pancakes in record time.

"Seconds, Professor?" The waitress smiled her question as she gathered up the empty plates. "Or how about a piece of Black Forest cake, baked fresh this morning?"

Carl was clearly torn by the invitation. He looked at Caroline, but she shook her head. "I guess not, Jenni," he said somewhat sadly. "Another time maybe. Right now I'm off to see the Archangels."

"Say 'hi' to the guys for me." The girl tore a sheet from her order pad and handed it to Carl. "Have a nice day, miss." She waved at Caroline and moved on to the next table.

"Everyone but I seems to know the Archangels," Caroline complained. "You said the Bruck brothers provide security for the university, but you never explained their nickname. Why do you insist on calling them the Archangels?"

Carl wrenched his frame out of the wooden chair, stretched his back muscles, and headed for the cashier's desk. "You'll find out soon enough," he called over his shoulder. "I want you to come along and meet them. Nothing gets by the Archangels. If they're willing to share what they know, we may get a better handle on last week's events."

Outside the restaurant, Carl turned and laid a hand on her arm. "There's one thing I have to know before we go any further," he said. "How in the world did a woman who claimed to know nothing about cars suddenly turn into an expert on Jeeps?"

Caroline laughed mischievously. "Do you remember that brother I mentioned earlier? Well, Al's been in love with automobiles since he was five years old. I phoned him this morning and he advised me on exactly what questions to ask."

"I should have known!" Carl shook his head in exasperation. "I'll never again underestimate your abilities."

"That, my friend, would be a big mistake," she responded. "I may not be Superwoman, but, like the Brucks, I run a close second!"

Carl parked next to the campus security building and glanced at his watch. "Perfect!" he exclaimed. "We should be able to catch two of the boys. The shift changes at three and it's 2:45 now."

Caroline followed him into the one story pink stone structure. Fashioned of the same fine grained rhyolite as the surrounding university buildings, it appeared more modern in design than the others. She guessed it was a recent addition to the stately campus, built to accommodate a force that took its business seriously. Inside, the utilitarian nature of the facility was starkly apparent. State-of-the-art computers and television monitors occupied most of the visible space while electronic gadgets sprouted from the walls like acne on a teenager's face. The only evidence of frugality lay in the two scarred and battered desks placed back to back in the center of the room.

Two men stood together near one of the TV monitors, sipping coffee and observing the black and white picture on the small screen. As Caroline and the Professor approached, first one, then the other, turned towards them.

"Afternoon, Carl!" they said simultaneously.

Caroline blinked. Either she was experiencing double vision or she was staring at the most perfect set of identical twins ever born to woman. Deeply tanned with hair the color of stone-ground mustard, the Brucks appeared to be in their early thirties. Both men possessed the physique of a boxer in training.

"Hello, Mike! Gabe!" Carl shook hands with the brothers, then introduced Caroline. "I'd like you to meet Caroline Rhodes, the mother of my research assistant, Martin Rhodes."

"And the new housemom at the nursing dorm," Michael replied.

"And the victim of a suspicious accident," added Gabe.

"Which only goes to show that a witness in a murder case ought to be more careful of her personal safety," concluded his brother.

Dumfounded, Caroline turned to the Professor. "You've talked to them already, right?"

"Oh no!" Carl said, shaking his shaggy head in delight. "I told you these guys are special, Cari. If there's news to be heard, it reaches their ears."

"Most of the time that's true, Professor." Mike pulled up a chair. "Sit down, Mrs. Rhodes. We were hoping you'd come visit us."

"Yeah," agreed Gabe. "Since we're not supposed to be involved in this mess, we couldn't quite go knocking on your door. President Hurst wouldn't approve at all."

"But we've got a lot of questions only you can answer. We hope you'll cooperate with us." Michael flashed a dazzling smile meant to win Caroline's heart. It did exactly that.

"Fire away," she said, totally captivated by the pair. "Anything you want to know..."

"Hold on there a minute," Carl interrupted. "Are you telling me Hurst put a muzzle on you fellows? Why?"

"Not just a muzzle," Michael retorted. "He's practically chained us to our desks! We're to cooperate fully with all police agencies, but investigate on our own? No way!"

"As for why," added Gabe, "that's a mighty interesting question with any number of answers. Unfortunately, the problem is coming up with the right one."

Carl frowned. "Garrison has always been obsessed with the university's public image. He's probably terrified the school will be crucified by the press."

"That'll only happen if the bomber turns out to be a student or a university employee."

"We doubt it could be a student, Mike," Caroline said. "Carl is convinced there are no misfits enrolled at Bruck. And it would take a misfit, a very disturbed young person, to commit this sort of crime."

"We agree it's highly improbable, Mrs. Rhodes, but the police think otherwise. They're going over student records with a fine tooth comb, looking for anyone with a history of trouble."

"They'd like to pin this on a local," Gabe told them. "Either a student terrorist or someone with a grudge against the hospital. They know how difficult it is to catch a madman. Look at the Unabomber. He got away with murder for over a decade."

"If our bomb was planted by an outsider, some psycho craving attention, he's long gone by now. And apparently he was an efficient son of a gun. The cops have few clues to go on," Mike said grimly.

"But you would know if there was a troublemaker at Bruck." Carl had reverted to his argument against the bomber being a student. "Angry kids take out their frustrations in class, or at the dorm. I know for a fact that not one professor pointed a finger at a student when they were questioned by the police. Has there been any gossip on campus?"

"Not a whisper," Mike replied. "But then, most of the kids have gone home for the holidays. I didn't expect to hear anything."

"Which is exactly the point," Caroline stated. "Everyone seems to have forgotten the holidays."

All three men appeared puzzled by the statement. She hurried to explain.

"The bomb was in the artificial tree, wasn't it?"

Gabe nodded. "The trunk was packed with plastic explosives. The tree itself was one of those fancy jobs where the lights plug into a fixture on the trunk. An electric cord extends from the fixture."

"The tree was rigged with an electrically activated detonator," Mike continued. "The bomb exploded when the cord was plugged into the wall outlet. It was very cleverly done."

"Would it take long to assemble this type of bomb?"

Mike shook his head. "Not if you knew what you were doing. And where to get your hands on some plastic explosives."

"Finding it wouldn't be easy, would it?" Caroline persisted.

"You'd be amazed at the amount available for the right price," Gabe said. "The Bureau of Alcohol, Tobacco, and Firearms recovers loads of stolen military explosives every year. There's one called Composition C-4. A half pound of that would level this building."

"You won't find it floating around Rhineburg. But it's definitely on the market," added Mike. "Go to any large city and you can connect with a source. It might take time and effort..."

"But time is precisely what the bomber didn't have!" Caroline insisted. "The damaged tree was found only three days before the explosion!"

"What are you talking about, Cari?" Carl asked sharply. "What damaged tree?"

Caroline realized the men had been caught totally off guard. Evidently they hadn't heard about the mice and the chewed up tree. She wondered if, like herself, the other ward personnel had failed to mention this bit of information to the FBI.

"Every unit has its own Christmas decorations stored down in the hospital basement," she began. "In December the maintenance men deliver the boxes to the various units, and then the staff does the decorating. This year the psych nurses got off to a slow start because the rec room was being painted. I think it was December 11th when they finally unpacked their tree. What they found caused a minor commotion on the ward. Rodents had chewed holes in the box and gnawed whole chunks out of the tree trunk. It was impossible to keep the branches in place."

"They needed a new tree," Carl said slowly.

Caroline nodded. "And the Administration refused to pay for another one. They claimed the unit's budget was stretched to the limit."

"Cheapskates!" Gabe muttered. "I'll bet the nurses were up in arms."

"Of course they were. Think how dreary it would have been for the patients without some Christmas cheer. The nurses immediately began collecting for a new tree. Their little disaster was no secret at St. Anne's. A lot of hospital employees dropped by the unit to donate to the cause."

"But the psych staff never did buy a tree, did they?"

"No, Mike, they didn't have to. Three days after the discovery of the damage, a huge package arrived on the ward. It contained the most beautiful artificial tree I've ever seen."

"No sender's name, though. No return address."

"Well, Carl, everyone just assumed some doctor had donated it anonymously. The staff was so thrilled they put it together that very morning. And you know what happened after it was decorated by the patients."

Michael strolled over to the coffee machine and poured four mugs of the thick brew.

"So our killer had only three days to set his plan in motion," he said as he handed a cup to each of them. "And if the ruined tree was unpacked on December 11th, our students are home free."

"Of course!" Carl exclaimed. "Semester break started that day. Most of the kids were leaving town!"

"I suppose you could try to tie the bombing to a local student," Caroline suggested. "But that's pretty far fetched. It seems a more likely suspect can be found inside the walls of St. Anne's."

"I agree." Gabe sipped his coffee thoughtfully. "The bomber had to have inside knowledge of the situation on the ward. It was the only way he could guarantee the rigged tree would be assembled."

"Three days isn't much time to build a bomb unless you're an expert with a ready source of explosives. Tell me, Mrs. Rhodes, do the FBI know about the ruined tree? They're in charge of this case since the the bomb was sent by mail."

"Was it posted in Rhineburg?" Carl asked Michael.

He shook his head. "That's one of the few things they're sure of. The package originated in Chicago." He turned to Caroline. "I still need to know if you've told the authorities about this. The time element changes everything."

Caroline shrugged. "I never even thought of it until today. As for the others who were questioned, I can't say. I haven't seen much of them since the explosion, and that day we were all in a state of shock."

"I wonder if that's why he tried to kill you, Cari," Carl said suddenly. He turned to the Bruck brothers. "I'm convinced the bomber was responsible for Caroline's accident. She's somehow a threat to him, and it may be because she's aware of the time frame involved."

"I doubt it," Mike responded. He added two teaspoons of sugar to his coffee, then flashed another of his brilliant smiles in Caroline's direction. "I actually hate coffee, but they won't let us install a pop machine in here. Sugar helps to hide the taste."

Caroline laughed. Michael seemed to know instinctively how to put one at ease. No wonder he was good with the students, she thought; he avoided the heavy-handed approach to authority.

"Why do you say you doubt it?" Carl was still concentrating on the attack on Caroline.

"Because Mrs. Rhodes isn't the only person who knows about this," Michael replied reasonably. "Everyone working on that ward is aware that only three days elapsed between finding the ruined tree and receiving the rigged one. Eventually, someone beside your friend will remember and tell the police."

"He would have to kill all of us to keep it a secret."

"That's true," Gabe agreed. "Our man isn't worried about this particular piece of information. It may narrow the field of suspects, but only as far as the students are concerned. It still leaves almost everyone at St. Anne's open for questioning."

"And we'll make sure the FBI are informed. They'll probably want to talk to you again, Mrs. Rhodes," added Mike.

"We're back to square one," Carl grumbled. "Cari must know something, but I'll be damned if I can figure out what it is!"

"We agree with the Professor, Mrs. Rhodes. What happened to you yesterday was no accident. I suggest you jog your memory a little bit harder. Until you come up with whatever it is you've forgotten, you're in grave danger of another attempt on your life."

Caroline shivered involuntarily. Michael's tone was gentle, but his words were deadly serious. She was suddenly very afraid.

That evening Caroline had dinner with Martin and Nikki in their apartment above Kelly's Hardware Store. The building faced the town square on Wilhelm Street, and while Nikki busied herself in the kitchen, Caroline and her son admired the panorama below.

"I'm beginning to understand why you love this place," she told him. "You have a great view of the square."

"It is pretty, isn't it?"

"'Pretty' isn't the word! Between all that snow and those little lights sparkling in the trees, it resembles a winter fairyland."

"Nikki says it reminds her of a picture by Currier and Ives."

"An apt description. I was thinking more along the lines of 'It's A Wonderful Life'. Any minute now I expect to see Jimmy Stewart come strolling through the door!"

The words were hardly out of her mouth when the bell rang. Martin grinned mischievously. "Well, mother," he said in his best imitation of the famous actor. "Sounds like another angel got his wings!" He opened the door with a flourish.

"Professor Atwater!"

"Hello, Marty. I hope I'm not disturbing you." Carl staggered in, his arms piled with books which he transferred to a bewildered Martin. "Can't you find a first floor apartment? Those stairs will be the death of me yet."

"Hi, Carl!" Caroline relieved her son of part of the load. She glanced at the top title. "What are these? Reference books?"

The Professor brushed past Martin. "I didn't expect to find you here. You were all tuckered out when I dropped you at the dorm."

"I napped," she said with a smile. "I'm feeling much better."

"Would anyone like to fill me in on what's happening?" Martin grumbled. He had a pretty good idea what the books meant and he didn't like it one bit. As for why the Professor had been out with his mother, he hadn't a clue.

"Oh! I'm sorry, Martin," Carl apologized. "My publisher called this afternoon. He needs the first draft of my new book by January fourth. Unfortunately, there are a few facts that still need to be referenced, but I figured you could do it between now and then." He pulled a folded sheet of paper from his pocket and handed it to Martin. "Mostly they're minor details, but important nonetheless. It wouldn't do to have mistakes show up in print."

Martin looked at the list and groaned. "How many 'details' are we talking about? I had kind of hoped to relax a bit over the holidays."

"It won't take you long," Atwater assured him. "A few hours a day and you'll be done in no time."

Martin glowered at the Professor but held his tongue. It sure wouldn't do to antagonize his boss; he'd only come up with a longer list of demands. "I think I'll check if dinner's ready," he said glumly and took himself off to find his wife.

Carl winked at Caroline. "That should keep him out of our hair for awhile. He'll be so busy he'll never notice we're investigating the bombing."

"Oh, Carl! That's cruel!" Caroline tried not to smile but she couldn't hide the amusement in her voice. "But I must tell you, Nikki will not be pleased with this."

At that very moment the subject of her warning came flying out of the kitchen, a bowl of greens clutched to her chest.

"What's all this about Martin working during the holidays?" The salad bobbed in the air as Nikki gestured her exasperation with both hands. "We planned to spend time with mom since it's her first Christmas in Rhineburg! Now what'll we do?"

Lettuce leaves and shredded carrots sailed past Nikki's shoulder and floated to the carpet. Caroline decided the girl was perilously close to dumping the entire bowl on Carl's head.

"I think that's sufficiently tossed, dear!"

She rescued the salad bowl and placed it on the table. From the corner of her eye she saw her daughter-in-law standing hands on hips glaring at a stammering Professor Atwater. It was definitely time to intervene.

"I for one am absolutely famished! Don't you think that lasagna is done by now?" She propelled Nikki towards the kitchen, throwing an 'I-told-you-so' look at Carl before adding, "I'm sure the Professor will reconsider his decision after a good hot meal."

Thus forced into staying for dinner, Carl did his best to mollify his hostess. Caroline aided and abetted him by refilling Nikki's wine glass each time she took a sip. Before long, Martin's wife grew mellow with food and drink.

"I suppose it won't be all that bad," she mused. "We could go shopping while Marty works on the book."

"There goes the bank balance," Marty grumbled. He was not so easy a nut to crack.

"Cheer up, lad!" Carl said heartily. "Think of the extra money you'll make on this."

Martin laid down his fork and stared at the Professor. "You're going to pay me for my time?"

"Of course!" the Professor bellowed. "Didn't I mention that earlier? I could hardly expect you to work during semester break without compensation!"

The atmosphere lightened considerably. Between December's tuition payment and Christmas presents, Martin and Nikki's bank account had taken a beating. This unexpected windfall would keep the hounds at bay for a while longer, and the two of them practically fell over each other trying to make amends for their earlier behavior.

Carl waved off their apologies. "Enough already! Let's talk about something else."

Caroline happily complied by introducing the subject of her new car. The purchase came as a surprise to the younger couple and they listened avidly as she touted the many features of the Jeep.

"I got a very good deal," she said. "This car was previously owned by Martha Schoen, the mayor's wife."

"She was killed in the explosion!" Marty exclaimed. "I read all about her burial yesterday."

Caroline's eyebrows rose. "Seems like her husband wasted no time in disposing of her belongings."

"Well, the two of them weren't exactly on friendly terms. At least not lately," confided Martin.

"Really?"

"You probably didn't hear about it, mom," Nikki said. "I think it all started before you arrived in Rhineburg."

"It really began years ago," Carl reminded them. "It only came to a head in late summer."

Caroline was intrigued. "So what happened?"

"Mrs. Schoen attacked the mayor right in the middle of a city council meeting! That's why he had her committed to St. Anne's."

"Oh, Marty! It was hardly an attack!" Nikki grinned at her husband. "Now tell your mother the truth."

Martin hovered somewhere between good taste and accurate reporting before falling victim to Nikki's affectionate chiding. He turned to Caroline, the shadow of a smile softening his all too proper expression. "Actually," he admitted, "she pelted him with a couple of cream pies!"

"Right before a packed audience," Carl added. "The local rag captured the event for posterity and plastered the picture smack dab on the front page. Teddy Schoen was a sight to behold with all that whipped cream on his face."

"And the headline read, 'Coco-Nut Creams Mayor'!" exclaimed Nikki. "You can guess what kind of pies they were, can't you?"

Caroline bubbled over with laughter. She saw the entire incident in her imagination and couldn't help but admire a woman with guts enough to attempt what Martha Schoen had done. "Did the good mayor deserve such a shellacking, or had Mrs. Schoen gone over the edge?"

"A bit of both," Marty replied.

"Oh, come on! You know he got exactly what was coming to him! If you ever paraded around with another woman on your arm, I might do more than throw a few pies at you!"

Martin back pedaled a bit, but managed to tease his wife at the same time. "There are those who say Martha Schoen has always been weird, Nikki, but of course you're right. If I ever act like the abominable Teddy Schoen, you have full permission to shoot me where it hurts the most."

"Let's hope it never comes to that!" Nikki remarked dryly.

"I take it the mayor is a lady's man."

"I've known Teddy for years. He's a good business man and an excellent mayor for Rhineburg. Unfortunately, his proclivity for philandering wrecked havoc with his marriage and alienated a good many female voters. Martha was only reacting to his latest adventures in the Land of Lust when she heaved those pies at him." Carl tugged at his beard, his great white eyebrows drawn together in concentration. "You know, her death may prove beneficial to the mayor."

"How so?" Caroline asked.

"For one thing, almost all the women in town were on Martha's side at the time of the council meeting incident. They became even more sympathetic towards her after Teddy had her committed. Teddy usually doesn't make political mistakes, but he did that time. He was running for re-election and he almost lost when ninety-nine percent of the women voted against him. It was the closest race of his life."

"He won't have to worry about her effect on the next election, will he?"

"No, Caroline, he won't," Carl agreed. "Martha was always an embarrassment to his political aspirations. She had a passion for oddball movements. Once she led a campaign to protect the rights of the ring-tailed raccoon. She wanted to have it named the official town animal because she thought the little critters were so adorable!"

"Another time she spearheaded a drive to outlaw all tattoos in Rhineburg. That was back when I was a junior at Bruck," Martin said. "Boy! Did the students get riled over that one!"

"Nobody, least of all Teddy, knew what she'd do next," added Carl. "I always thought her antics were meant to keep her husband in line. As long as he was faithful to her, she behaved herself, but if she got wind of an affair in progress, she was off to the races. Politically speaking, Teddy's better off without her."

"Why didn't they just divorce?" Caroline asked.

Atwater shrugged. "Believe it or not, Martha truly loved Teddy. As for the mayor, I'd say he loved Martha's money. She inherited a considerable holding in the quarry outside of Rhineburg when her father died. The Schoen wealth was settled in Martha, not Teddy, although no one would have guessed it. Teddy made all the business decisions for his wife. He not only kept her fortune secure, he saw that it grew."

"So Martha Schoen was a wealthy woman," Caroline mused. "I suppose the mayor was the chief beneficiary of her will."

Carl shrugged "I'd imagine so. Teddy's often talked of running for county commisioner. Now that he has access to all that money, he's a shoo-in for the party nomination."

"And he'll make a nice profit from the re-hab of the high school stadium," Nikki added. "He could never have negotiated a deal with the college while Martha was alive, but all that's changed too."

All heads turned to Nikki. She obviously knew something none of the others had heard.

"Who told you that?" her husband inquired.

"I have my sources!" Nikki responded archly. She gave Martin a wink, then relented when she saw the expression on his face. "Oh, all right! I'll confess if I must. I had a hair cut yesterday at the Dip-N-Do. The place was overflowing with the pre-Christmas crowd and the subject up for discussion was, of course, the bombing at St. Anne's. Somebody mentioned Mrs. Schoen's funeral and that got the ball rolling. First there was some speculation over who the mayor was currently fooling around with. Once that topic was exhausted, the issue of the inheritance came up. According to a woman who teaches at the high school, Martha Schoen attended a PTA meeting back in September. She made a speech opposing renovation of the stadium based on the cost, saying that the money could be better spent on educational needs within the school. A lot of people agreed with her, and she ended up pledging that the quarry would never be a party to any new stadium construction as long as she was the major stockholder in the company."

"I'll bet President Hurst was boiling mad when he heard the news!"

"Apparently the mayor wasn't too pleased either, Professor," Nikki replied. "One of the hairdressers pointed out that he was all for the improvements since the quarry, and he himself indirectly, would make a bundle on the deal. With Martha dead, the mayor is free of his chief opposition to the plan. He'll push it through the city council and you'll see: by next September Rhineburg will have a spanking new pink football stadium."

"We're talking big money here," Caroline commented. She glanced at Carl to see if he was thinking the same thing she was. Money had always been a motive for murder. What if the mayor himself was behind the bombing? Or the mayor and President Hurst together? Now that was a blood curdling thought!
"What else have you heard over at the beauty shop, Nikki? Any ideas on who the bomber is?"

"Oh, come on, mother!" Martin complained. "You can't be serious!"

"I'm very serious, Marty. A beauty salon is a storehouse of knowledge. If you want to know what's happening in a town, that's the place to go."

"You've got to be kidding! The Dip-N-Do is nothing but a hothouse of gossip. The beaticians probably vote each morning on a new 'Victim of the Day', some unlucky soul whose life they can dissect between haircuts!"

Caroline shrugged. "Seems fair to me. An hour under the dryer can be deadly boring without someone to talk about!"

That was too much for Martin. He suggested they continue the discussion some other time, then stood up and started gathering plates from the table. Caroline winked at an amused Nikki before asking Carl for a lift back to the dorm. Within minutes the two of them were bundled into their coats and headed out the door.

"You enjoy goading your son, don't you?"

The remark astonished Caroline and she glanced over at the Professor to see if he was serious. Carl had his eyes on the road but his lips were twitching in suppressed mirth.

"Martin tends to be pompous at times. When he treats me like the town idiot, I consider it my duty to take him down a notch or two."

"He's a bright young man."

"And he knows it!" Caroline retorted. "Don't get me wrong, Carl. I thank God my son is intelligent, but occasionally he forgets that not all knowledge resides in the university setting. Nikki's hairdresser probably has a greater appreciation of human nature than many of your colleagues at Bruck. I wouldn't take what she says lightly."

"I must confess I never imagined Teddy Schoen as a murderer before tonight. He certainly had a lot to gain from his wife's death, though."

"I'd say so. Not only will he inherit her money, but he may also end up with a juicy political job." Caroline frowned. "I wonder who gained from the deaths of the other bombing victims?"

Carl swung off the highway and took the road leading to Bruck.

"I'll bet the FBI is asking that same question."

"I suppose so," Caroline agreed. "But they may be looking for answers in the wrong places. I doubt their agents have visited Rhineburg's beauty parlors."

"I see what you mean," Carl said slowly. "There's a gold mine of information out there, but if you're not plugged into the local grapevine, you might overlook an important clue."

"Exactly. The authorities have so much ground to cover that they'll never have time to check out all the gossip flying around town."

"But we could do it!" Carl pulled up in front of the dormitory and shifted into park. He turned in his seat to face Caroline. "If you're still committed to finding the killer, that is."

"I wish you'd believe me when I say I mean to go through with this. I won't pretend I'm not afraid, especially after Michael Bruck's warning this afternoon, but I refuse to be a sitting duck for some murderer."

Carl grinned broadly. "That's my girl, Cari! I knew you had it in you! Now let's decide where to start this investigation."

Caroline had firm ideas on that subject. "We don't have the resources of the FBI, so it's useless to copy what they're doing. Let's leave the physical evidence to their lab people. We can rely on the Archangels to keep tabs on any progress in that direction."

"Agreed."

"Since we've discounted the 'mad bomber' theory, we have to assume there was a motive for the murders. As far as I can see, there are only two. First, someone may be out to ruin St. Anne's. An explosion not only destroys property, but it also frightens off people. The hospital census has fallen considerably since the bombing. Folks are driving south to Newberry for everything but emergency care."

"I didn't know that," Carl responded. "Has it reached the crisis point yet?"

Caroline shook her head. "No, but it will if this keeps up much longer. My shifts have been cancelled twice since the explosion. The hospital doesn't need floaters when their patient-nurse ratio is four to one."

"I still find it hard to believe St. Anne's was the real target. It just doesn't make sense to me."

Caroline didn't argue with him. Privately, she thought anything was possible, but she knew Carl's thoughts on the issue. She wasn't going to sway him with logic.

"Of course, the motive may be a personal one. The murderer could have been out to kill someone on that ward. And whether or not he accomplished his mission is still unknown."

"Seven people died that day, Cari. Certainly his plan was a success!"

"Not necessarily," Caroline said. "He didn't manage to destroy the entire ward. Only the rec room was damaged, so maybe the person he was after escaped."

Carl shifted uncomfortably. "You're saying the bomber may strike again."

"If needs be. We can't be sure of anything, Carl, but I believe our best chance of uncovering the killer lies in investigating the people who were on the ward that day. We should work on the premise that someone wants one of them dead, and then look for the reason why."

Carl thought about it for a moment, then nodded. "It seems the most sensible approach to take. Let's concentrate on the victims first. We can tackle the survivors later."

"I'll speak to Jane Gardner, the unit manager. She may be able to help us with background information."

"And I'll put out some feelers in town. I'm more or less of a fixture in Rhineburg, so folks are apt to be open with me."

They left it at that. Caroline promised to call Carl if she learned anything, and he agreed to do the same. Neither of them mentioned the danger they were courting, but when the Professor pulled away from the dorm, Caroline watched him go with a certain sense of dread. Two nights ago she had sneered at his Holmesian attempts, and now here she was, an active participant in the game. It was a contest without rules where someone was playing for keeps; it scared her to think they might easily lose. She shivered as she unlocked the lobby door. When it closed behind her, she made doubly sure the deadbolt was pushed home.

FOUR

December 22

1 a.m. Caroline looked at the clock and groaned. Exhausted and still sore from the accident, she'd gone to bed only minutes after arriving home, sleeping soundly until midnight when she awoke with a start from yet another disturbing nightmare. This time she'd been roving a deserted hospital, searching aimlessly for her coworkers and calling their names. Walking down one corridor after another, she'd finally come to a dead end at a door marked 'Recreation'. She'd flung open the door and chunks of plaster and stone had come tumbling from the room. They kept spilling into the corridor, threatening to bury her as she stood rooted to the floor. She'd panicked, unable to drag herself from under the growing pile of debris, and that's when she saw the Buick racing towards her from the other end of the hallway. It was almost upon her when she woke up screaming.

Wrapping herself in a terry-cloth robe, Caroline headed for the apartment's tiny kitchen where she poured two fingers of creme de menthe into a glass, added a dash of cold milk, and downed it in two gulps. Now, an hour later, she sat staring out the bedroom window, sipping slowly on a second drink. She'd stopped shivering, but her mind raced with memories of the explosion at St. Anne's.

She could recall every detail of that day. It had begun at 6:55 a.m. when she'd arrived on the psychiatric ward.

"Hey, Caroline! Glad to see you again!" The unit manager, Jane Gardner, was an athletic looking young woman with short chestnut hair cut in a casual style. She was quick to smile and undisturbed by the emotional hotbed in which she worked. "You didn't seem enthralled with us the last time you were here, so I was surprised when Samantha called from the staffing office with your name."

Caroline blushed. "I confess this isn't my favorite place to work, but when you commit to the float pool, you go where you're needed." Actually, Caroline had almost turned the assignment down. Her first tour of duty on the ward had been a disaster. She'd been tense with the patients, whose problems she related to, and wary of the doctors, whose methods she abhorred. It was only after she'd completed the shift that she realized the source of her discomfort. 'There but for the grace of God go I!' she'd thought, and decided then and there she couldn't risk another day on the unit. But when Sam had called, practically begging her to fill in for an absent nurse, Caroline relented and agreed to work.

"Well, we appreciate your help. We're shorthanded with two nurses out sick. I promise we'll give you the easier patients."

Caroline smiled her thanks, then followed Jane into the lounge where the night shift had started report. The evening had been uneventful and Caroline hoped her eight hours would be equally quiet.

Breakfast had been cleared away and morning exercises begun when the intercom crackled into life. Caroline listened to the general summons for all staff to report to the desk.

"What's up?" she asked as she approached the others.

"Look what just arrived!" one of the RNs said excitedly. She pointed to a large rectangular box leaning against the desk. "Someone's sent us a tree! We're going to have one after all!"

Seeing the blank look on Caroline's face, the other nurse hurried to explain about the damage the mice had done to the unit's decorations.

"Our cheapskate Administrator refused to buy us a new one. He said it wasn't in our budget!"

"But some kind soul's donated this," Jane gloated. "I can't find any message so I assume one of our docs is playing Santa Claus. Let's put it up this morning, then the patients can decorate it this afternoon."

"We really should have a party," an orderly suggested. "I've got a great recipe for punch."

"Sure you do!" Jane retorted. "One-fourth lemonade and three-fourths Jack Daniels!"

"We could invite Charles Paine," another nurse joked. "I say we slip a little arsenic in his drink and be done with him!"

The discussion dissolved into a series of ribald remarks aimed at the unpopular administrator. Jane had some difficulty regaining control.

"OK, everybody. Let's get back to the subject of a party. I think it's a great idea and I don't see why we couldn't take the money we collected and spend it on a cake and ice cream now that we have a Christmas tree."

The plan was immediately approved and Caroline chosen to do the staff's shopping.

"If you call Meyer's Bakery, I'm sure they'll whip up some kind of cake by one o'clock," Jane said. "And we'll need candy and cookies and maybe some cider too. Let me go get the money, Caroline, and you others divvy up her patients."

Cash in hand, Caroline happily set off for Rhineburg. Not only was she relieved to be off the ward, but she also appreciated what the staff was doing. The patients would benefit from the party.

The roads were clear and she made it to town in just under ten minutes. Her first stop was Pregenzer's, the local grocery store, where she picked up ice cream, cider, and cinnamon sticks. A quick trip next door to the Fudge Shoppe netted her two pounds of chocolate creams. Then it was on to Meyer's Bakery. The owner smiled broadly as she entered the shop.

"Ah, Mrs. Rhodes! I have just finished the last flower." The old baker held up the sheet cake for Caroline to examine. "You will agree it is a work of art?"

"It's perfect, Mr. Meyer!" she exclaimed, and it was. Shiny red poinsettias filled the corners, their green leaves pointing to the center of the cake. Tiny chocolate reindeer strutted across the top pulling a miniature Santa in an ebony sleigh. Below them the words 'Merry

Christmas' were inscribed in a paler shade of red on the white buttercreme frosting. Caroline grinned like a kid in a candy shop; it was exactly what she'd ordered.

She purchased five pounds of cookies before leaving the bakery, then nosed the Buick out of its parking spot and headed back towards the hospital. Once outside of town, she accelerated past the speed limit.

'What the hell,' she thought as the speedometer inched towards sixty. 'If I get a ticket, at least it will be for a good cause.'

Caroline rinsed the last dregs of creme-de-menthe down the sink and wandered back to the bedroom. She still wasn't sleepy and memories of the explosion continued to plague her. So far she hadn't remembered anything unusual that would account for the attempt on her life. Disgruntled at her lack of progress, she returned to the window and gazed up at the stars glistening above Bruck Green. Their number and brilliance never failed to amaze her. In Chicago they had competed with the city lights and only the brightest stars could be seen summer or winter. Ed had loved the stars. He'd tried to teach her the names of the constellations, pointing out Orion the Hunter and Lyra spread across the northern skies. She remembered Vega, the brightest of the night stars, but the rest had been lost on her. It wasn't that she didn't appreciate them -- was there a soul alive who hadn't at sometime gazed in wonder at the Milky Way? -- but she rebelled at placing them in tidy little groups. The supreme need for order in man's life impelled him to organize everything he saw, to name it as if it belonged to him. The stars belonged to no one. She preferred it that way, claiming no other link to the heavens than a common Creator.

Thinking of Ed had always caused pain in the past. Tonight as she stared up at the stars she felt only a fondness for his memory. Perhaps she'd turned a corner in her life when she met Carl Atwater. His objectivity allowed him to be brutally honest, whereas her family and friends had been all too ready to coddle her. She'd needed a good kick in the butt to jump start her back into life. Figuratively speaking, Carl had done exactly that with his blunt assessment of her behavior. Now it was her turn to take the bull by the horns and move on.

With that thought in mind, Caroline picked up the list of names she and Carl had drawn up. The seven victims of the explosion were virtual strangers to her, still she had access to someone who was familiar with all of them. Jane Gardner, the unit manager, would of necessity know the histories of the six patients. Hopefully, she could also tell Caroline something about the student nurse who'd been killed.

The youth of the last victim was particularly disturbing to her. The girl was barely out of her teens and now she was dead, murdered by someone who probably didn't even know her name. Caroline recalled she'd been impressed by the young woman as she watched her move about the ward that fateful day. She'd been in the rec room when Caroline entered it around one-thirty.

"The food's ready," she'd told Marina, one of the regular ward staff nurses. "It's set up on carts in the kitchen."

"Thank goodness! Things are getting out of control in here." Marina nodded towards the people clustered around the tree. "They've been at each other's throats ever since they started decorating the damned tree."

"Getting their feelings out in the open?" Caroline joked. "Where are the rest of the patients?"

"They'll all show up when the cake is served. These are the only ones we could coerce into decorating. Of course, Mr. Canty was no help at all. He just bounces around on that couch and makes up nutty rhymes that aggravate the others. He really is out of it! But then," Marina remarked with a grin, "as the Cheshire Cat said, we're all mad here!" She motioned to the tree. "Looks pretty good, doesn't it?"

Caroline surveyed the splendid balsam in the corner. It was a graceful tree, perfectly proportioned for the size of the room.

"I think it's great! Although," she said as she cocked her head to one side, "that angel on top is a bit crooked."

Marina laid a restraining hand on Caroline's arm. "Please don't mention it to Martha Schoen! She'll bite your head off if you criticize her masterpiece."

Caroline laughed. "I'll watch my tongue!" she replied before drawing Marina's attention to Gail Garvy. "Our student is doing a good job, don't you think?" She watched as the young woman deftly interposed herself between two male patients who were glaring at each other. The girl said something to one of the men and his reply brought a gasp from a matronly woman standing near the tree.

"Now what?" Marina grumbled. An argument had erupted over who was to light the tree. Voices were raised, then someone called out a name and Gail moved away from the group. She walked towards a solitary figure standing near the fake fireplace.

Caroline frowned. The student was trying to coax a thin gray haired man into joining the group around the tree. It was obvious he was reluctant to go with her. He raised a closed fist, bringing it close to the young nurse's face. Caroline took a step forward but the man made no attempt to hit Gail. Instead, he uncurled first his index finger, then one by one the others. The gesture reminded Caroline of children counting on their hands and she watched with growing interest when the man leaned forward to whisper something in Gail's ear. Unfortunately, she was too far away to catch the words.

Marina nudged her on the arm. "Let's go get the goodies."

"Hum? Oh, sure. I'll be with you in just a minute." Caroline continued to observe the scene unfolding before her. The patients were now gathering around the Christmas tree. Gail Garvy began to sing 'Silent Night' and slowly the others joined in. The man Gail had guided across the room stood forlornly by her side. He said nothing when she placed the tree's electrical cord in his hand.

'Time to go,' Caroline decided and she turned to leave, promptly colliding with a man who was walking briskly towards the doorway.

"Sorry!" she apologized. "Didn't mean to run you down."

The patient glared at her but strode out of the room without a word. Caroline followed a few steps behind. The corridor was empty and the man headed for the exit, then hesitated as if he knew he was being watched. He made a sudden about face and slipped into a classroom across the hall.

"That's right, my friend," she muttered. "There'll be no patients escaping the ward today!"

"Caroline? Are you coming?" Marina wheeled a cart out of the tiny area that served as a kitchen for the staff. She pushed it in the direction of the rec room. "Once we're set up in there..."

It was then that the explosion occurred. The noise of the bomb was deafening and Caroline instinctively covered her ears and crouched down against the wall. She felt it shake as debris erupted from the rec room. Chunks of plaster flew across the corridor, slamming into the chart desk and careening off the ceiling. Thick gray dust filled the air. It coated Caroline's lungs and she fought for breath in the suddenly darkened hallway. Burying her face in her scrub shirt, she crawled backwards until her foot touched an open doorway. She twisted around and fell into the room, then struggled to her feet, coughing convulsively. It took several seconds before her lungs cleared and she was able to breathe easily again. By then she could hear shouts coming from the hallway. Someone was screaming in pain and fright. The sound roused her nursing instincts and she plunged back into the corridor. The dust was already beginning to settle. Caroline could see shapes beyond the desk area moving towards the elevator. She heard Jane shouting orders to her nurses as they hustled patients to safety, then suddenly the unit manager was by her side.

"Marina's hurt!" she yelled. "Help me!"

Caroline and Jane hurried back towards the ruined rec room. Marina lay on the floor, conscious but groaning in pain. Her left leg was twisted at an unnatural angle and blood ran from a ugly gash above her knee. Together, the two nurses lifted her to her good foot and half dragged, half carried her down the hall. Staff from the floor below were already arriving to help. They assisted Marina into the elevator, leaving Jane and Caroline free to return to the rec room. What they saw there caused them to retreat in horror.

"Are you two OK?"

The first firemen to reach the hospital were emerging from the elevator. One of them had seen the two women huddled together in the corridor, the older one comforting the younger. Now, standing over them in the silence of the deserted psych ward, he repeated his question.

"Are you all right? Is there anyone left down there?"

Caroline continued to hold the sobbing Jane in her arms. She looked up into the eyes of their rescuer and slowly shook her head.

"Not alive," she murmured. "Not alive."

Caroline crawled back into bed at 2 a.m. and willed herself to sleep. Recalling the explosion hadn't helped one bit. She was still as puzzled as ever over the attempt on her life. She set the alarm for seven, and when it rang, she awoke with a fierce headache.

Aspirin was useless. What Caroline needed was eight hours of undisturbed sleep, but she'd made plans for the day and refused to change them. She made a phone call, then showered, dressed, and left the apartment by 7:45. Minutes later she entered the hospital cafeteria where she found Jane Gardner waiting at a table.

"Sorry to call so early," Caroline said as she slid into a chair. "But the only time I can catch you is over breakfast."

Jane grinned. "My life is not my own any more. Since the bombing, I seem to spend more time with the police than with my staff." She took a sip of coffee. "Glad to see you're in one piece. I heard about your accident."

"It was no accident," Caroline responded soberly. She gave the other nurse an edited version of the past days' events, omitting only

Carl's part in them. It wouldn't do to give the hospital grapevine any more business, she reasoned. Jane listened silently, her chin cupped in one hand, her brows furrowed, while Caroline explained her theory of the killer's familiarity with the hospital and the victims.

"You're playing with fire, you know. If your theory is correct!"

Caroline shrugged. "Somebody's out to kill me, Jane, and I don't know why. I figure I better do something about it."

Jane nodded but made no comment.

"I need your help, Jane," Caroline continued. "You knew those patients better than anyone on the unit. If the motive for the bombing lies with one of them, you could help me discover it."

"Clients," Jane murmured absently.

Caroline frowned. "What did you say?"

"Clients!" Jane repeated heatedly. "We don't call them patients any longer. They're known as clients!"

"Sounds very businesslike."

"Why shouldn't it? Medicine has become big business. You'd better use correct terminology if you want to be in sync with the times."

"Like 'unit manager' instead of 'head nurse'?"

"You've got it!" Jane exclaimed. "We're big on techno-talk here since Charles Paine became Administrator. Before his arrival nurses were allowed to concentrate on patient care. Now we have to endure endless policy meetings and quality improvement seminars."

"If it's any consolation to you," Caroline said mildly, "the same thing is happening all across the country. Some people call it 'progress'."

"Bull! Don't get me started, Caroline!" Jane crushed her empty coffee cup angrily. "Let me tell you something. You've reached your own conclusions concerning the explosion, but I have a very different theory. I think somebody got sick and tired of being manipulated by the bigwigs in this joint. I'll bet that bomb was planted as revenge for all the havoc wrought by Charles Paine."

Caroline was taken aback. "I don't know much about the new

Administrator," she said. "He may be a villain to some..."

"Oh, he is!" Jane responded vehemently. "He's a tightfisted businessman brought in by the Board to boost St. Anne's financial standing. He's done that all right, but at the expense of every worker in this hospital. He's cut the number of staff so drastically that we can hardly handle the patient load any more. People are overworked to the point of exhaustion. As a result, patient care has suffered."

Caroline frowned. She hadn't anticipated this twist to the conversation. Still, Jane's view of the situation at St. Anne's merited attention. If the unit manager had vented her spleen to the authorities, it was no wonder the investigation was going so slowly. The FBI was being forced to search for a malcontent among the hospital employees.

"Tell me more about Charles Paine. Exactly what has he done to make everyone so angry?"

Jane settled back in her chair and stared at the ceiling. "Number one, he took the place of a very popular administrator. Sister Ambrose was a woman who cared about people first and finances second. That's not to say she wasn't sharp when it came to money. She knew how to keep us out of the red, but she didn't push St. Anne's far enough into the future to suit the Board. They had dreams of glory and she was a down-to-earth kind of leader."

"How do you mean?" Caroline asked.

"Well, she understood the limitations we face. St. Anne's is not a big city hospital. We don't serve a community that can support a wing for open heart surgery, or a dialysis center for kidney patients. Sure, there are some wealthy families in Rhineburg, but ordinary working people make up the bulk of the population. They're not the kind of folks who leave bequests to hospitals in their wills!"

"So Sister Ambrose ran the hospital on a shoestring."

"The budget was tight," Jane admitted. "But the practice of medicine was excellent. Health care is a community thing here. Why, half the town works at St. Anne's. We're more than just a hospital;

we're part of the life blood of Rhineburg."

"And Charles Paine is a threat to that role?"

Jane sighed. "We had to send some patients to other hospitals when we couldn't treat their conditions here. Like I said before, we couldn't afford the same kinds of services offered at larger facilities. Unfortunately, the Board of Directors didn't share Sr. Ambrose's vision of a small town hospital. I don't know if it was an ego thing or if the Board simply didn't understand the high cost of modern medicine, but they felt Sister was preventing St. Anne's from growing. They voted her out as Administrator and hired Charles Paine to replace her."

"Could they do that? I thought St. Anne's was owned by a religious order."

"Oh, no!" Jane responded. "The town built St. Anne's a little over eighty years ago, but the powers-that-be back then made a deal with a German order of nuns to run it. They figured the sisters were old hands at operating hospitals, so they gave them a free rein in decision making. The Board of Directors was mainly a rubber stamp outfit put in place by the Mayor. Since the initial funding for the hospital came from the town, it only seemed right that the City Council be kept aware of its financial standing."

"But somewhere along the line, all that changed."

"Different times call for different approaches. At least that's what the Board decided." Jane shifted in her chair. "To be perfectly honest, I can understand their concern. Government involvement has turned health care upside down. Medical advances have added to the confusion."

"We're doing procedures never thought possible fifty years ago," Caroline said. "That means people are living longer and requiring a different kind of health care system."

"In a way, Sr. Ambrose represented the past." Jane gazed over Caroline's shoulder as if she was privately recalling another way of life. She was quiet for a moment or two, then resumed her rambling discourse. "I started here fresh out of nursing school. Back then, the staff held picnics on the back lawn and Ambrose was as familiar a face as any in the hospital. She was a nurse herself, you know. She used to come up on the wards just to see how we were all doing."

"A personable woman," Caroline remarked.

Jane looked her straight in the eye. There was a hard edge to her voice when she said, "A caring Administrator, unlike Mr. Paine! He sits locked away in his office all day, handing out memos and thinking up new ways to cut staff! The Board thinks he's a financial wizard, but the nurses hate him. He laid off a lot of people the first month he was here. The economics of medicine, he called it. Then he came up with plans to consolidate units and form new ones without cutting into the hospital's revenue. The psych ward was his brain child, you know."

"I heard it was a new addition to the hospital."

"Relatively speaking, yes." Jane hastened to explain. "Paine came from a hospital in Chicago. He still has financial connections in the city and he went there to drum up support for his ideas. Shortly after that trip, he closed down a medical ward, refurbished it completely, then reopened it as a psychiatric unit. In its brief existence it hasn't done a booming business, but it seems to pay for itself."

"Your Administrator sounds like the consummate businessman. But I still don't understand why you consider him a target for a bomb."

Jane leaned forward and stared hard at Caroline. "I told you, Paine fired a lot of people here. I saw which way the wind was blowing so I updated my education at the university. When the position opened, I was qualified for hire as the psych unit manager. But most of the med-surg nurses from the now-closed unit hadn't been able to return to school. Some had families to support, and others couldn't afford the tuition. They were great at their former jobs, but they didn't know beans about psych nursing!"

"So they were out on their ears."

"Without any place to go. Paine had promised to shuffle them onto other medical floors, but with the general layoffs, there weren't any positions open. A lot of careers went straight down the drain."

"You think someone who lost a job at St. Anne's planted that bomb in the Christmas tree."

"It's possible," Jane agreed.

"But the ward opened last summer!" Caroline objected. "If there was going to be trouble, it should have happened back then, not now. Six months is a long time to hold a grudge."

"You never know, do you?" Jane replied. "Working in psych has taught me that people can explode long after the precipitating event. Who's to say one of our displaced staff members didn't finally go over the edge? Not that I want to be right about this, but I'd say my theory is a great deal more believable than yours!"

The light was blinking on Caroline's answering machine when she returned to the apartment.

"Mrs. Rhodes? My name is Tom Evans. I'm with the FBI and I'd like to talk to you about your auto accident. Apparently there are some...suspicious aspects to the crash that need to be discussed. I understand you also have something to add to your statement about the bombing at St. Anne's. I suggest we meet this morning at the hospital. I'll be there by nine thirty and you can reach me through the operator."

The message ended abruptly and another one began. This time it was a woman's voice on the recording. Unlike the FBI agent, the caller's tone lacked both confidence and sophistication.

"Mrs. Rhodes? Mrs. Caroline Rhodes? The police...they told me you're the dormitory house mother and if I wanted to, I should call you. About Gail's things, that is. They said you've got the keys, and seeing as how they're done in the room, you can let me in. I guess you're not home now so I'll call again later today. Umm...I'd like to come over there tomorrow, if that's OK with you. To pick up Gail's...to pick up...

everything. Well...I...I guess that's all for now."

The answering machine beeped twice, then rewound the tape. Caroline paid no attention to its whirring as she considered the two very different messages. There was something in the first she found disturbing. Agent Evans' voice held a note of cynicism akin to disbelief. He'd hesitated before uttering the word 'suspicious' and emphasized it ever so slightly. Then again he'd sounded rather demanding, almost egotistical, as he'd instructed her to meet with him. 'A man used to getting his way!' she thought. The woman was a different kettle of fish. Her voice had broken several times before she'd managed to get her message on the tape. She'd also been so upset she hadn't left a name.

Caroline opened a desk drawer and rummaged through it until she found her student resident file. She scanned the two page list, searching for the name of the dead student. There it was: Gail Garvy, room 206, Stromberg. An Elvira Harding was identified as next of kin. The last names were different but Caroline assumed the mother was either widowed or divorced and had remarried, leaving Gail with her father's name. She guessed this was the woman who had called her. Mrs. Harding was probably so devastated by her daughter's death that she wasn't thinking clearly yet. Forgetting to leave a name wouldn't be unusual under the circumstances.

Caroline sat down at her desk and considered what to do next. She really wanted to talk with Carl, tell him what she'd learned from Jane Gardner, but her report would be incomplete without some information on the Garvy girl. She'd forgotten to ask about her when she'd talked with Jane.

'But now I know the police have unsealed the dorm room,' she thought to herself. 'I'll just have a look in there before I call Carl.'

She pulled her keys from her pocket, selected the master key to the dorm rooms, and nodded in satisfaction. It was difficult to imagine a young nursing student as anything other than an innocent victim of the explosion, still it never paid to be sloppy. Excluding Gail Garvy from the investigation might be a grave mistake. With that thought in mind, she left the apartment and took the stairs down to the deserted second floor.

Just as she'd been told, the police tape had been removed from the door of 206. Caroline used her key to unlock it and stepped inside. The room was much as she expected. Posters covered the walls, mainly colorful ones of rock bands with strange names like Grapevine Homage and Battle Me Back. The two beds were made, but sloppily, and various articles of clothing were scattered over the rumpled blankets on both of them. Gail had shared the room with another student and it took Caroline a few minutes to discover which of the twin desks belonged to the girl. It turned out to be the neater of the two. She sat down at it and started pulling out drawers. The FBI had probably done the same thing a couple of days ago and found nothing of interest. Still, Caroline was curious about the student nurse. Perhaps there was something in the desk that would shed light on Gail's character, on her background.

"Bingo!"

Caroline had opened the lower most drawer and discovered a stack of rubber-banded letters. She lifted them out and laid them on the desktop, then swept the empty drawer with her fingertips, aware that something was not quite right. The drawer seemed about ten inches deep on the outside but the inside appeared much smaller. She ran a fingernail along the edge of the plywood base and found a groove separating the back of it from the drawer wall. Inserting the tip of her nail into the groove, Caroline pried up the false wooden bottom.

"Now what have we got here?" she muttered. She placed the plywood base on the floor and reached into the drawer, withdrawing a slim leather notebook from its depths. It appeared to be Gail's diary. Caroline flipped through the book, tempted to read it right then and there, but in the end opted to take it back to her apartment where she could examine the pages more closely. She replaced the false bottom and closed the drawer.

Six blue spiral bound notebooks lay on the left side of the desk.

Caroline leafed through them but found nothing of interest; they were obviously Gail's classroom notes. She put them down and glanced around the room, determined not to overlook anything that might provide a clue to the student nurse's brief life. On the dresser lay a small jewelry box half hidden behind a photograph in a carved wooden frame. Caroline walked over and picked up the photo first. It showed a young woman, probably in her early twenties, seated on a porch swing and smiling. She was wearing a plaid flannel shirt and jeans, and cradled a baby in her arms. It was impossible to date the picture; the clothes were timeless and the woman's haircut neat and simple. Caroline turned the photo over but there was no writing on the back.

Placing it back on the dresser, she opened the jewelry box. Two antique cameos rested on the velvet lining along with a gold wedding band. The ring looked almost new and inscribed on the inside were the letters 'MGH'. Caroline guessed the 'G' stood for Garvy, but it couldn't be Gail's since the first initial didn't fit. Her mother's then? But wasn't Elvira Harding her mother? Maybe it had belonged to her grandmother. No, Caroline decided. It would have been thin and worn from wear. Another little mystery to solve.

Caroline replaced the ring and closed the jewelry box. Just to be thorough, she checked the closet, then took a quick peek under the bed and beneath the pillow. She even slid her hand between the mattress and springs, coming up empty handed again. She wasn't sure what she was looking for but the false drawer bottom bothered her. If Gail had gone to such lengths to conceal her diary, she might have hidden other personal items as well. The question was, what and where were they?

'This is silly!' Caroline thought suddenly. She straightened up self-consciously and dusted her hands on the legs of her jeans. 'What would Martin think if he saw me rummaging through this room like some nosy old biddy?' She pictured her son shaking his head in disgust. He would certainly disapprove of her attempts at detection. But then Carl's face replaced Marty's in her imagination. 'Why do you care what

Martin thinks of you?' he was asking.

"Why indeed?" Caroline grumbled, annoyed now with herself and her son. She gathered up the items on the desk and took one last look around. On the surface, the room appeared no different than when she'd entered. No one would ever know she'd been there, and she'd return the diary and letters before Mrs. Harding arrived tomorrow. Content that she'd investigated as best she could, she left the room, locking the door behind her before taking the stairs back up to her apartment.

She was barely inside the door when the phone began to ring. Hoping it was Carl calling, she dumped the diary and letters on the coffee table and grabbed the receiver.

"Hello, Carl?"

"Sorry, Mrs. Rhodes. Wrong man! This is Jim Morgan." Pause. "From Stromberg and Morgan." Another pause. "The car dealership, remember?"

"Oh! I'm so sorry, Mr. Morgan!" Totally flustered, Caroline babbled on brightly. "I'd almost forgotten about you. I mean to say, I'd forgotten about the car! Not actually forgotten I'd bought it, but..."

"Oh, dear!" Morgan broke in with a roguish laugh. "And here I thought I'd swept you away with my charm. Must be losing my touch if you've dismissed me from memory so easily."

Caroline relaxed. The man's wry sense of humor swept away her embarrassment. "I haven't exactly dismissed you, Mr. Morgan."

"Please! Call me Jim. Or James, if you prefer to be formal like the Professor."

"Jim," Caroline continued, "My mind's been elsewhere this morning. I do apologize. I hope you're calling with good news?"

"Definitely!" the salesman responded. "Your Jeep is ready to go! My mechanic just pronounced it fit for any and all action, and knowing how badly you need it..."

"Oh, I certainly do!" Caroline assured him. "But I probably

can't pick it up until later this afternoon." She'd have to call Carl and ask him to drive her to town.

"No problem, Mrs. Rhodes. I'll be here all day. Just stop by before six o'clock, all right?"

Caroline agreed and hung up a happy woman. Having her own car again meant freedom from begging rides off the Professor. Not that she minded his company, especially since they had so much to discuss, but still, she preferred the independence of her own automobile. She picked up the phone and dialed Carl's number.

"Hello?"

"Hi, Carl. It's Caroline. I was wondering if you could meet me some time today. I have news for you."

"Anything wrong, Cari?"

Caroline was surprised by the intensity in Carl's voice.

"Relax," she answered. "No more attempts on my life, at least not yet. I met with Jane Gardner this morning and what she had to say was a little surprising. I thought we should discuss it."

"Great! I have some news for you too, so how about I pick you up in ten minutes and we can grab a light lunch at McGinty's?"

Caroline surmised that any working relationship with Professor Atwater would involve food. No wonder he and Martin got along so well. Her son was also a devotee of restaurants. She only hoped Marty had the good sense to curb his appetite more firmly than Carl did his. Nikki might not appreciate a roly-poly husband eating them out of house and home.

"I'm not really hungry," she said tentatively. "But if you are..."

"Woman!" the Professor roared. "You're practically skin and bones! I'll bet you didn't even eat breakfast today."

Caroline briefly considered her 140 pound frame and her lame attempts at dieting, but decided not to argue with Carl. "I'll be in front of the dorm in ten minutes," she said with a sigh. "I don't intend to freeze out there, so be on time, OK?" She hung up the phone before he could reply.

Caroline stared at the plate the waitress had set before her. The reuben sandwich was at least three inches thick, and the mound of french fries resembled a small volcano. Even the stein of beer was enormous; she figured the glass held a pint of the home town brew.

"You call this a light lunch?" she asked, her eyebrows arched in disbelief. "This is enough to last me all day!"

Professor Atwater dismissed her complaint with a wave of his hand. "You city types are bent out of shape over food. You think bean sprouts and wheat germ constitute a well rounded meal."

Caroline grimaced.

"They're not high on my list," she replied archly. "But now an occasional vegetable wouldn't hurt your cholesterol level, would it?"

"I ate my vegies yesterday," Carl protested. "Just tell me, what are potato pancakes made from?"

"Lots of starch deep fried in oil!" Caroline shook her head. The man was simply impossible. The reuben sandwich, on the other hand, grew more attractive by the minute as the aroma of fresh corned beef and sauerkraut tickled her nostrils. A few bites wouldn't hurt, she reasoned. After all, breakfast had been over three hours ago.

Twenty minutes later Caroline polished off the very last french fry and sat back contentedly. Carl politely refrained from commenting on the speed with which she'd devoured her sandwich. Instead, he simply ordered apple pie and ice cream for the two of them.

"So what were you up to this morning?" Caroline kept her tone light. She'd seen the twinkle in Carl's eyes when he'd ordered dessert, but she'd be damned if she allowed him the satisfaction of knowing how much she'd enjoyed the meal.

"I made a few phone calls. Then I went over the obituaries of all the victims of the bombing. Thought I might get a clue as to motive, but no such luck."

Mention of the murders sobered them both. Food was now the last thing on their minds.

"James Belding was born in Rhineburg," Carl continued. "But he was buried yesterday in Chicago. It was a private funeral, family only. His was the last of the services."

"You were at a funeral the day of my accident."

Carl nodded. "May Eberle was an old timer around here. She and her sister April were the unofficial town criers of Rhineburg. They made sure we were all aware of each other's sins."

"Puritans at heart? Or just busybodies?"

"More like Victorians I'd say. Full of self-righteous indignation, although I suspect they secretly enjoyed exposing their neighbors' faults. They certainly spread some scandalous tales!"

"Could be a motive there," Caroline suggested. "Perhaps May put her nose in the wrong place one too many times."

Carl frowned. "I don't know about that. April took a fall back in August and died of a brain hemorrhage. Then in September, May's father became ill and died. That was surprising since old man Eberle was healthy as a horse and strong for his age. May didn't tell a soul about it. She kept his body right there in the house for weeks on end."

"How macabre!" Caroline remarked. "But she finally did have him buried, didn't she?"

"Actually, it wasn't May's idea at all. Eberle had a rigid routine for all his activities, and when he stopped showing up at his regular haunts, people began to wonder what was wrong. For instance, he used to stop by the bank every Monday morning to withdraw cash for the week's shopping. When he missed two Mondays in a row, the teller reported it to the bank president. He in turn mentioned it to the chief of police, and Chief Moeller thought it strange enough to warrant a visit to the old man's house. Jake Moeller is a conscientious officer and it's a good thing he is! He discovered May in an upstairs bedroom chattering away to her dead father. He took Mr. Eberle to the morgue and May to

St. Anne's. She was committed to the psychiatric ward that very day."

"How sad!" Caroline commented. "She lost both her father and her sister within a matter of weeks. It must have been simply too much for her to handle." She was silent for a moment, remembering her own weakness in dealing with death. "Didn't May have any other family?"

Carl shook his head. "She was the last of her line. And because of her tendency to gossip, she had no real friends. I guess that's why I went to her funeral. It seems wrong to be buried without any mourners present."

The apple pie and ice cream arrived and Carl dug in with gusto. Caroline picked at her dessert, her mind occupied with thoughts of May.

"Now tell me about your meeting with Jane Gardner," Carl said between mouthfuls. Caroline pulled herself back to the present and related her discussion with Jane. She emphasized the nurse's concern that an ex-employee might be the bomber. Carl considered the idea, but then discarded it as improbable.

"Can you really believe some nurse had the skill to build such a device?"

"No," Caroline answered truthfully. "Bombmaking 101 wasn't on the curriculum back when I was in training, but not everyone laid off was a nurse. Some male orderlies lost jobs too."

"And you really think one of them might have waited this long to strike back at the hospital."

"I said practically the same thing to Jane. But she pointed out that people sometimes explode long after what she called 'the precipitating event'. Frankly, I believe the police must have gone over the personnel records of employees fired or laid off. That only makes sense, doesn't it? Yet I suppose one of those ex-orderlies could have found work at the quarry. If so, maybe he was trained in the use of explosives there, and then used that knowledge to take his revenge on the hospital."

"Remember, Cari, that tree was packed with plastic explosives.

I'm not positive about this, but I think they only use dynamite at the quarry. I could ask the Archangels to look into it if you like."

"Would you?" Caroline asked. "Jane would be relieved if we could prove none of her old friends is the bomber."

Carl swallowed his last piece of pie before answering. "I'll call Michael this afternoon. It won't take long for him to hunt down the answer."

"Oh! One more thing, Carl. Jim Morgan called this morning. My Jeep is ready to be picked up. Could you give me a lift over there?"

Carl stroked his beard to hide his pleasure. "I'd be delighted! But first, will you come with me to visit Jim's grandmother? We're invited to her home at two o'clock."

Caroline's eyebrows shot up. "Alexsa Stromberg Morgan? I don't think I'm dressed for the occasion!" She gazed ruefully at her jeans and hiking boots. Why hadn't Carl mentioned this when they'd talked on the phone? She would have worn something more appropriate. Honestly! The Professor was absolutely maddening!

Atwater reached across the table and picked up Caroline's piece of pie. "You're not going to finish this, are you? Good," he said happily after she shook her head 'no'. "It's really quite delicious." He paused, his fork half raised to his mouth, then lowered it quickly when he saw the expression on his companion's face.

"What's wrong?" he asked in surprise. "You're not worried about your clothes, are you? Don't bother! Alexsa won't even notice what you're wearing. She's not that kind of person."

All women are 'That Kind of Person', Caroline reflected but refrained from saying. True to his gender, Carl possessed an abysmal lack of understanding of the opposite sex. She would be wise to remember that whenever they discussed the female victims of the explosion. Hopefully, Carl's observations about the men in the case would be more accurate.

"What a lovely pullover! A fisherman's knit, isn't it?" Alexsa Stromberg Morgan fingered the soft wool of Caroline's sweater. "From Ireland, of course."

Caroline murmured assent while glaring at Carl over the elderly woman's bent head. "I bought it in Chicago, but it is imported."

"How I'd like to go there again!" Alexsa sighed. "Chicago, I mean. I've not been to Ireland. The continent, of course, but never to Ireland. Too much fighting going on. You never know what you might get caught up in." She beckoned with a bejeweled finger and they fell in step, following their hostess down a carpeted hallway leading to the back of the house. "But Chicago...of course, that's another story altogether. Quite safe now with Capone dead. I'd visit all the shops on Michigan Avenue and buy absolutely tons of clothing!"

Stopping abruptly, Alexsa turned to Caroline, lowered her voice and said confidentially, "Don't know where I'd wear them, of course. I hardly go out any more since I broke my hip." She tapped her left leg with the ivory handled cane she carried. "The doctors said it would be good as new after the surgery, but you know how they are. Promise you anything as long as you pay the bill! They do try..."

"Of course!" Caroline said, finishing the sentence for Alexsa. She was amused by the old lady's disingenuous behavior, yet doubted she was as scatterbrained as she made herself out to be.

A glimmer of annoyance flashed in the eyes of the Morgan matriarch. She recovered quickly though, and signaled towards a set of double doors with her cane. "Carl, I thought we'd sit in there. Would you please lead the way?"

The Professor strode past and swung open the heavy oak door. "After you, madam," he said with a bow. He ushered Alexsa into the room and Caroline followed. Once inside she stopped dead in her tracks. They'd entered what appeared to be a modern gymnasium. Exercise equipment lined the windowless walls like ranks of silent soldiers standing at attention. A square blue mat occupied the center of the floor while a maze of rings and ropes dangled from the high ceiling. A balance beam stood off to the left next to a suspended punching bag. Beyond that at the far end of the room was a lounge area with soft chairs and end tables gathered in a semicircle around a large screen TV. In the corner was a five foot long wet bar flanked by a pool table.

"Come along, dear. No need to gawk," Alexsa chirped. She reverted once more to a sort of rambling chatter, clearly meant to disarm her guests. "This is the boys' room, but I sneak in on occasion when I want privacy for my visitors. The servants tend to eavesdrop, you know. With this excellent sound proofing," she gestured around the gym, "I can talk to my heart's content and not worry that my conversation will be repeated all over town."

Caroline grinned despite herself. 'Clever old girl!' she thought as she followed her white haired hostess across the room. Carl was already in the lounge area drawing three chairs close together. He winked at her as she sunk into the plush elegance of a brocaded recliner. 'So this is how the rich live!' she marveled, stroking the tightly woven material on the armrest.

"Whiskey or beer?"

"Um, what?" Caroline snapped out of her reverie to find Alexsa standing over her. The other woman's eyes bore into her.

"I said, whiskey or beer? There's not much choice in here. The boys are rather limited in their tastes."

"Nothing for me, thank you." Caroline was determined to keep a clear head. She had to figure out the game Alexsa was playing since she was convinced the 'granny act' was a put-on. "How many children do you have, Mrs. Morgan?"

"Only one, dear. When I speak of the boys, I mean my son Bill and his son James. They may be grown men, but they still enjoy boys' games, as you can see." She waved a hand languidly towards the exercise equipment. "They retreat to this room every evening on the pretext of 'shaping up'. In actuality, they sit in here drinking and watching whatever sport the TV has to offer. Carl! Take whatever you want but bring me a whiskey, large and neat." She sank down on the middle chair, leaning her cane against the arm before commenting cheerfully, "I'm so glad to see you're not dead, Mrs. Rhodes. It would have been a shame to have missed meeting you."

"Alexsa!" Carl's voice was heavy with disapproval.

"I feel the same way about you, Mrs. Morgan," Caroline replied with a wicked smile. Two could play this game, she decided.

"Cari!" The Professor was practically sputtering.

"Do be quiet, Carl. And please sit down. You're distracting me with all your bustling around." Alexsa accepted her drink, raised it in silent toast to Caroline, then downed half the whiskey in one swallow.

For her part, Caroline did her best to maintain an expression of total disinterest. She mentally applauded Alexsa's display of showmanship, still it didn't intimidate her in the least. As far as she was concerned, it was only the second inning; the score was tied one to one.

"Let's get down to business," Alexsa said brusquely. "You've come to discuss this affair at St. Anne's, haven't you? What exactly do you want to know from me?"

"How did you guess?" Carl asked in surprise.

"Servants work both ways," Caroline answered shrewdly. "They may repeat what they hear in this house -- although I doubt it; you wouldn't put up with that, would you, Mrs. Morgan? -- but I suspect it's mainly the other way around. They probably report in to you on a daily basis, right? How else would you have known about my accident?"

Alexsa threw back her head and laughed. It was not the titter of a frail old lady any more, but the hearty laugh of a woman in firm control of her life. Alexsa Stromberg Morgan was nobody's fool, and she wanted Caroline to know it.

"You'd make a worthy opponent if we were enemies," Mrs. Morgan stated. "Thank goodness we're not! You may call me Alexsa, and I shall call you Caroline. 'Cari' is much too diminutive a name for a woman with your powers of perception."

Caroline nodded graciously. She was still puzzled by Alexsa's strange behavior, but obviously a truce had been granted. She would take advantage of it while it lasted.

"What in the world is going on here?" Carl looked from one woman to the other. He was clearly mystified by the conversation.

Alexsa patted his arm. "Nothing, dear Carl. I'm just being obnoxious today. Now that I'm ninety, people expect it of me."

"Not I!" Carl responded heatedly. "I expect your help!"

"And I'll try to give it, but you must tell me what you want. I'm not a mind reader, although I've been accused of that in the past."

"We were wondering about the people killed in the explosion. The Professor," Caroline smiled sweetly in his direction, "assured me you know the folks in this town better than anyone else."

"And why shouldn't I?" Alexsa sniffed. "I've outlived practically everyone born in Rhineburg! I must also admit to an inquisitive nature. But," she added solemnly, "I know how to keep a confidence."

"Unlike May Eberle?"

Alexsa nodded. "Poor May. She didn't deserve to die that way, even if she was a gossip. May was basically a timid woman, as was her sister, April. The two of them clung to each other like the proverbial orphans in the storm, which, in fact, they were."

"What do you mean?" Caroline asked.

"Their mother died soon after May was born. The girls were raised by their father, a brutish, strong willed man who cared for no one but himself. He treated the girls like slaves, allowing them no friends, no pleasures, just a life of drudgery and devotion to his whims."

"He never remarried?"

"No woman in her right mind would take Albert Eberle for a husband! He was furious when his wife died leaving him without a son, and he certainly courted far and wide, but he never persuaded another girl to marry him."

"It's just as I told you, Cari. May was the end of her line."

"Not exactly, Carl," Alexsa responded, a twinkle lighting up her dim blue eyes. "Albert was, shall we say, a dabbler in the sexual arts. He left progeny scattered in his wake much like a child eating cookies scatters crumbs. There's many an inhabitant of this county with Albert's genes in his blood."

Carl was dumfounded. "I never knew that! We've discussed Albert Eberle before, but you never told me about his philandering."

"Of course not, dear," Alexsa retorted. "You might have been tempted to mention it in one of your books. Even if you'd omitted his name, people would have known you were writing about Albert. Just think how that would have hurt his daughters."

So Alexsa hadn't been boasting when she'd claimed she could keep a secret. Caroline wondered how many other scandals the old woman was aware of. Plenty, she'd bet.

Carl was still put out by Alexsa's lack of confidence in him. He ignored her totally as he addressed Caroline. "That means someone stands to inherit a hefty piece of change now that May is gone. If he, or she, can prove paternity, that is."

"If it's a motive you're after," Caroline replied, "you'd do better to check out Albert's grandchildren. May's half-brothers-and-sisters must be at least as old as she was."

Carl grunted. "Hadn't thought of that."

"The Eberle girls were odd little creatures," Alexsa continued. "Albert taught them no manners, no social graces. When they moved about in public, they were either ignored or ridiculed by the townspeople. I suppose that's why they took to telling stories about their neighbors. It was a form of revenge on Rhineburg."

"Were their stories believed?"

Alexsa smiled sadly. "Small towns thrive on gossip, Caroline. While there were grains of truth in some of the tales, mostly they were pure fabrication. Still, the Eberles told their awful lies to anyone who'd listen and the stories spread exactly as they wished. They did a great deal of damage in Rhineburg. They broke up marriages, destroyed friendships. There were those who lived in real fear of what the women would do or say next." Alexsa gazed down at her blue-veined hands, her mood suddenly pensive. Caroline wondered if she was recalling a time when she herself had been touched by the sisters' vicious gossip. It was always a possibility, given the old lady's standing in the community, that she'd been a prime target for talk.

"April died in August, didn't she? I suppose May was pretty devastated by her sister's death."

"Wouldn't you be," Alexsa said softly, "if your father murdered your best friend and only companion?"

Carl bolted upright in his chair. "Are you accusing Albert of killing his own daughter? Come now, Alexsa!"

Alexsa met his frown with a steady gaze. "April didn't fall down those steps on her own, Carl." She turned to Caroline. "Albert said she slipped at the head of the staircase and tumbled headlong down its entire length. But Elvira Harding was cleaning there that day. She told me Albert was in a terrible mood over some money missing from the household fund. He accused both of his daughters of theft, then stalked upstairs to search their rooms. April ran up after him, begging him to reconsider what he was doing. Elvira didn't see it happen but she heard Albert slap her, and then April screamed. Elvira ran into the hallway just as April came hurling down the stairs."

"Why didn't Elvira tell this to the police?" Carl groaned. "They would have arrested Albert Eberle."

"If they'd have believed her! I told you, Elvira never actually saw what happened. She only heard what sounded like a slap and then April was falling to her death. There was no proof of murder, Carl, but I trust Elvira's account of what occurred that day. Albert killed his daughter as sure as I'm sitting here. And furthermore, May poisoned him in revenge."

Now Carl was really stunned. Caroline observed the interplay between her two companions as they squared off for battle.

"I can't believe you'd say that!" Carl roared. "May was a pest and a gossip but she certainly didn't murder her father!"

"She hated him all her life," Alexsa maintained. "April's death brought it all to a head."

"Nonsense! Everyone knows Albert was an old bully, but May stayed and took it, didn't she? She waited on him hand and foot."

"Bah! For an intelligent man, Carl, you're talking like a fool! May had no choice but to stay! She'd never learned how to make a choice living with that tyrant!"

Caroline interrupted the two. "Excuse me, but we're getting off the track, don't you think? The real question is, was there any reason for someone to want May dead also? Did someone hate her enough to blow up the psychiatric ward?"

Carl glanced at Caroline, then returned his attention to Alexsa. "And just how did May poison her father?" he demanded to know.

Alexsa shrugged. "I suppose she slipped something in his food. May was a gardener. She had lethal compounds at her disposal."

"You're reaching, Alexsa! You've absolutely no proof of what you're saying."

"Perhaps not, Carl, but I know that Albert was a strong, healthy man until the day April died. Then suddenly he expired also. May allowed no one in that house for weeks. When the body was finally discovered, it was thought he'd had a heart attack. No autopsy was performed, you know. May was clearly 'round the bend by then, so no one really cared to pursue the matter of her father's death. She was carted off to St. Anne's and Albert was quietly buried alongside his wife."

Carl was silent as he considered the possibility that Alexsa spoke the truth. Caroline saw he was upset, but she suspected it was because his ego was badly bruised. The Professor considered himself an insider in Rhineburg, a man who was knowledgeable of the happenings there. He'd suddenly been shown how little he knew of his neighbors' lives.

"Ahem!" Caroline cleared her throat. "May I remind you again that we're discussing the explosion at St. Anne's? May Eberle is important to us only if she was the bomber's target. Alexsa, I'd like to ask you again if anyone hated May enough to plant that bomb in the Christmas tree."

Alexsa pursed her lips and stared up at the ceiling.

"Certain people are greatly relieved May is no longer around to spread her ugly rumors," she said after a moment. "But of course, Caroline, you can hardly blame them. It's only natural to rejoice over the defeat of one's enemies."

The old woman's comment sent shivers down Caroline's spine. More chilling, though, was the thought Alexsa failed to put into words: the ultimate defeat for anyone was death. Of course.

Carl and Caroline were alone in the gymnasium. Alexsa had been called away to the phone, leaving the two of them free to discuss her odd behavior.

"I don't know what's gotten into her today," Carl said. A frown darkened his usually jovial features. "Her manners are always impeccable, and she never drinks like that! Something very strange is going on here."

"I knew that the minute the maid took our coats."

"What do you mean?" Carl's expression changed from one of irritation to utter bemusement. He was clearly perplexed by his friend's statement.

"You were speaking to her as she hung up our things," Caroline explained. "You said something about her brother in the Army, I think. Anyway, while the two of you were talking, I happened to glance in the mirror hanging in the hallway and I caught a glimpse of Alexsa standing up at the head of the staircase. She was watching us. Actually, it was almost like she was sizing us up. Then she started down the stairs, moving very spryly I thought for a woman her age. But when she was about halfway down the steps, she suddenly stopped and her entire demeanor changed. It was as if she shrunk right before my eyes. She bent over and her hands began to tremble. She gripped her cane like she couldn't take another step without it. When I first saw her, she resembled a healthy seventy-five year old woman. But by the time she reached the foot of the stairs, she was a frail ninety year old grandma."

Carl snorted. "There's certainly nothing frail about Alexsa. She broke her hip three years ago, but I was at her last birthday party and she danced with every man in the room. She hasn't used that cane since she came home after the surgery."

"There has to be a reason for the act. Perhaps Alexsa knows something about the bombing that she'd rather not tell."

"Impossible!" Carl retorted. "If anything, she'd want to get to the bottom of this business. Martha Schoen was, after all, her cousin."

"I knew she was a Stromberg before her marriage, still I wasn't sure how closely related she was to Mrs. Morgan."

"Close enough for Alexsa to come to her defense after the pie throwing incident."

"Then Alexsa didn't approve of Martha's hospitalization?" asked Caroline.

"Certainly not!" Carl replied. "The mayor got his cousin, a GP in Newberry, to sign the commitment papers. Martha Schoen annoyed a lot of people, including Alexsa from time to time. But on the subject of Teddy's philandering, Alexsa backed her cousin a hundred per cent. I'd say she hates that man with a passion."

Caroline recalled what Alexsa had said about rejoicing over the defeat of one's enemies. If she thought the mayor was behind the bombing, she'd surely make her feelings known.

A door clicked shut behind them. Caroline turned to see Alexsa crossing the room.

"I'm sorry to have kept you waiting," she called out. "That was Jim on the phone. I told him you'd stopped by to visit." She smiled charmingly as she settled back down in her chair. "Now where were we?"

"You mentioned the relief felt by some people now that May Eberle is dead," Caroline said. "Would you care to say who's celebrating her passing?"

Alexsa cocked her head to one side. "You certainly are the curious one, aren't you? Perhaps you'd better explain first why it is you want to know all this."

Carl heaved himself out of his chair and walked over to the bar.

"I'll answer that," he said as he pried the cap off another bottle of beer. "You know that Cari wrecked her car outside of town the other day. I'm sure you heard it was an accident..."

"Actually," Alexsa interrupted, "I've been told someone fiddled with your brakes. You were fortunate to escape with so few injuries."

Even Caroline was surprised now. Alexsa certainly seemed to have a wide network of informants.

"I was very lucky," she responded. "Carl has a theory that the attempt on my life was a result of my presence on the psychiatric ward the day of the bombing. He believes that the same person who planted the bomb also tampered with my car, and I've come to agree with him."

"So the two of you have set out to unmask the killer." Alexsa made it sound like they were a couple of kids playing 'Clue'. Caroline blushed but Carl's anger flared. He strode over to where Alexsa sat and glared down at her.

"See here, Alexsa! Caroline could have been crippled, or even killed, in that accident! We have every right to try to find out who's behind these murders."

Alexsa remained unruffled. "Put that way, I suppose I must agree with you. Sit down, Carl. I'm not attacking the two of you, but you're asking a great deal of me. If I were to reveal names and you two mentioned them to the police, a lot of innocent people could be dragged into this investigation. You obviously believe the bomber was after one of the patients on that hospital ward. I'll tell you what I can about those I knew, but I won't point a finger at one of my neighbors and say, 'There he is! He's the murderer!'"

"Fair enough," said Caroline. She dug a small notebook out of her pocket and flipped through the pages. "I think we can dismiss Richard Canty from our list of likely targets. The man's been in and out of psychiatric hospitals for the past ten years. He arrived at St. Anne's four weeks ago after being picked up by the state police. They found him wandering down the highway stark naked."

"Brrr! Maybe he belonged to the Polar Bear Club."

Alexsa was referring to a group of Chicagoans who swam the icy waters of Lake Michigan each winter. Caroline smiled at her hostess, aware that she was trying to ease the tension in the room, but Carl's face remained set in a scowl. He wasn't going to forgive the old lady that easily.

"Jane Gardner gave me what information she could without breaking the rules on patient-nurse confidentiality. A lot of this was public knowledge, still she saved me from having to scrounge through the newspaper files for it. She said Richard Canty's body wasn't claimed after the explosion. Apparently he had no family."

"He wasn't from around here," Alexsa stated. "That's an English name and we have few Rhineburgers of British descent."

"The police traced his fingerprints when they picked him up. He had a minor record dating back several years ago. In-between hospitalizations, he did some shoplifting in grocery stores. If it hadn't been for that, the cops might not have discovered his identity."

"He doesn't sound like he was a threat to anyone. It's safe to cross him off the list." Carl motioned towards the notebook. "What else do you have in there?"

"Next comes Thomas Adrian. A man in his early seventies, he'd suffered from paranoia for years before admitting himself to St. Anne's. Jane felt he was improving under treatment."

"I doubt it," Alexsa remarked dryly. "Thomas was a fine actor. I'll bet he simply played the role of recovering patient to test his doctors. Probably wanted to see how smart they really were!"

"You knew him then? He wasn't from Rhineburg."

"No, but my husband and I were acquainted with him. In fact, he was a guest in this house several times."

"Of course!" cried Caroline. "Now I know why his name was so familiar! He was a Shakespearean actor, wasn't he?"

Alexsa nodded in Caroline's direction. "You continue to amaze me, Mrs. Rhodes. Thomas's stage career was well before your time."

"Actually, my daughter told me about him," Caroline said with some embarrassment. "Kerry is a theater major. I believe she studied his work." She refrained from repeating what Kerry had said about Adrian: he was a nut case of the first degree!

"Thomas was one of the best," Alexsa recalled. "Unfortunately, his career was all too short. You see, he couldn't get through a run without demanding that someone, either another actor or a member of the crew, be fired. He was convinced people were out to destroy him. He would fixate on somebody, then imagine that person was plotting against him. His paranoia knew no limits."

"How did you meet him?" Carl asked.

"My late husband was a great supporter of the arts. He backed several of Adrian's plays and was intrigued by the man. You see, Thomas was extremely unnerving, but brilliant in his interpretation of Shakespeare. He had a rare power about him, the ability to focus so completely on his role that he actually became the character he played. I sometimes thought his madness derived from too close an association with Hamlet." Alexsa allowed a smile to cross her lips. "Although he was never as melancholy as the young prince. Thomas was a combination of fire and ice, a most difficult man to comprehend. Over time," she said after a pause, "Directors became wary of hiring him. His paranoia and odd habits made for strained relationships both on and off stage, so he was offered fewer and fewer parts. His was a forced retirement, not one that he was happy with."

"What a pity," Caroline remarked. "I wonder how he ended up at St. Anne's?"

"That was my doing," Alexsa admitted. "I recommended it to him, although I never imagined my advice would lead to his death."

"I'm confused," said Carl. "I thought you knew the man years ago when your husband was still alive."

Alexsa smoothed the wrinkles in her skirt, avoiding Carl's eyes as she answered, "I've had no real contact with Thomas for years. Still, last spring I came across an article about a home for retired actors out in California. It mentioned that Thomas was living there, but had been asked to leave due to his constant accusations against the other residents. In particular, he was convinced someone was trying to poison him. I realized Thomas was still delusional, so I wrote to him and suggested he come to St. Anne's. He didn't answer my letter, but I discovered he'd checked into the hospital in October."

"Well, you can't blame yourself for Adrian's death," Carl said gruffly. "You were only trying to help the man."

"Are you sure these attempts on his life were all in his mind?"

"Well..." Alexsa temporized as she stared off into the distance, "I've wondered about that ever since the explosion. Thomas made many enemies in his heyday. People lost their jobs because of his demands, and some of them did threaten to do him harm because of it."

"Those folks would have to be the same age as Adrian," Carl reminded them. "I can't see some septuagenarian building a bomb just to knock off an old rival!"

The Professor's words rang true to Caroline. She turned to Alexsa.

"Can you think of any other reason someone might want to see

Adrian dead?"

Alexsa's eyebrows puckered in concentration. "The most likely motive is money, of course. Thomas had plenty of that since he invested every cent he ever earned. My late husband advised him on certain companies worth watching and I know Thomas always listened to him. Even though he stopped working at a relatively young age, he had no financial worries. He was quite a wealthy man."

"Any heirs?"

"Like I told you, Carl, I lost track of Thomas some time ago. He may have married; I really wouldn't know."

Carl grunted. "It just doesn't sit right with me. I can visualize someone taking a knife to Adrian in the heat of the moment, but blowing him up with a bomb? No, it doesn't make any sense."

"Unless you consider his mob connections."

"What?" Carl nearly jumped from his chair. "Adrian was mixed up with them?"

Alexsa shrugged. "There was some talk of it," she responded. "Thomas knew the most unlikely people. He adored the gambling casinos and spent a great deal of time in Las Vegas. In fact, after his retirement from the theater, he relocated to that city. He said he had friends there he could stay with."

"That doesn't necessarily mean Adrian was involved with the Mafia," Caroline said gently. She wondered why Alexsa had withheld this bombshell until now. Obviously, any ties with organized crime would be considered important by the police; the mob wouldn't be above planting a bomb to rid itself of a troublesome character.

"Well, my husband always thought he was! That might not be evidence to you," Alexsa snapped, "but then, you didn't know Thomas Adrian the way we did!"

'Methinks the lady doth protest too much,' Caroline decided, but she let the matter drop when she caught sight of Carl's face. He looked ready to explode, and that would be no help at all.

She quickly consulted her notes. "Now William Chappel was a resident of Rhineburg before his commitment in late September. Jane told me he suffered a nervous breakdown after the deaths of his wife and brother in a house trailer fire."

"I remember that case," said Carl. "Supposedly the brother was romancing the wife behind Chappel's back. Her family insisted that Chappel himself set the fire. They pushed the police to press charges against him, but he cracked up before anything came of it."

"A guilty conscience," Alexsa stated.

"Perhaps. Chappel and his brother worked opposite shifts at the quarry, which was convenient if there was an affair being carried on. Chappel's father-in-law was employed there also." Carl considered the significance of what he'd just said. He shot Caroline a meaningful look. "There might be something in that, you know. Maybe the wife's father was skilled in handling explosives."

Caroline wrinkled her nose. "I don't like it. If the father-in-law wanted revenge, he would have taken it immediately, not waited three whole months. And anyway, how would he have learned about the damaged tree? That seems to me to be the sticking point in this entire affair. Someone had to have known about the tree!"

"Teddy Schoen probably did," Carl remarked. He turned to Alexsa and explained about the ward's ruined Christmas tree. It was the first she'd heard of it, which meant her spies had missed something.

"Teddy kept a close eye on Martha," Alexsa told them. "It's more than likely he heard about the tree, although I'm not sure he'd have paid attention to it. Much as I despise Teddy, I don't see him as a murderer. He hasn't got the guts for it."

Caroline didn't know what to say to that. She doubted Alexsa's objectivity when it came to the mayor. After all, he was related to the old woman by marriage. She might not be willing to point a finger at someone so closely tied to her family.

"That leaves James Belding," she said. "Do you know anything about him, Alexsa? He was born in Rhineburg but buried in Chicago."

Alexsa appeared deep in thought. She took her time answering. "I don't recall anyone by that name," she finally said. "He might have come from one of those transient families that work off and on at the quarry. Jobs are always changing hands there."

"There must be someone around town who remembers Belding. Carl, maybe you could..."

"It seems to me these were all quite ordinary people," Alexsa snapped as she rose from her chair. "It's true May Eberle was a thorn in the side to several people in town, and as I said, Thomas Adrian had some dubious acquaintances. But I think the police are better equipped to carry out an investigation than you two. Why not leave all this detecting to them?"

With that, she picked up her cane and started towards the door. Caroline and Carl had no choice but to follow. They weren't exactly being pushed out of the house, yet clearly, the interview was over.

"Mrs. Morgan!"

Alexsa stopped in her tracks and turned to face Caroline. Her lips still held a smile but it was devoid of warmth. "What is it, dear?"

"Is there anything you can tell us about Gail Garvy? She was a student nurse who also died in the explosion."

Alexsa looked at her queerly, her dim blue eyes reflecting no emotion at all. She hesitated, then replied quite firmly, "I'm afraid not, Mrs. Rhodes. Elvira Harding is an old and valued friend, but I hardly knew her niece." She shifted the cane to her right hand and, leaning heavily on it, walked away from them. When she reached the double doors, she looked back. "Elvira is in mourning," she told them. "I hope you have the decency to leave her to her grief."

Carl began to protest, but Caroline laid her hand gently on his arm. "Let it go," she murmured. "She's upset enough."

Carl frowned, still he said no more. The two friends stood in silence as their hostess swung open the heavy door and, without another word, disappeared into the quiet emptiness of the old house.

Carl yanked open the car door and stood aside while Caroline climbed in. She'd barely settled into her seat when he slammed it shut and strode around to his side.

"My! Aren't we in a fine mood?"

Carl shot her a look of pure fury. "It's not funny, Cari. I didn't appreciate Alexsa's rudeness."

"I wouldn't say she was rude; just cautious. After all, Alexsa doesn't know me from a hole in the wall. Perhaps she thinks I'm the one who planted the bomb."

"Come on!" Carl sputtered. "Alexsa knows I'm a better judge of character than that. I'd hardly come waltzing into her house with a murderer on my arm!"

Caroline's eyes twinkled mischievously. "You yourself said the killer had to be someone like me. Someone with a little knowledge of the town and the hospital. Alexsa's a pretty sharp woman. If she's fallen for that stuff about a 'mad bomber', she might also suspect it's no coincidence I arrived in Rhineburg just about the time all those victims were admitted to St. Anne's."

The Professor pounded the steering wheel with a closed fist.

"That's ridiculous!" he exclaimed. "In fact, it's libelous! And if Alexsa dares to say even one word in public..." Carl shifted uncomfortably. A new thought had struck him. "I hope she doesn't share that theory with the police. They may be desperate enough to believe her."

"I wouldn't worry about the police," Caroline reassured him. "After all, they know someone tried to kill me too." She explained about the phone call from the FBI.

"You shouldn't be alone when you meet with that agent," the Professor said grimly. "I'll go with you."

"Sure, if you want to. Say, Carl, who's that woman down by the fence?" Caroline pointed to a solitary figure standing several yards away. She had her back to them and was staring off into the distance, her arms wrapped about her and her long blond hair blowing loosely in the wind.

"That's James' wife, Elizabeth."

At that moment the woman turned and began to walk their way. Her head was bent, but as she approached the driveway, she looked up and saw the Jeep. She stopped abruptly, gazed at them for a moment, then changed course and vanished around the side of the house.

"I guess she didn't want to say 'hello'."

Carl shook his head. "Elizabeth is a strange woman," he said. "Very withdrawn, very cool. She seems an odd match for James."

Caroline thought of the jovial salesman with his boyish good looks. Even from a distance she'd noticed the woman appeared older than him.

"Do they have any children?"

Carl nodded. "Two girls. Teenagers."

That could account for it then. If Jim was the typical husband, Elizabeth did the lion's share of parenting. Kids at that age were known to cause gray hairs and age lines in mothers.

"We'd better get to the dealership." Carl started the Jeep and threw it into gear. He was still preoccupied by thoughts of Alexsa. "You know, there's one thing I don't understand. Why would someone who'd been out of touch with a man for years suddenly up and write to him? And about something as personal as his mental condition?"

"You're talking about Adrian. Frankly, Carl, that's a very good question. It could be Alexsa wasn't telling us the whole truth."

"What do you mean?"

"Well, there may have been a romantic connection between the two. Not lately perhaps, but back when he was a dashing young actor and she was a middle-aged matron lacking excitement in her life."

Carl huffed through his mustache. "You're jumping to some big conclusions there!"

"Maybe I am. But think about it now. Apparently her husband introduced Alexsa to the theater scene when he first backed Adrian's plays. If she traveled to Europe, she certainly visited New York and Chicago. Consider her life there compared to here in Rhineburg. Much more attractive, I'd say!"

"Perhaps," Carl said reluctantly.

"It wouldn't be the first time a bright, beautiful woman from a hick town -- pardon me, but Rhineburg isn't the Hollywood of the midwest! -- became entranced by the glitter of the big city. Under the circumstances, she could easily have fallen for a New York Romeo."

"She did use the word 'unnerving' to describe Adrian."

Caroline nodded. Atwater's defenses were breaking down. "I suspect Alexsa was drawn to Adrian, but being a sensible woman, she opted for life with her husband over a romantic interlude with an unstable Thespian. Still, memories have of way of deluding us." 'And don't I know!' she mused. Shaking off a sudden surge of melancholy, she continued. "Alexsa read about Adrian's predicament and probably felt compelled to renew the relationship. Now she genuinely regrets having written to him."

"Do you suppose he really was the target of that bomb? Could there be some Mafia connection there?"

Caroline shrugged. "I think we should inform the FBI of the possibility. They could look into it better than we. I do think, though, that I'll call my daughter tonight. Kerry studied Adrian in acting class, and she's acquainted with all sorts of theater people in Chicago. Perhaps one of her friends will remember him. Better yet, maybe Kerry knows an old actor who worked with him on stage."

"Alexsa didn't have much to say about William Chappel," Carl noted. "Do you think she's hiding something there also?"

"I doubt it. Wealthy women generally don't hang around with quarry workers. Surely the social rules apply in Rhineburg as well as in

Chicago! I'm surprised she didn't know James Belding, though. He grew up in Rhineburg and was close in age to her grandson."

"That was pretty odd. You know, there was a preacher in the area by the name of Belding who died a few years back. The two were probably related."

"The Archangels would know, wouldn't they?"

Carl nodded. "It's worth asking them. What struck me as odd was Alexsa didn't seem to know Belding's sister. According to the newspapers she's the CEO of a company in Chicago and one rich lady!"

"And wealth generally knows wealth. Unless Alexsa no longer has a role in the family business, I'd guess she'd at least have heard of the woman. Jane told me the sister brought Belding to St. Anne's in September. He was a Viet Nam veteran who suffered a nervous breakdown. I understand he was pretty much out of it."

"Doesn't seem a likely candidate for murder, unless the bomber had something against the sister or her company."

"Do you think that's possible?" Caroline queried. "Wouldn't it be better to blow up the corporate headquarters if you're plotting revenge on the CEO? But again, I'm sure the FBI are investigating that scenario. I wish we had a little more background information on both of the Beldings. Alexsa's reference to the family was vague at best."

"We need a better local paper," Carl replied. "The 'Rhineburg Rag' hardly mentioned him at all."

"I haven't had much time to read the 'Tribune', but I've kept all the copies printed since the explosion. I'll take a look at them tonight. Belding's obituary must be in one of them."

The conversation died as they reached Rhineburg. Carl slowed the Jeep and drove cautiously down busy Wilhelm Avenue. Caroline stared out the window absently, her thoughts still on the victims of the bombing. They knew so little about any of them, least of all Gail Garvy, the student nurse Alexsa had refused to acknowledge. She suddenly remembered the diary and letters she'd taken from Gail's dorm room. She'd better look them over as soon as she got back to the apartment.

"You seem to be a million miles away, Cari."

"Hmm? Oh! We're here already!"

"Yep. Stromberg and Morgan..."

"Purveyors of Fine Automobiles!" Caroline glanced at the sign above the doorway of the dealership and slowly shook her head. "I just hope my new Jeep lives up to Jim Morgan's standards!"

"It better," Carl growled. "Or I'll have that young squirt's head on a platter!"

"I've been waiting for you." James greeted them at the door with his boyish grin. "You're going to love her, Mrs. Rhodes!"

Caroline always wondered why men automatically genderized automobiles as female. Ed had named all his cars Annie, and during his lifetime he'd owned Annie I, II, and III. She had no intention of carrying on the tradition. She'd start a new custom; she'd call her Jeep Clyde, or Abe, or Rudolph.

"We've just come from your grandmother's," Carl said as they followed Jim across the showroom.

"Really, Professor? I'll bet she enjoyed your visit."

"Actually," Caroline replied, "I think we may have upset her."

Jim frowned, his blue eyes darkening with displeasure. "How so, Mrs. Rhodes?"

"We were discussing the people who died in the explosion at St. Anne's Hospital. Evidently Alexsa was friends with one of the victims, a man called Thomas Adrian."

"Oh? I've never heard mention of him." Jim seemed genuinely surprised by Caroline's statement. She decided to spring another name on him; maybe his reaction would be more revealing this time.

"There was another man, a James Belding.." She hesitated as if reluctant to pursue an unpleasant subject, then shrugged and gave Jim a beguiling smile. "Your grandmother appeared somewhat distressed when his name came up. I got the distinct impression her memories of him weren't happy ones."

"I don't know why," Jim responded cautiously. "Belding left town when he was a teenager. I doubt Grandmother even knew him."

"But you did, right?"

Jim walked over to the coffee maker and poured himself a cup. He was so distracted that he forgot to offer any to his customers. With his back still turned to them, he said, "Not really. He was ahead of me in high school."

"What about his sister?" Carl persisted.

"His sister? I don't know...yeah, I guess maybe she was in my class. It's hard to remember that far back."

Caroline exchanged a puzzled glance with the Professor. Jim was as reticent as Alexsa. Either evasiveness ran in the Morgan family or they'd stumbled onto something important. She tried another tack.

"I take it Alexsa and Elvira Harding are close friends. Gail Garvy's death must have come as a shock."

"Elvira is my grandmother's housekeeper. Has been for years." Jim suddenly swung around. "Why all these questions, Mrs. Rhodes? What are you looking for?"

Caroline decided the time had come for honesty. She told Jim about the Buick having been tampered with and was not surprised by his calm acceptance of her statement. Apparently the story had already reached the salesman, just as it had reached his grandmother. What did astonish her was the way he brushed it off.

"Probably some college kid out to get his kicks. I wouldn't give it a second thought if I was you."

"Oh, really?" roared the Professor. "Attempted murder doesn't seem to bother you at all, James!"

Jim's jaw jutted forward. His eyes blazed as he replied tightly, "Mrs. Rhodes survived that crash, didn't she? No broken bones, no internal injuries. Just a little cut on the head." He drew in a deep breath, then turned to face Caroline. "Not at all like Gail Garvy, right? She had no chance at all, poor kid." He put down his coffee cup and checked his watch. "You'll have to excuse me but Liz is waiting dinner. The Jeep is around back." He pulled open a desk drawer and came up with a set of keys. "I'll drive it up front and meet you there. If you have any problems with the car, you know where to find me, Mrs. Rhodes."

He escorted them out the door, locking it firmly behind them. Caroline saw the fury in Carl's eyes as he glared through the plate glass at Jim's retreating figure. The Professor clamped down hard on his pipe.

"If you're not careful, you'll bite that stem in two."

Carl snatched the pipe from his mouth and grimaced. "That's twice today I've been thrown out of places by old friends! What the hell is going on?"

"Alexsa got to him," Caroline answered. "Don't you remember she took a call from Jim while we were at her house? I'll lay you odds she warned him not to talk to us. She probably shared her suspicions with him, and he took it from there."

"This is downright ridiculous!" Carl fumed. "Jim practically accused you of sabotaging your own car!"

Caroline nodded. "If I were the bomber, it would be a smart move. I'd blame someone else and draw the attention away from myself."

At that moment Morgan pulled up to the curb in Caroline's new Jeep. She smiled despite herself as she ran her hand over the sparkling clean forest green Cherokee. It was perfect, just as Jim had promised.

"Thank you, Mr. Morgan," she said as he handed her the keys. "It's exactly what I asked for."

"Remember to read the owner's manual, and if there's anything you don't understand, just give me a ring." Jim had slipped back into his salesman's persona. He smiled automatically before jogging off to his own car. They watched in silence while he made a U-turn and drove rapidly away.

"In a real hurry, isn't he?"

"Probably rushing over to Grandmama's place to find out what she really told us."

"I'd say you're right about that, especially since Jim's house is back that way." Carl jerked a thumb over his shoulder.

Caroline smiled at him grimly. "Well, Sherlock," she said as she moved towards her Jeep. "We seem to have stirred up a hornet's nest in Rhineburg. It'll be interesting to see who gets stung next!"

The Professor's tone was light, but his words cut to the quick. "Hopefully, my dear Watson, it won't be us!"

FIVE

December 23

Caroline pulled her Cherokee over to the curb and depressed the switch for the side window. It slid down silently and she waited while Carl stopped alongside and did the same.

"Call me in the morning!" she shouted above the wind. It was snowing again, thick wet flakes whipping about the cars as the full fury of the latest blizzard hit Rhineburg. Caroline could barely see Professor Atwater through the curtain of whiteness separating the two Jeeps, but then he leaned across the passenger seat and gave her the thumbs up. She waved back and signaled him to go ahead of her. With the four wheel drive in gear, she followed him as far as the hospital before he turned off for home.

The day had ended pleasantly enough. Caroline had wanted to show off her new car, so when they left the dealership, they drove directly to Martin and Nikki's place. Martin insisted on celebrating what he called his mother's 'Christmas toy', and promptly order pizzas from a local eatery near the campus. After dinner, Nikki dragged out a box of ornaments and dragooned the pair into decorating the Christmas tree. Carl bellowed his way through an assortment of carols, substituting bawdy limericks for the original lyrics as he tossed tinsel over the pine branches. Marty did his best to harmonize. His clear tenor blended nicely with the Professor's deep bass, but Nikki and her mother-in-law shunned any attempt to match their boisterous singing. Content to be the audience, they cheered enthusiastically each new version of an old favorite.

It was nearly midnight when the party broke up. Now, as she turned into the hospital parking garage, Caroline checked her watch one more time. 12:22. In another fifteen minutes she'd be tucked up in bed enjoying a well earned rest. Just thinking about sleep made her yawn.

She left the Jeep in a slot on the third level, exited the garage, and followed the snow covered sidewalk to the ER entrance. Inside, the hospital was comfortably warm and Caroline loosened her coat and scarf as she passed the triage area attached to the emergency room.

"Hi, Caroline! Quite a storm out there." Paul Wakely was the doctor on duty that night. He waggled a chart in her direction from his chair behind the main desk. "How you feelin'? Any more headaches?"

Caroline smiled at the man who'd sewn her up after the crash. "I'm fine," she called out. "But these stitches are beginning to tickle."

"That means you're healing nicely. Come see me when it's time to take them out. And don't overdo it, OK?"

"Of course not. I'm getting my share of rest."

"That's not what I hear!" Paul retorted jovially. "You've been running around ever since you were released from the hospital. Even bought a new car I was told."

Caroline frowned. If her movements were so easy to follow, her attacker knew what she'd been up to also. She shivered at the thought.

"What's wrong, Caroline?" Paul started to rise, but she waved him back into his chair.

"Nothing. I'm just surprised at how quickly news travels here."

Paul laughed. "That's what you get for moving to Rhineburg. You ought to know there's no privacy in a small town."

Caroline forced a laugh and hurried on. She passed X-ray and the Cast Room, then turned left, her wet boots squeaking noisily on the polished floor of the hospital's south corridor. Paul's words echoed uncomfortably in her mind as she followed the hallway towards the courtyard nestled in the center of the four-winged complex. When she tugged open the plate glass door and stepped into the enclosure, she was met by a blast of wind and wet snow. This shortcut to the dormitory was anything but inviting, the path crossing it unlit and thick with drifts. Caroline hesitated, but then the snow suddenly thinned to a flurry. She gripped the hood of her parka and plowed on, keeping as her goal the dimly lit windows on the other side of the yard.

Halfway to her destination, a curious scene unfolded before her She saw two figures outlined in one of the far windows. Locked in an embrace, they swayed in and out of view in the shadowy north corridor. Caroline slowed to a halt, her curiosity piqued by the strange movements. A sixth sense told her she wasn't watching the romantic scuffling of two employees. She knew she should go back for help, but instead she started running towards the north wing door. She was only steps away from it when a sudden gust sent snow swirling through the courtyard. Icy pellets slapped her cheeks and she ducked her head, shielding her eyes with an arm. When she looked up again, the corridor before her was dark and the couple had vanished from sight.

Caroline stumbled through the last of the drifts and re-entered the building. It was pitch black inside and she paused for a moment to get her bearings. An exit lamp glowed above the elevators at the far end of the corridor, but all the overhead lights were turned off. She turned to her right, her hand sliding along the wall as she moved cautiously down the passageway. Her eyes quickly accommodated to the darkness and she began to make out shadows ahead of her. One particular shadow thickened into a still gray mass on the floor. Steeling herself to recognize it for what she instinctively knew it to be, Caroline approached the corpse.

The man lay huddled beneath a window, his knees drawn up, his left shoulder propped against the wall. His head was twisted crazily upward and to the right, and a sudden burst of moonlight captured the look of surprise in his open staring eyes. Caroline bent down for a closer look. A lock of silver hair hung down over the man's forehead and she gently smoothed it back into place alongside its copper brothers.

Charles Paine had been fastidious about his appearance; hopefully, the undertaker would do him justice.

"Damn!" she said as she rose to her feet. She looked up and down the corridor but saw no one else there. The cafeteria entrance was only a few feet away and Caroline knew there was a house phone just inside the door. Even in the dark she found it easily enough.

"Code 88," she told the operator. "Near the cafeteria. And call maintenance. There are no lights down here."

She disconnected, then hit 9-0 for an outside line. The operator was announcing the code over the loudspeaker system when she dialed Carl's number. He picked up on the second ring.

"Thank God you're home!"

"I just got in. What's the matter, Cari? What's happened?"

"Can you come back to St. Anne's right away? Charles Paine is dead. Murdered."

"Where are you?" Carl asked crisply.

Caroline told him. "Will you call the Archangels? I'd feel much better with one of them here."

"Right! Stay where you are and I'll be there soon."

Caroline hung up the phone with a feeling of relief. She didn't want to be alone when the police arrived with their endless questions. With Carl for support, she could face the coming unpleasantness.

"Where the hell are the lights?"

The code team had arrived. Caroline could hear the sound of running feet and the crash cart being trundled down the hallway.

"Down here!" she called as her fingers swept the wall near the phone for a switch. It was only inches away and when she flipped it up light spilled out from the cafeteria into the corridor.

"Be careful!" she warned the newcomers. "He's been murdered. The police will want to see everything just as it is."

"Not you again!" Dr.Paul Wakely motioned the rest of the code team back. He gave Caroline a quick smile that vanished from his face when he bent over the body. He felt for a carotid pulse, then placed his stethoscope on Paine's chest. After a moment he straightened up and turned to her.

"You called the code?"

Caroline nodded. "I knew it was useless as soon as I saw him there, but I didn't want security messing around with the body before the cops arrived. It seemed best to call you people first."

"We'd better notify them now." Paul glanced over at one of the nurses. The woman nodded and moved quickly away just as the overhead lights came back on. At the entrance to the cafeteria, she passed an employee in a brown uniform hurrying their way.

"Who the hell's been fooling with the lights down here?" The man glared at Paul and Caroline before catching sight of the body on the floor. His face went suddenly pale. "Oh shit! Is that guy dead?"

Paul stepped in front of the corpse, blocking it from the man's view. "Don't worry about him. What's wrong with the overheads?"

The maintenance man took a step backwards. He dragged his eyes away from the body and addressed Dr. Wakely gruffly. "Somebody opened that panel." He pointed to a metal cover on the wall at the end of the corridor. "He blacked out the entire hallway."

"Was it unlocked?" Caroline asked.

"Hell, no!" the man replied angrily. "You think we leave it open so some damn fool can play games down here? It was jimmied! Now we'll have to replace the entire panel!"

"Did you touch the door when you turned the lights back on?"

"Look, lady! Are you into dumb questions, or what? Of course I touched the door! I had to swing it open to get at the switches inside."

Paul drew the fellow off to one side and cautioned him to stick around; like it or not, he'd have to talk to the cops. Left alone, Caroline found herself engrossed with the behavior of the code team. None of them were expressing regret for the administrator's sudden demise. Despite the circumstances, a couple of nurses were actually smiling.

'I guess I can't blame them,' she mused. Paine had been a real hatchet man during his years at St. Anne's. All of these nurses must know someone affected by his cuts. She turned to Paul, about to ask him if the cause of death was what she suspected, when the elevator bell jingled.

"OK! You all hold it right there!"

A tall broad shouldered man in a blue military type uniform had emerged from the elevator. He strode towards them, a gun gripped dramatically in both hands and pointed square at the code team.

"Holy shit!" Paul swore softly. "The cavalry has arrived."

"Let's go over this one more time."

Tom Evans, FBI, unlaced his stubby fingers and placed both palms flat on the table. With pursed lips and furrowed brow he gazed solemnly at the spot between them. Caroline might have bought the act if she hadn't seen it coming.

"You know what?" she said. "You've got the Columbo bit down to a 'T', but it's beginning to get on my nerves. Why don't we stop playing these silly games. I don't intend to confess to murder, and you've haven't any real evidence against me, so why don't we call it a night?" She stood up and stretched her muscles. After forty-five minutes of sitting on a straight-backed chair, her spine was screaming in pain. What she wouldn't give for her own soft recliner.

"Please sit down, Mrs. Rhodes. This won't take much longer."

Angry with the agent's officious manner, Caroline turned on the man vehemently. "No way, my friend! I've said everything I could about what happened tonight. Why don't you question President Hurst? I told you I heard him arguing with Paine during the faculty party at Bruck Hall. Something was going on between the two of them."

"Mr. Hurst will have his chance to explain that conversation," Evans replied smoothly. "I intend to speak with him next."

"Good! Then you won't be needing me any longer!"

Caroline grabbed her coat off the chair and stalked away. Just as she reached the door, Evans called out to her.

"Don't leave town, all right Mrs. Rhodes?"

Caroline looked back and shook her head in exasperation.

"You really should work on your lines, Mr. Evans. Your whole performance is rather outdated."

She walked out of the room, restraining herself from slamming the door behind her, and crossed the hallway to the Administrator's office. There in the waiting room she found Carl deep in conversation with one of the Bruck brothers.

"Are they done with you?" the Professor asked. He pushed his rotund frame out of the thickly padded sofa and guided her over to an easy chair, a sympathetic gleam in his eyes.

"It's more like I'm done with them," Caroline responded wearily. "I couldn't take it any more. Evans kept going over and over the same things, trying to trip me up on my answers." She looked around the little room. "Where's Hurst? He's next in line for a grilling."

"The President waits for no man!" Carl grinned. "He bullied one of the officers into taking him downstairs for coffee. They should be back any minute now."

"Then let's get out of here. I don't think I can stomach any more of that man tonight." Caroline rose and headed for the door. "Are you guys hungry? Why don't you come up to my apartment and I'll fix us some sandwiches."

The two men were quick to take her up on the offer. Together they tramped through the empty hospital corridors down to the tunnel connecting St. Anne's to the nursing school dormitory. Five minutes later they were in Stromberg.

"Welcome to my humble abode." Caroline ushered them into the apartment. "Make yourselves at home while I check out the frig."

"Let me help you," Carl insisted, making a beeline for the tiny kitchen. He opened a glass cabinet and took out three plates.

Caroline pulled up a chair to the kitchen table before diving into the refrigerator. "Have a seat, Mike," she said while searching the shelves for sandwich ingredients.

"I'm not Michael," the young man said sheepishly. He pushed a strand of blond hair off his forehead and smiled.

Caroline straightened up in embarrassment. "I'm sorry, Gabe. You two are so identical..."

"I'm not Gabe either." Another quirky grin lit his face. "My name is Rafael, Mrs. Rhodes, but you can call me Rafe. I'm the youngest, and last, of the Bruck brothers."

Caroline was speechless. She stared at the security man for a moment, then broke into laughter. "I should have known!" she said, shaking her head. "There are three Archangels mentioned in the Bible: Michael, Gabriel, and Rafael. So you're the most junior of the Brucks. By how long, Rafe?"

"About a minute and a half," he answered with a chuckle. "Mom had a C-section."

Caroline didn't know what to say to that. She motioned to the chair again, still shaking her head in amazement. The three brothers looked incredibly alike; hopefully, they were equally intelligent.

"I was on duty when the Professor called," Rafael said, getting back to the business at hand. "Unfortunately, we didn't get to talk to you before the FBI arrived. The hospital security people sealed off the ground floor and we had a heck of a time persuading them to let us down there."

Caroline handed Rafe a package of sliced roast beef, a jar of mayo, and a loaf of rye bread. She turned back to the frig for lettuce and cheese. "It was more like a three ring circus than a crime scene after that gun toting guard stepped off the elevator. He refused to holster the damned thing until his boss showed up!"

"He'll be out of a job tomorrow!" the youngest Bruck assured her. "Harns is a good security chief. He doesn't put up with stupidity."

"I hope not! Do you know, that fellow actually asked Dr. Paul Wakely for his identification card? And he wanted to search the code team for weapons!"

"Damn fool!" Carl grumbled. "Just when did Hurst show up?"

"He came trotting down the hall behind Chief Harns. He said he'd had an appointment with Paine, and when the Administrator didn't show up in his office, he got worried. He notified security and they were searching the first floor when the code was called. He swore he didn't suspect anything was really wrong until he overheard the message on the guard's two way radio. Harns put out a general alarm after he was phoned by one of the nurses down stairs."

"Then he called the FBI."

Caroline nodded. "Mr. Harns seems to know his business. He figured Paine's murder might be related to the bombing."

"That's a pretty good guess," commented Rafe. "Tell us about the interrogation, Mrs. Rhodes."

Caroline finished making the last sandwich and sat down. Carl handed her a bottle of beer, and she took a swallow of the cold liquid before answering. "It was unnerving, to say the least. Evans seems to think I'm the murderer."

"What?" Carl almost dropped his sandwich. "Don't tell me..."

Caroline nodded. "Alexsa spoke to them. She just wanted to share a few thoughts with Agent Evans, he said, and he appeared quite grateful for her help."

"Dammit!"

"Now, Carl, don't get so upset. I told you she didn't trust me. Anyway, Evans had already been digging into my past. He started his own investigation after the accident."

"And what did he come up with?"

Caroline glanced at Rafe and blushed. The Professor knew of her emotional problems, but she wasn't happy discussing them with strangers like the Brucks. She realized anything she said tonight would be repeated to the other brothers.

"He was aware of Ed's accident. And my hospitalization," she finally admitted. "The Chicago police sent him the file on the hit-and-run. It contained a lot of background information on Ed, including the fact that he'd been in the Army reserves and was adept at judo and karate. Evans wanted to know if Ed had taught me any special moves." She took another sip of beer but she didn't miss the glance exchanged by her two guests. She slammed the bottle down angrily. "Look, you two!" she snapped. "I'll tell you exactly what I told that damned fool from the FBI: Ed was the expert, not me! I was too busy taking care of the kids to fool around in some gym with a bunch of grown up boys in white togas! My husband was the one who needed that outlet. He enjoyed the physical training and the company of the other guys in the class. You know -- the male bonding bit!"

Rafe silently studied his sandwich while Carl huffed and puffed through his mustache. Caroline had embarrassed them both with her outburst, and she wasn't done yet.

"If it's any comfort to you," she continued bitterly, "I swear that although I can recognize a broken neck when I see one, I have neither the ability nor the strength to twist someone's head until their spine snaps!"

"Nobody here suggested that, Mrs. Rhodes," Rafe protested. "It's just that you have the unfortunate habit of being in the wrong place at the wrong time. You were working on the psychiatric ward the day of the explosion. Then tonight you were the one who found Paine's body. Evans may be hard-nosed, but he's a street smart cop. He doesn't go in for coincidences.

Carl allowed her a moment to calm down before asking, "What did Evans say about your accident?"

"He had one of his men check the Buick. He acknowledged the brakes were tampered with, still he pointed out how it is the nineties. As he put it, women do know something about cars today."

"He thinks you cut those hoses yourself!" Carl groaned. "I was afraid of that, Cari. The FBI is stuck and Evans is looking for anyone to pin this bombing on."

"That anyone just might be me if we don't come up with some answers pretty quickly!" she retorted. "I tried to tell him about the argument I overheard between President Hurst and Charles Paine, but he didn't bat an eyelash. He kept concentrating on the fact that I arrived in town around the same time as all the victims were admitted to St. Anne's. And my past history apparently doesn't lend to my credibility."

Rafe frowned at her. "I guess I'm missing a part of the story, Mrs. Rhodes. What do you mean by your 'past history'?"

Caroline pondered the situation she was in. If she was going to rely on the Brucks for help, she had no choice but to be honest with them. In for a dime, in for a dollar, she told herself.

"I had a nervous breakdown some months ago," she conceded. She told him briefly about Ed's death and her plunge into despair. "Evans suggested I never truly recovered my sanity. He thinks I'm a nut case out to punish the world for the loss of my husband."

"That's ridiculous! And you said this man had brains, Rafe!"

"He does, Professor. Evans has one hell of a reputation when it comes to breaking big cases. That's why he was assigned to this one. You have to remember he's under a lot of pressure from various sources. There's politics involved here, as well as big money."

"You mean Mayor Schoen," Caroline stated.

"For one," Rafe agreed. "Politically, this could ruin him. Folks won't forget he dumped his wife in St. Anne's shortly before the explosion. Already the gossips are suggesting he had a hand in it."

"His opponents must be jumping for joy."

"You bet, Professor! There's nothing like a rumor of murder to drag down a potential candidate."

"And the fact that her death made him a wealthy man doesn't help his cause."

"There you're wrong, Mrs. Rhodes," Rafe replied. "The Mayor can only claim property they held in joint tenancy. Martha Schoen's personal fortune was tied up in a type of tontine."

"A tontine? With whom?" Carl asked incredulously.

"Her blood relatives." Rafe chewed on his lip as he wrestled for the words to explain the convoluted dealings of the Stromberg family. "Mrs. Schoen's great-grandfather set up an arrangement by which only blood relatives would benefit from his wealth. In order to inherit, his children had to sign a binding agreement designating their own children as sole beneficiaries of their wills. His grandchildren were required to do the same, and their children also. Marriage partners were not considered suitable to inherit. The money was meant to stay within the bloodline."

"So Teddy got nothing?"

Rafe shook his head. "Not a red cent, Professor. This all came out at the reading of the will. Since Martha died childless, her share of the family fortune reverts to her closest living relative."

"That would be..."

"Alexsa Stromberg Morgan," Rafe concluded with a grin. "The old lady is rolling in money as it is, and now she'll get even more!"

"What about Martha's shares in the quarry?" Caroline queried.

"She inherited them from her father. They'll go to Alexsa also."

"Then the Mayor will still have problems pushing through the stadium construction project." Caroline outlined what Nikki had said about Martha's opposition to the plan. "Since Alexsa despises Teddy, she'll probably follow her cousin's lead. It appears Schoen gained nothing but trouble from his wife's death."

"Maybe that's why he sold her Jeep so quickly," Carl mused. "Teddy may be looking for cash to invest on his own."

"Perhaps," Caroline agreed. "What's most important about this is that it rules out Martha Schoen as the target of the bomber. The only person to profit from her death is Alexsa Morgan. And Alexsa doesn't need Martha's money."

"That leaves us with Chappel, Adrian, Belding, and May Eberle. The motive for the bombing must lie with one of them." Carl turned to Rafael Bruck. "Is there anything you can tell us that would indicate which of these people was the intended victim of the killer?"

"I don't know anything about Thomas Adrian," Rafe said with a shake of his head. "Chappell's father-in-law threatened to kill the man after his daughter died, but then he up and had a stroke right after the funeral. He's been bedridden ever since. There were no other male relatives, and frankly, I can't think of anyone else in town who hated him enough to do this."

"Then we should cross him off the list too. How about May Eberle? Alexsa hinted she'd caused trouble for a lot of people. Could there be a motive there?"

Rafe shrugged. "She and her sister spread some ugly rumors in their day, Mrs. Rhodes. I know of at least two divorces they had a hand in. Now if May'd been found dead with a knife in her chest, I could give you a whole list of potential suspects, but somebody bombing St. Anne's for revenge?" He shook his head. "I doubt any of her victims would have gone to such extremes."

Caroline frowned. "Alexsa might disagree with you there. By the way, she accused May of murdering her father. Carl thinks that's a lot of nonsense."

"She's probably right." To Carl's amazement, Rafe appeared totally serious. "Old man Eberle was a real, pardon my language, bastard. He treated his daughters like trash, which may be why the sisters resorted to their gossipy ways. They couldn't lash back at their father, so they took out their frustrations on the town."

"To tell you the truth, I always felt sorry for the two of them," Carl interjected.

Rafe nodded agreement. "Elvira Harding came to see Mike the same day April Eberle died. She told him what she'd seen and heard, but it wasn't evidence of murder. It would have been her word against Eberle's as to what actually happened on that staircase. Still, I wouldn't put it past the old guy to hit his daughter in a fit of anger. When he himself died so suddenly, I figured May helped him along to the grave. She was devoted to April, and her death was the straw that broke the camel's back."

"But no one investigated Mr. Eberle's death."

"Why should they? What good would it have done?"

Caroline was forced to agree. With May safely ensconced in St. Anne's, what was the point of creating a scandal?

"Who inherits May's money?" Carl asked.

"There's absolutely no money," Rafe told them. "The house is a run-down monument to miserliness. Eberle pinched pennies when it came to upkeep on the place. The roof is falling in, the wiring is a fire hazard, and the foundation is crumbling. No one ever visited, except for Elvira who went once a month to clean, so no one ever saw what a mess it was inside. May willed the place to the Historical Society, but they don't want it. I expect the town council will have it torn down."

"I knew Eberle was a skinflint," Carl said. "Still, I thought he'd left a wad of dough to May."

Rafe shook his head. "Nothing to speak of. God knows where his money went! There was only a few hundred in his bank account."

"Alexsa told us May's father had several children outside of marriage. Do you think it's possible one of them, or one of his grandchildren, might have thought there was something to be gained by getting rid of May?"

"Are you kidding, Mrs. Rhodes?" Rafe grinned. "No decent Rhineburger would own up to being related to the Eberles!" The look on Caroline's face sobered him. "I'm sorry. I know you're worried about this, but I'd say Alexsa Stromberg exaggerated Eberle's sexual prowess. I've never heard the slightest hint of anyone other than his daughters being fathered by the man."

"Hmm!" grunted Carl. "So Alexsa was playing games with us!"

Caroline glanced at her watch. It was close to three a.m. "You must be tired, Rafe, but could you please tell us what you know of James Belding before you go?"

"It's very little, I'm afraid." Rafe drained his bottle of beer and stood up. "There was a preacher in these parts by the name of Ty Belding, but he died years ago in a hunting accident. He was James Belding's uncle, and James and his sister Janice lived with him for a while outside of town. The Belding kids attended high school here but dropped out of sight after graduation. Mike is trying to find out more about them both. We know Janice went to Chicago and married the son of a business tycoon. As for James, he entered the Army and served in Viet Nam. That much we learned from the newspapers, but they haven't printed a whole lot on his background. I'll let you know if we dig up anything further." He shrugged on his coat but stopped midway to the door. "By the way, what was that you said earlier about an argument between Hurst and Paine?"

Caroline told them both what she'd overheard at Bruck Hall the night of the faculty party. "I didn't realize Paine was talking to Hurst until tonight when the President introduced himself to Paul Wakely. He used his first name, Garrison. Then I remembered hearing Paine call the other man in the room 'Gary'. It had to be Hurst he was talking to."

"That's a pretty good guess, Mrs. Rhodes. I don't know of any other Garys associated with Bruck U. It sure would help, though, if we knew what that conversation was about."

"They might have been arguing over university business," Carl suggested.

Caroline shook her head. "I don't think so, Carl. Charles Paine sounded very angry. He said something like, 'a maniac did it!'. I'm sure he was talking about the bombing."

"Well, if you remember anything else, gives us a call." Rafe flashed the signature Bruck brothers' smile and left. Carl hugged

Caroline before heading for the door also.

"Don't worry, Cari. We'll figure this thing out sooner or later."

Caroline doubted it, still, she didn't voice her misgivings. After the two men were gone, she laid down fully dressed on her bed, setting the alarm for five o'clock in case she fell asleep. Her eyes were burning from fatigue but her mind was racing as she remembered her interrogation by the FBI agent. Evans had accused her of creating the story about Hurst and Paine, calling it 'a convenient memory'. She feared he'd settled on her as his prime suspect.

"How in the hell did I get into this mess?" she muttered. Her life had taken a definite downhill slide ever since Ed's death. Now her future seemed more precarious than ever. 'It's all your doing, Ed!' she thought irrationally. 'If you hadn't gone and left me...'

'Cut it out!' she told herself angrily. Tossing the blankets aside, she stood up and began to pace the room. 'It's your own fault if Evans questions your mental stability! You acted like a fool back in Chicago, so why expect people to think you're sane now?'

"Thank goodness May Eberle's dead," she grumbled aloud. "I'd be in jail by now if she was still around spreading gossip."

It was typical ER black humor, still it roused Caroline from her doldrums. She stretched out on the bed, a smile tugging at her lips as she pictured herself in prison blues begging for mercy from a tight-lipped May Eberle. The absurdity of the scene brought perspective to her problems and soon Caroline was back in control. She closed her eyes and began making plans for the morning.

The sky was crowded with a veritable fleet of battleship gray clouds when Caroline made her first phone call at five a.m.

"Kerry? Hello, honey! I'm sorry to wake you so early in the morning, but I wanted to catch you before you left the apartment."

Her youngest daughter mumbled something incomprehensible before dropping the phone back on its cradle. Caroline dialed again, and this time when Kerry answered, she shouted into the receiver.

"Kerry! Don't hang up on me! This is your mother!"

"Who?" a sleepy voice replied. "My mother doesn't live here."

Afraid she'd hang up a second time, Caroline placed two fingers to her lips and whistled shrilly. That got the girl's attention.

"What the hell! Who is this?" Fully awake now, Kerry sounded hopping mad.

"My goodness, dear! What was that noise? Are you having trouble with your phone?"

"Is that you, mother?" Kerry demanded grimly. "What in the...world...do you want at this time of the day? Don't you know it's only... Wait a minute! Is anything wrong? Are you OK?"

Caroline assured her that all was well in Rhineburg. Both Kerry and Krista knew of her accident -- Martin had called them from the hospital -- but they were as unaware as he of her latest troubles.

"I know it's an ungodly hour to be calling, but I need some information about an actor and of course I immediately thought of you." Caroline's rapid fire delivery was intentionally aimed at arousing her daughter's curiosity. She knew the girl well. Once intrigued by a problem, Kerry would go to hell and back to find the solution.

"This is really important, dear, so listen carefully." She told her as much as she could about Thomas Adrian. The stun-gun approach worked well; Kerry was overwhelmed into silent attention. "I'm also looking for a connection between Adrian and a woman called Alexsa Stromberg Morgan. If you can dig up anything on the two of them, I'll be forever in your debt. And Kerry," she added without a pause, "I need you to get back to me by eight o'clock."

She realized she was asking a lot, and her daughter confirmed that appraisal in no uncertain terms. After a bit of haggling, they settled on a more reasonable time frame. Caroline hung up with a smile, confident Kerry would come up with some answers for her.

At six o'clock she placed another call to Chicago. Her brother answered on the third ring.

"Caroline! Hey there, how's the new Jeep?"

"I love it, Al. It handles as nicely as you said it would. And with all the snow we've had, the four wheel drive comes in handy."

"That's great," her brother stated. "But you wouldn't be calling this early in the day just to talk cars. What's on your mind, sis?"

"I need your professional help, bro. I'm in trouble, big trouble!" Caroline didn't beat around the bush. She explained the situation as concisely as possible. Alan was horrified when he learned the auto accident had been engineered to permanently eliminate his sibling.

"Why didn't you tell me this before?" he demanded to know.

"I didn't want to worry you, Al," she replied. "I really am fine, except an FBI agent named Evans thinks I'm the one who planted the bomb at St. Anne's. He also suspects me of Charles Paine's murder."

Alan indulged is several graphically colorful statements before regaining control of his temper. "Would you care to explain his reasoning on the matter?"

"The FBI heard about my nervous breakdown. Apparently I fit their profile of a 'mad bomber'."

Alan swore for a second time. "So this Evans guy figures you're a loose cannon traumatized by Ed's death. I suppose he thinks killing people is your way of handling grief!"

"Something like that," Caroline agreed. "But I don't intend to sit by quietly while they build a case against me." She told him about Professor Atwater and their joint effort to track down the murderer. That alarmed her brother even more than the FBI's accusations.

"Holy shit, Caroline!" he roared. "Don't you know you could get killed playing that game?"

"Listen to me!" she replied with equal vehemence. "This man has already tried to put me in my grave! I refuse to give him a second chance. I could use your help, Alan, but if you'd rather not get involved..."

"Don't be a fool!" Alan said gruffly. "Of course I'll help you. Tell me what you need."

Caroline knew she could count on her brother. She told him about James Belding and his sister, Janice. "According to the newspapers, her name is now Honeywell. She married the head of some company in Chicago."

"Honeywell Industries."

"That's the one. Do you happen to know her?" As the V.P. of a commercial bank, Alan's social circle ranged far beyond hers.

"Not personally, though I've met her at various functions. An attractive woman, and bright too. You know, Caroline, I read about her brother's death in the papers here, but I never suspected you were involved until now."

"Everything's happened rather quickly," she said in apology. "Before last night, I had no idea the FBI were even interested in me!"

"OK, sis. It's no use beating a dead horse. Now let me get this straight. You want background info on both Beldings, right?"

"And their uncle, if possible. His name was Ty Belding, and he was a preacher here in town. James and Janice lived with him at one time, but he's dead now."

"We may have some difficulty with him, but I'll get my people on it right away. Anyone else on your list?"

"Just one more person," Caroline replied. "Alexsa Stromberg Morgan is a very rich woman who knows everything about everybody in Rhineburg. Strangely enough, she can't seem to remember the Belding family, even after all the newspaper coverage."

"That's odd," Alan admitted. "Money usually knows money. You'd think she'd keep tabs on a home town girl who married a millionaire. So when do you want the results of this little investigation?"

"Would yesterday be too soon?"

"Of course not!" Alan laughed. "I'll shake a few bodies out of bed and call you back later this morning."

"Thanks a lot, Alan! I'll appreciate anything you can come up with."

"Listen up, doll," Alan drawled in his best Edward G. Robinson imitation. "Don't worry about a thing. The cops ain't got nothin' on us big time bankers. We've got stool pigeons everywhere!"

"Don't I believe it!" Caroline laughed.

"Believe this too," Alan said more seriously. "I love you and I'm concerned for your safety. Tell me you won't do anything rash."

"Of course not, Alan. I give you my word I'll be careful."

Little did she know in a matter of hours she'd be breaking that promise.

"Hi, Jane." Caroline placed her breakfast tray on the table opposite the unit manager and sank wearily into a chair. The effects of sleeplessness were evident in the dark circles under her eyes.

"You don't look so good," Jane commented between mouthfuls. "I suppose I wouldn't either if I'd stumbled over a dead man last night."

"So you've heard."

"Who hasn't! Word spreads quickly in these hallowed halls." Jane sipped her coffee as she watched Caroline pick gingerly at the food on her plate. "Didn't anyone warn you to avoid the omelets? Half the ingredients are rejects from the lab."

Caroline grimaced and pushed her plate aside. "Now you've made me lose my appetite. Oh well. I was going on a diet anyway." She leaned back and grinned at the other nurse. "So tell me, what's the gossip on our late Administrator? Any bets on who killed him?"

"I don't know about bets, but the staff is ready to proclaim you Employee of the Year!"

"Keep your voice down," Caroline joked. "If the FBI hears you talking like that, they'll pull me in for further questioning. Speaking of questions, I have a couple for you."

"As long as they're original, my friend," Jane responded. "I'm so sick of answering the same ones over and over again!"

"I take it you've been worked over by the Feds also."

"I've talked to more different police than I ever knew existed. Every time I think they're done with me, they come up with a new angle to explore."

"Have they questioned you about the tree the mice destroyed?"

"Funny you should ask. I forgot all about that when I made my first statement, but yesterday a very annoyed FBI agent visited me. He wanted to know why we put up a brand new tree in the rec room and, more importantly, why I withheld that information from the police."

"What did you tell him?"

Jane shrugged. "I said it slipped my mind in all the excitement after the explosion. Since then, I've been too busy trying to get the ward back in order to worry about mice."

"How soon before you can reopen the unit?"

"God knows!" Jane answered grimly. "The rec room is sealed off for repairs, but Paine was adamant we'd start admitting patients again right after Christmas. Now that he's dead, I'm not sure where we stand."

Caroline changed the subject. "What kind of a student was Gail Garvy?"

"Why are you interested in her?"

"Just curious, I guess," Caroline lied. "She seemed to work well with the patients."

"So she impressed you, huh?" Jane smiled and shook her head. "I must be the only one who didn't like the girl."

Caroline was taken aback. "Why not?"

Jane stared at the table before answering. When she looked up at Caroline, her expression was sober. "I suppose one shouldn't speak ill of the dead, but frankly, Caroline, I always considered Gail to be a queer one. She really didn't give a damn about any of the patients except one."

"Who was that?"

"James Belding."

"Belding!" Caroline suddenly recalled the scene in the rec room just before the explosion. Someone had called out Belding's name and Gail had approached him, coaxing him into joining the others around the tree. He had whispered something to her after raising four fingers to her face.

"Why was she interested in James Belding?" she asked in bewilderment.

"I really don't know, Caroline. No matter who we assigned her to, she always drifted away from that patient and ended up with Belding. I got the impression she was studying him, but not like a student studies an intriguing case. There seemed to be something personal about her fascination with the man." Jane paused to gather her thoughts. "I can't put my finger on it, but I swear she was after something. What that could be, I don't know since Belding was almost catatonic from the day he arrived on the ward. He never spoke a word and he..."

"What do you mean, he never spoke!" Caroline interrupted. "I saw him talking to Gail right before the explosion."

"What!" Jane almost spilled her coffee in her excitement. "He actually said something to her?"

Caroline nodded. "I was too far away to hear his words, but I certainly saw his lips move. And Gail answered him as if it was a perfectly normal exchange between patient and nurse."

Jane was stunned. She leaned back in her chair and stared at Caroline. "Do you know how hard we worked to get that man to communicate? Everyone on the unit knew they were to report directly to me if he said even one word! His sister was very concerned about his progress, and Mr. Grove ordered us to contact him immediately if Belding responded in the least little way to treatment."

"So you thought James Belding was totally mute."

"Not just totally mute, but totally out of it!" Jane drummed her fingertips on the table and frowned in concentration. "Why in the hell would Gail have kept this to herself?" she fumed. "She was informed of the situation when she first came on the unit. She should have reported his behavior at once."

"Who's this Mr. Grove you mentioned?" Caroline asked.

"He's Mrs. Honeywell's personal representative. He acted as a liaison between her and the hospital concerning Belding's care. He used to fly into town every couple of weeks to check up on things."

"That's a lot of checking up. Didn't the sister trust you?"

"Of course she did!" Jane replied indignantly. "Mrs. Honeywell provided the money to establish the psych ward."

Caroline's eyebrows shot up. This was news to her. "You told me Charles Paine had financial backing from connections in Chicago, but I never guessed they were so impressive. According to the newspapers, Janice Honeywell is rolling in money."

"I believe she bankrolled the unit so she'd have a safe place to keep her brother. Safe from publicity, I mean."

'But not from a killer,' Caroline thought. She tactfully skirted the issue.

"Did you ever mention Gail's behavior to her instructor?"

"Sure. She talked to the girl twice, and both times Gail had an excuse for hanging around Belding. She seemed prepared for any objections I raised." Jane smiled wryly. "Gail was a smart cookie. She knew only qualified staff were supposed to work with Belding. Whenever Tony Grove appeared, she'd drift back to her own patients. But between his visits, she gravitated to James like a bee to honey."

'I'd love to know why,' Caroline mused.

"Mrs. Honeywell intended to make another large donation to the hospital. I suppose she'll cancel it now."

"Hmm?"

"Sorry, Caroline. I was thinking out loud." Jane took another sip of coffee. "James Belding's death hurts St. Anne's in more ways than one. Paine had persuaded his sister to fund a major renovation project involving the outpatient department. Tony Grove was handling the details, which is one of the reasons we saw so much of him on the ward the week before the bombing."

"And now the deal's off?"

Jane shrugged. "Grove's still hanging around, but Paine's murder certainly makes negotiations difficult."

Caroline considered that the understatement of the year.

"But then again, I may be wrong." Jane pointed to the doorway of the cafeteria. Caroline swung around in time to see two men carrying empty trays step into line by the breakfast bar.

"Who are they?" she asked.

"The older man is Bill Bruck, grandfather of the Archangels and presiding officer of the Board of Directors. The short one in the five hundred dollar suit is Tony Grove."

The Honeywell representative was a well built man in his late forties or early fifties who carried himself with a confidence born of success. Caroline recognized his type immediately. He was the sort of man to whom winning meant everything, be it in business or at play. She suspected his cool demeanor concealed an ego of huge proportions.

She was about to turn back to Jane when Grove looked over in her direction. His eyes seemed to bore straight through her, and it suddenly occurred to Caroline that she'd seen his face before.

"I've met that man," she said slowly. "Only I can't place where it was."

"Impossible!" Jane countered. "If you'd ever dealt with Grove you'd remember him. He's a real tough customer, the kind who always gets his way and never makes a mistake. Still," she grinned, "I think he made one today!"

Caroline gazed at the other nurse in puzzlement but Jane's smile only broadened as she gestured towards Grove's tray.

"He ordered the omelet!" she laughed.

Back at the apartment, Caroline fielded a couple of calls from reporters who'd learned she'd discovered Charles Paine's body. She dealt with them swiftly, but wasn't so lucky handling her own son's call.

"It's been on the news all morning!" he exclaimed. "You should have called me, mom. I would have come right over."

"Professor Atwater was here," Caroline told him. "And Rafael Bruck arrived also. I managed quite well with their help."

"So you met the third Archangel. Are you impressed?"

"Rafe seems as bright as his brothers. They're young, though, to be in charge of security at the university."

"I guess so," Martin replied. "But they were trained by their father, and he's was the best Chief of Security Bruck ever had."

"He's not working any longer?"

"He had a heart attack a while back. Since then he only advises the boys when they need it. Has Nikki told you about their wives?"

"No. Is there something special about them, also?"

"Well...you can judge for yourself when you meet them. They'll all be here for our New Year's Eve party. Speaking of parties, are you coming to the one in town tonight?"

"The Winter Festival? Nikki mentioned it to me. I'll try, dear, but I can't promise you I'll make it." Caroline didn't mention she might be busy hunting down a killer with the Professor. The less Martin knew of their adventures, the better.

No sooner had she hung up on her son when Kerry called.

"How you doin', mom?"

"Fine, Kerry. What have you got for me?"

"My goodness! You're certainly businesslike this morning. Not even a 'Hi! How are you?' for your favorite daughter?"

"Hello, dear. How are you?" Caroline answered automatically. "Now, what have you got for me?"

Kerry sighed in exasperation. "Whatever's going on there better be good. I woke up quite a few friends to get this information!"

"I do appreciate it, Kerry, but please! Just tell me what you've uncovered. I don't have time to explain right now."

There was a moment of silence, then Kerry sighed again. "I expect a full account when I come to Rhineburg for Christmas. OK, now, let's see what I have here." Papers rustled on her end of the line. "Ah, yes. Thomas Adrian was considered a rising star in the early fifties, mainly due to his roles as Hamlet and Macbeth. You know, mom, Shakespeare wrote so many other fine plays, yet producers always seem to go for..."

"Kerry! Can we please stick to Mr. Adrian and his career?" Caroline pleaded. Discussions with her youngest daughter were often tricky since Kerry's thought processes tended to be erratic at best. Like a butterfly in a garden of wildflowers, she flitted from subject to subject, enamored by them all.

"Sorry about that, mom. Sometimes I get carried away. As I was saying, Adrian was a pretty good actor, but he had this thing about trusting people. He was convinced his co-stars were out to steal the show."

"Is that so unusual in the theater?" Caroline asked. "I thought most actors were peculiar in one way or another."

There was dead silence on the line before Kerry answered, her voice dripping with sarcasm. "Thanks for that vote of confidence!"

"I didn't mean you, dear," her mother said hastily. It wouldn't do to ruffle Kerry's feathers. After all, the girl had worked hard for all this information and deserved Caroline's thanks. "I meant some actors."

"Forget it, mom. Actually, you're right in a way. There's a lot of ego involved in acting. Still, Adrian pushed ego to the limits. He was positively impossible, and that's why directors stopped hiring him."

"I was told Adrian was so paranoid that he actually believed his coworkers were out to kill him. Is that true?"

"Well, I have a marvelous book written by Frederic Gordon, the theater historian. He lists Adrian as one of the finest interpreters of Shakespeare known to America, but he also calls him 'erratic' and 'temperamental'. Gordon doesn't go so far as to call him paranoid, still I guess he couldn't write that while Adrian was alive. Defamation of character, and all that rot. I wonder if he'll update the chapter now. I should call the publisher and get Gordon's address and then I could..."

"Kerry! You're wandering again."

"Oh. Where was I?"

"Adrian made a lot of wild accusations against his coworkers. Was anyone really gunning for the man?" Caroline closed her eyes and forced herself to be patient.

"Anna's uncle would have gladly strangled him, but he's been dead for years. The uncle, I mean. Not Adrian. He's only been dead a few days."

Count to ten and start over. "Who is Anna, dear?"

"Mother! How many times have I got to tell you? Anna is my inspiration in the theater, my mentor, my..."

"Professor. Now I remember, Kerry. We met at 'Hamlet' last year. So you're telling me her uncle knew Adrian, right?"

"Not only did he know the man, he also directed three plays in which Adrian had the lead. Mr. Karasov left his diaries to Anna and she let me look at them this morning. There were several references to Adrian's unstable mental condition, all written in no uncertain terms. Apparently the guy was a real fruit cake!"

"Fruit cake or not, Kerry, did anyone other than Mr. Karasov want to kill him?" A long dead director hardly seemed a likely suspect!

"Fruit cake. That's a traditional Christmas gift, isn't it? I can't think of anything to give Anna this year, and I really should stop by her place with a present."

Caroline sighed. This conversation was going nowhere.

"It's a wonderful idea, dear. Now what about Alexsa Stromberg

Morgan? By any chance, did Mr. Karasov mention her name in his diary?"

"How'd you guess?" Kerry exclaimed. "Who is this mystery woman, mom?"

"She lives here in Rhineburg," Caroline said shortly. "Tell me about her, Kerry."

"Well, according to Anna's uncle, the only reason Adrian was given the lead in his last play was because Mrs. Morgan was footing all the bills. She demanded that he be given the role."

Caroline perked up. "You're positive it wasn't her husband who backed the play?"

"Definitely not, mom. Mr. K. made a notation next to an entry concerning payments to the theater. He wrote, 'Foolish woman!', then underneath it he scribbled her name."

Was this confirmation of a romantic link between Alexsa and Adrian? Or was the director referring to the woman's spending habits?

"Maybe it means she was talked into bankrolling a bad play," Caroline thought aloud.

"Shakespeare didn't write bad plays," Kerry replied indignantly.

"Sorry, dear. You're right, of course. What I meant to say was, perhaps the production was poor."

"God only knows!" Kerry responded. "It never even made it to opening night. Evidently, all kinds of things went wrong. A set collapsed, injuring a crew member, and it had to be totally redesigned. Then there was a mix up with some keys. Somehow Adrian got locked in the wardrobe department, and because he was claustrophobic, he practically tore the place apart before they found him. The head seamstress walked out on the play after that little scene. Finally, the leading lady had a heart attack and died right on stage. Adrian claimed she'd been poisoned, but by mistake, the intended victim actually being himself. He insisted that all the accidents were aimed at him. Of course, his accusations created quite an uproar in the newspapers."

"And that's when the production shut down?"

"Yep! Karasov called Mrs. Morgan and told her to get a new director. She said forget it, the play's off. I guess she was sick and tired of all the ruckus. She simply withdrew her financial backing."

"Sounds like it was a disaster from the start."

"Well, mother, what do you expect?" her daughter replied matter-of-factly. "They were doing 'MacBeth'!"

Caroline recalled the old superstition concerning Shakespeare's famous play. Actors believed it bad luck to mention its name before opening night. Considering all the calamities that had occurred, either someone had shouted 'MacBeth' at each and every rehearsal, or Adrian wasn't quite as crazy as people thought.

As a likely target for murder, Thomas Adrian just moved to the top of the list.

"Mrs. Rhodes? Mrs. Caroline Rhodes?"

The female voice on the other end of the line sounded too unpolished to belong to a reporter. Still, Caroline responded cautiously.

"Yes, this is she. May I ask who's calling?"

"My name is Elvira Harding. I'm Gail Garvy's aunt and I left a message for you yesterday on your machine."

"Of course, Mrs. Harding! I'm sorry I didn't get back to you. I was out most of the day."

"That's OK, Mrs. Rhodes. I know how busy a person can get around the holidays."

"I'm so sorry about your niece," Caroline said. "She was a fine young person."

"So you knew my Gail?" There was a hint of hopefulness in Elvira's voice.

Caroline hesitated. "Not very well. But I worked with her the day of the explosion." If she was to get anything out of this woman, it seemed best to appear knowledgeable about the girl. "She'd developed quite a good rapport with the patients on the psych unit. Very attentive to their needs."

"That was my Gail all right!" Elvira boasted. "Always listened to people, cared about their problems. She was like her mom that way."

"Please give my condolences to Gail's mother. I wasn't able to attend the funeral."

Since her words were met by dead silence, Caroline assumed she'd blundered in some way. "Mrs. Harding? Are you still there?"

"I'm sorry, Mrs. Rhodes. I guess there's no way you could have known about Monica. Gail's mama died when Gail was just a baby."

"Oh! Forgive me, please!" So that's why the Harding woman was listed as next of kin. Still, it didn't explain the initials on the ring she'd seen in Gail's room.

"Don't give it another thought," Elvira said kindly. "My sister, Albina, is simply shattered by what's happened to her granddaughter. She couldn't bring herself to call you, so I said I'd do it for her. Can I stop by today and pick up Gail's things?"

Caroline thought fast. She hadn't yet read Gail's diary, but she could hardly refuse the woman's request.

"Of course," she agreed reluctantly. "What time would be good for you?"

"I'd like to come by now, if that's convenient."

Caroline stalled for time. "I've an appointment in ten minutes," she lied. "But I could meet you in the dormitory lobby at noon."

Mrs. Harding agreed without hesitation and Caroline hung up considering her next move. She needed to read Gail's diary before the aunt arrived, but she also wanted to talk to Carl. After a moment's hesitation, she picked up the phone and dialed the Professor's number.

"Damn it!" she swore when it continued to ring unanswered. "Where are you, Carl?"

Replacing the receiver, she turned to the coffee table and found Gail's diary and letters right where she'd left them the day before. She was just about to open the slim leather book when the phone rang again.

"Hello, Carl?" she said hopefully.

"Sorry, Mrs. Rhodes. Wrong person."

The voice was unfamiliar to Caroline. "I'm sorry," she said. "I was expecting someone else. Who's this?"

"Bill Morgan, over at Stromberg and Morgan. If it's Professor Atwater you're looking for, he just left my place a minute ago."

"Oh. Well, I'll catch him later, I guess. So now, what can I do for you?"

"My son Jim told me you bought Martha Schoen's Jeep. I just thought I'd check in and see if everything was OK with the car."

"It's running beautifully, Mr. Morgan. It's nice of you to ask." Caroline wanted desperately to be rid of the man but he appeared intent on continuing the conversation.

"That's good, Mrs. Rhodes. I'm glad to hear it. There's, ah, something else I need to say to you. It's, ah, kind of difficult to know how to start though!"

Caroline waited, surprised by the embarrassment in the man's voice. When he didn't go on, she finally said, "What's wrong, Mr. Morgan?"

"Well, like I said, Carl Atwater was just here. He told me about my mother's actions yesterday when you visited her. He also said Jim was behaving strangely."

"Did he mention that Mrs. Morgan spoke to the FBI about me?"

"Yes, ma'am, he did, and I want to apologize for that. Actually, it was Jim who called them. Mother was upset about it, still she had no choice but to cooperate when they came to the house."

That put a new twist on things. Caroline had thought it was Alexsa who'd contacted Evans.

"I tried to explain the situation to Carl, Mrs. Rhodes. I hope you'll be as understanding as he was."

"Why don't you just say what's on your mind, Mr. Morgan?"

Caroline attempted to keep the anger out of her voice. Alexsa and her grandson had caused her nothing but trouble so far.

"Please call me Bill, Mrs. Rhodes. And don't judge my family too harshly. This whole mess has us tied up in knots."

Morgan certainly sounded distraught. His sincerity touched Caroline and she relented. "Go on, Bill," she said more kindly. "And it's Caroline, OK?"

"You see, we thought this Jim and Monica stuff was behind us. I never realized my son would go off like a loose cannon when Gail died."

"I don't understand what you're talking about, Bill. Maybe you'd better start at the beginning."

The man heaved a sigh. "It all happened so long ago," he said. "Jim dated Monica Garvy before he married Liz. She was a damned little gold digger, and I told him so, but Jim just couldn't see through her. He thought the sun rose and set in that girl."

"Maybe he was in love with her," suggested Caroline.

Bill snorted. "She was a hussy if I ever saw one! Dollar signs big as saucers in her eyes. Hate to admit it, but I was relieved when she died in the fire at St. Anne's. At least she was out of Jim's life."

Caroline recalled there'd been an inferno in the dorm back in the '70's. "Monica was a nursing student here?" she asked.

"Yeah. She was Elizabeth's roommate, but that was after Gail was born. You see, Monica got mixed up with some rich guy from Chicago. She dropped out of school to have his kid, then went back again when her aunt said she'd look after the baby. Her own mother threw her out of the house, and the baby's father turned out to be married already, so Monica was left holding the bag."

"That's unfortunate," Caroline commented. "And the father refused to help her?"

"Worse than that," Bill explained. "The guy up and died in a car crash right after Monica found out she was pregnant. She claimed they'd tied the knot a week before the accident, but her marriage certificate was phony. At least that's what Rev. Belding said, and he was the preacher who supposedly performed the service."

"Would that be Ty Belding you're talking about? A minister from this area?" Caroline felt the hairs rise on the back of her neck.

"Yeah, that's him, although I'm not sure he was a real minister. Had a farm outside of town where he held revival meetings under a big striped tent. Lots of whooping and hollering and passing the plate."

"Did he have relatives in town?"

"Sure he did. That fella who got killed in the explosion..."

"James Belding."

"Right. He was the preacher's nephew, and there was a niece too. Can't say I remember her name."

Caroline did though. And Bill should have, if he'd been reading the newspapers lately. "Why did your mother pretend not to know the Beldings?"

Bill groaned. "Monica's aunt Elvira has been my mother's housekeeper for years. Alexsa feels a loyalty to her, so she didn't want her disturbed by your questions."

That seemed a poor answer to Caroline. "What about your son? He also answered evasively when we asked him about James Belding."

"Jim hates that entire family. He was sure the Reverend lied about Monica's marriage. When Albina Garvy disowned her daughter, my son became absolutely furious. It didn't help that the father's family refused their financial support. They wanted proof of paternity, but Monica wouldn't allow Gail to be tested. She said it was too humiliating. Jim figured Monica got a raw deal all the way around. He was set to marry her when she up and died."

"Was Jim close to Gail?"

"No, not particularly. Monica used to bring Gail up to the house back when she was a baby. Jim saw a lot of her then, but after Monica's death, they didn't have any real contact. The way I see it, the bombing brought back all those bad memories. Jim still thinks of Monica as some kind of martyr, and now he's placed Gail in the same category."

"So you're saying we opened a can of worms when we brought up the subject of Gail Garvy."

"Yeah," Bill agreed. "Mother's caught in the middle. She feels bad for Elvira, but she wants to protect Liz and Jim's marriage."

Caroline's eyebrows rose. "It's that bad, is it?"

Bill sensed he'd gone too far and tried to cover his mistake.

"Women don't like to hear about their husbands' old girlfriends. Jim wants justice for Gail, but sometimes he doesn't realize how it sounds when he rants and raves about the situation. He mentions Monica a little too often, and that causes tension in the family. Oh, hell!" he said heatedly, giving up any attempt at pretense. "The truth is, Liz is sick and tired of Jim's dramatics. If he doesn't cut it out, she's going to walk out on him."

Caroline recalled the haunted look on Liz's face when she'd seen her standing outside the Morgan house. She'd mistaken it for age, but now she knew better. Jim's wife was exhausted from contending with Monica's ghost, and Caroline doubted it was a recent phenomenon. She'd bet Jim had carried a torch for his dead flame all his married life.

"I appreciate your explanation, Bill. It couldn't have been easy for you telling me all this."

"Well," he replied gruffly, "everybody knows whoever left that bomb was some kind of nut. I'm just sorry my family caused you trouble by gossiping to the FBI."

"It'll all get cleared up," Caroline reassured him. She crossed her fingers and hoped what she'd said was true.

At quarter to twelve Caroline looked at her watch and frowned. She was curled up on the couch reading Gail Garvy's diary, but it was slow and tedious work. The girl had used a form of shorthand known only to herself and Caroline had wasted precious minutes unraveling the code. Now that she was fairly adept at deciphering the pages, she was skimming the book hurriedly. It had to be returned to Gail's room before Elvira arrived, just in case the aunt knew of its existence. She was halfway through it when the phone rang again.

'Oh, damn!' she thought, snapping the little book shut. She grabbed up the receiver with a curt "Hello?"

"Hello to you too!" her brother said in surprise. "Have I caught you at a bad time?"

"Forgive me, Alan, but the phone's been ringing all morning. I thought you were another annoying reporter."

"They've been hounding you, have they? I'm afraid I can't help you with that problem, but I do have the information you wanted."

"Great! I have to be somewhere at noon. Is ten minutes enough time? Or shall I call you back later?"

"Ten minutes should be just about right. I'll keep it brief, and if you have questions you can catch me at the office after lunch. Now let's see, where shall I start?" Alan could be heard shuffling papers on his desk. "I think I'll tell you about Honeywell Industries first. It's a relatively new company, formed during World War II by an engineer named Arthur Honeywell. Arthur parlayed a small government contract into a profitable postwar business designing and manufacturing airplane parts. He married well, but his wife died shortly after giving birth to a son. Peter Honeywell was his father's pride and joy. Arthur brought him into the company at an early age and the young man displayed a real knack for improving on his dad's ideas. Peter doubled the company's profits before his twenty-fifth birthday."

"Sounds bright enough, Alan, but where does Peter fit into the picture? I thought you were investigating Janice Honeywell."

"Patience was never your strong suit, little sister. Just stay with me and The Great Alan will reveal all!"

Caroline laughed. "Of that I have no doubt. OK, Alan, I'm all ears."

"As I was saying," her brother continued, "Peter had a head for business. Before long he was his father's right hand man, a full vice-president in the company. Apparently brains weren't his only asset; he was handsome to boot! One of our research people contacted an old friend who covered the society beat back in the '70's. According to this columnist, Peter was known as a lady's man until he suddenly dropped out of the social scene. Nobody could pin a name on the girl, but the general consensus was young Honeywell had settled down with one special woman.

"Then Arthur dropped dead of a heart attack. Peter was away on business, but he took the first plane home when he heard about his dad. He was on his way to Lake Forest when a truck swerved into his car. He slammed into a retaining wall and was killed instantly."

"How tragic!" Caroline exclaimed. "Father and son dead within days of each other."

Alan agreed. "But here comes the interesting part. Arthur left everything he owned to his son, but Peter never made a will. Two days after the funeral, the Honeywell relatives met with the family lawyers. There was a knock down, drag out fight over the division of the estate. It looked like the whole mess would be settled by the court, but then Janice Honeywell stepped forward. What happened next was enough to send shivers up the backs of conservative bankers like myself."

"Janice Honeywell, nee Janice Belding, produced a marriage certificate stating she was Peter's wife, right?"

"How clever of you, Caroline!" marveled Alan. "It seems you're one jump ahead of me!"

"Just a good guess," Caroline admitted. She told Alan about the earlier conversation with Bill Morgan. "Bill mentioned Monica Garvy had dated 'some rich guy from Chicago' who later died in a car crash. Monica claimed he'd married her shortly before the accident, but Rev. Ty Belding, who supposedly presided at the wedding, said the marriage certificate was a phony. Rev. Belding had a niece named Janice, and she had a brother named James. Two plus two still makes four, brother dear."

"So I've heard," replied Alan dryly. "Makes you wonder if Jim Morgan isn't right when he says Monica was cheated out of her inheritance. Maybe there was some hanky-panky going on between Janice Belding and her uncle."

"How did Janice explain her marriage to Peter?"

"According to my sources, Janice was Peter's secretary. She claimed they'd been seeing each other for months outside the office, and only married secretly after Arthur voiced his objection to the match. I suppose Arthur wanted his son to marry into his own social class."

"The court must have accepted her story."

"It decided in her favor," answered Alan. "The newspapers had a field day covering the legal battle. My people found loads of material on it and apparently the marriage was duly recorded with the state of Illinois. Your Rev. Belding swore on the Bible he performed the ceremony himself."

"If you ask me, the whole thing is very fishy. What did you find out about James Belding?"

"There's another interesting story!" Alan exclaimed. "My people are still digging into his past, but so far they've learned that he and his best buddy joined the Army right after graduation from high school. They served in the same unit in Viet Nam, and both were declared MIA after a particularly dicey mission in the Mekong Delta. James Belding was presumed dead until this past spring when he surfaced in Thailand."

"That must have come as a surprise to his sister."

"Surprise isn't the word! Janice Honeywell was placed in a very precarious position by his sudden appearance. Her company had taken advantage of the new trade initiatives with Viet Nam. Honeywell Industries was deep in negotiations to open a factory over there."

"And her brother's appearance was an unwelcome reminder of the war."

"It sure was! The Viet Namese were embarrassed as hell since he apparently lived in their country for twenty years without being found. They were supposed to account for as many of our missing men as possible, and here's one who slipped through their fingers. Our government was embarrassed for similar reasons. We sent a lot of officials to Nam to look for traces of our guys. They brought back no evidence of survivors, yet Belding proves there might still be soldiers alive over there. Honeywell Industries was in the middle of the whole mess. How was Janice Belding, the CEO of the company, suppose to react when she met with the foreign officials? She could hardly forget that her brother lost twenty years of his life, not to mention his mind, in the jungles of Viet Nam!"

"How'd you learn about this, Alan?" Caroline asked. "I don't remember reading a word about Belding's rescue."

"It happened around the time Ed died," he said sheepishly. "You weren't paying much attention to world news back then. Of course, all the facts weren't made public right away. The government whisked him out of Thailand and into a Army hospital where they could debrief him before sending him home."

"Debrief him? James Belding was emotionally destroyed! He couldn't tell the Army anything."

"I guess that's what they decided too, 'cause he was shipped to Janice Honeywell pretty quickly after his arrival in the states. Our people in Washington came up with this material only this morning. Folks are beginning to talk now that Belding is dead. He's no longer a threat to the negotiations."

"Isn't that a pleasant thought!" Caroline snapped. "A man's life doesn't hold much weight next to a business deal!"

"Don't take it out on me, Caroline," Alan responded in an injured tone. "I'm only relating what I've learned, not what I was involved in."

Caroline could have kicked herself. Alan was also a Viet Nam vet; if anyone would be upset by the tragic story of James Belding, it would be her brother.

"I'm sorry, bro. I wasn't thinking clearly."

"It's all right," Alan answered kindly. "You've got a lot on your mind at the moment." He changed the subject. "Last but not least, we come to Mrs. Alexsa Stromberg Morgan."

"By the tone of your voice I'd say you've discovered something interesting."

"Actually, I found it more puzzling than anything else. Alexsa Morgan has holdings in several major corporations, but it appears she prefers one particular company to all others."

"Honeywell Industries?"

"Exactly!" Alan exclaimed. "She holds 22% of that company's stock. Outside of Janice, Alexsa is Honeywell's single largest investor."

Caroline was dumfounded. "Then why was she so vague about the Beldings? Surely she knows Janice is James Belding's sister!"

"I put that same question to my staff and they came up with a quite logical answer. Alexsa was protecting her investment."

Caroline was unschooled in the finer points of the stock market. She waited for Alan to explain.

"Look at it this way, Caroline. What if someone was extorting money from Janice Honeywell, using her brother as ransom against industrial terrorism, and she refused to pay? To show he means business, the killer plants a bomb at St. Anne's and ka-pow! There goes James Belding! The implied message is: next time you'll be dead, or maybe I'll level a couple of your factories and simply kill your business. Honeywell Industries is publicly denying such a possibility, but I think the FBI suspects the company was the actual target of the explosion."

"And where does Alexsa fit in?"

"Investors are a notoriously conservative lot. Let a rumor start that someone is sabotaging the corporation and they'll pull their money out in a New York minute. Since the bombing, the market value of Honeywell stock has depreciated. If the slide turns into a nose-dive, the company could go under. Janice is doing her best to play down any connection between her brother and the explosion at St. Anne's. Still, her people have been quietly working to reassure the stockholders, and I remind you, Alexsa is the most important of those. I'm sure she's agreed to go along with the company's version of the disaster, which is there's a madman running loose in Rhineburg."

"That's the same explanation pushed by Charles Paine, our late Administrator." Caroline recalled what Jane had told her about Janice Honeywell's contributions to the hospital. No fool himself, Paine would have cooperated completely if asked by Tony Grove, Honeywell's representative in Rhineburg.

"Here's one last bit of information, Caroline. Without a doubt, Mrs. Morgan knew Peter Honeywell," Alan stated. "As V.P. in charge of investor relations, he courted the more prominent stockholders, keeping them apprised of the company's success. My sources say he was constantly on the move, flying around the country to report personally to these people."

"Then he must have come to Rhineburg!"

"And I'll bet he brought along his secretary, Janice Belding!"

Caroline pondered the situation for several minutes after Alan hung up. If Alexsa was in cahoots with Honeywell Industries, everything she'd told them yesterday might be a lie. Or at least a distortion of the truth. Caroline was forced to reconsider the importance of Thomas Adrian and May Eberle in the inquiry.

She also contemplated the pressure being placed on the FBI. Janice Honeywell would move heaven and earth to influence the investigation. She'd goad the police into arresting someone who presented no threat to the status quo, no menace to profits, and she'd want him in jail before the closing bell on the next day of trading. Not a lot to ask if you were a wealthy industrialist with friends in high places.

And Caroline had no doubt the CEO of Honeywell Industries had powerful allies. Just look at the effect of Alexsa's little talk with Agent Evans. In one day Caroline had gone from victim to suspect in the eyes of the police. She wouldn't be surprised if Evans wasn't out gathering proof against her at this very minute.

It was a sobering thought, not one that Caroline wished to dwell on. Determined to beat her opponents at their own game, she locked the door of the apartment and walked downstairs to await the arrival of Elvira Harding.

"Mrs. Harding? Hi! I'm Caroline Rhodes."

Caroline ushered the short, gray haired woman into the nursing dorm lobby. Elvira was stout but not fat. She held herself erect, adding dignity to her five foot three inch frame, as she nodded somberly at Caroline.

"This is my grandson, Jerry," she stated matter-of-factly. "He's come along to do the liftin' and carryin'."

Caroline smiled at the boy standing behind Elvira. Barely old enough to shave, he pulled off his battered Bears cap and bobbed his head in her direction, all the while chewing on his bottom lip. She sensed his discomfort and couldn't blame him one bit; packing up the belongings of a dead relative was no fun, as well she knew.

"Gail's room is on the second floor. We can take the elevator if you'd rather not tackle the stairs."

Mrs. Harding eyed the rickety open-cage lift with its wrought iron doors. "I'd feel safer with the stairs," she said. "After you, Mrs. Rhodes."

Caroline led the way up to Stromberg. Elvira was silent until they reached the room.

"I hope we're not botherin' you, showin' up like this after your trouble last night."

Caroline sighed as she unlocked the door. Word sure did

spread quickly in Rhineburg! "No problem, Mrs. Harding. It was a shock finding Charles Paine's body, but since I..."

"Oh, my!" Elvira exclaimed. "What a mess!"

Caroline smiled indulgently. "The students do tend to be a bit sloppy at times."

"I'd say this is a lot more than sloppy," drawled Jerry. He fixed her with a cold stare. "Looks like somebody tore the place apart."

"What?" Caroline turned to look through the doorway. "Oh no!" she gasped. The boy was right. The dorm room looked like it had been hit by a cyclone. Dresser drawers lay upended on the beds, their contents heaped around them. Posters had been ripped off the walls, and books were scattered everywhere. Resting against the leg of the desk was Gail's jewelry box. It was open and empty.

Caroline felt an equal mixture of anger and bewilderment. Who had done this? And how had he gained entrance to the room?

"We shouldn't go in," she told Elvira grimly. "I'll call for help." She walked over to the pay phone knowing she should notify hospital security first. Instead, she dialed the Archangels' number.

Michael Bruck arrived at the dormitory only minutes after her call. He took a swift look inside Gail's room before turning to Caroline.

"Was it locked when you arrived?"

She nodded 'yes'. Michael frowned, then squatted down on his heels to examine the door latch. He refrained from touching it.

"Who has a key to this room beside you?" he asked as he stood up again.

"I honestly don't know," Caroline replied. "Gail Garvy and her roommate had keys, and hospital security probably has a master. They'd know if anyone else has one."

Michael looked at her thoughtfully. "Gail should have had her key with her the day she died. She wouldn't have gone off to work and left the door unlocked."

"If she did, it must have been lost," Elvira replied. There was bitterness in her voice when she continued. "There wasn't much of Gail left to find, much less what she had in her pockets!"

Caroline glanced at a grim Michael.

"The FBI must have one," she said. "Perhaps it's Gail's key."

The security man nodded and gazed once more into the room. "Most likely our intruder didn't leave any prints, but Tom Evans will want the place dusted regardless. You go home, Mrs. Harding, and I'll call you if he discovers anything."

Elvira snorted in disgust. "The FBI won't be any help and you know it, Michael Bruck! They haven't caught my Gail's murderer yet, have they? You think they can catch a plain old thief? Come on, Jerry!" She motioned to the boy before stalking back down the corridor.

Caroline shrugged helplessly at Michael, then took off after the others. Catching up with them in the lobby, she laid a hand on Elvira's arm.

"Mrs. Harding, would you please answer a question for me?"

Elvira turned to face Caroline. "Seems all I've been doin' lately is answering questions. First the police, then the press, and today it was Alexsa Morgan." She shook her head and continued toward the door.

Caroline hesitated. What was Alexsa up to now? Investigating on her own, or trying to set up more roadblocks?

"Wait, Mrs. Harding!" she called out. She stopped the woman just as Jerry opened the door. Pushing him gently aside, she closed it again and barred the way with her body. "You have to listen to me, Elvira. If you don't, Gail's killer may never be found."

Elvira's eyes narrowed, but her attention was now riveted on Caroline. "What do you mean, Mrs. Rhodes?" she asked.

"Let's sit down." Caroline led the other woman to a couch in the lobby. When Elvira was settled, she continued. "The FBI isn't getting anywhere fast because this 'mad bomber' nonsense has totally confused the issue. They're being forced to investigate physics students at Bruck and ex-employees of the hospital, all of which is a waste of time. Mrs.

Harding, our murderer isn't mad in any sense of the word. He may be evil, but he's not insane."

"You seem pretty sure of yourself."

"Professor Atwater and the Bruck brothers agree with me."

That appeared to impress Elvira. Gail's aunt cocked her head to the side and studied Caroline's face. After a moment the indecision faded from her eyes.

"Go on," she said calmly.

"There are people in this town who would prefer the madman theory be accepted by the police. Charles Paine was one of them." Caroline had to proceed cautiously. She still didn't have a handle on Elvira's friendship with Alexsa, so she couldn't mention the old lady's name. "Others have muddied the picture with innuendoes and fabrications. And still more have simply refused to speak to the police at all."

"Folks in Rhineburg don't trust them FBI types. They twist your words around 'till you can't even remember what you really said!" Elvira looked up at her grandson. "Ain't that right, Jerry?"

The boy nodded furiously. "Cops practically called me a liar when I told 'em about that red Jag I saw parked in the woods. They said I was makin' it up to impress my friends at school."

"But Jerry saw that car, Mrs. Rhodes. And he saw that man walkin' away from it. My grandson wouldn't lie about such a thing!"

"I believe you," Caroline said. She turned to the boy. "Who did you see in the woods, Jerry? Someone you know?"

The teenager shook his head. "Never met him before. I was takin' a walk down by the river, tryin' to figure out things in my head. Like who'd blow up a hospital, and why it had to be Gail who got killed that day. I mean, things were finally startin' to look up for her, and then she goes and gets murdered!"

"And that's when you saw this person?"

"Yeah," Jerry agreed. "He came drivin' down the road and

parked near the old loggin' trail past the bridge. I thought maybe he had to..." He glanced at his grandmother and his face reddened. "Well, you know what I mean, Mrs. Rhodes. But that wasn't the reason he stopped. When he got out of the car, he just stood there lookin' into the woods. He didn't do nothin', just stood there."

"Then what happened, Jerry?"

"After a while he got back in the car and drove off. I wondered what he'd been lookin' at, so I crossed the road and walked over to where he'd parked. I couldn't see anything special about the place 'till I hiked up the trail a bit."

"Is that where you found the Jaguar?"

Jerry nodded again. "Yes, ma'am. It was buried in a drift about fifty feet down the path. I mean, it was really covered up! Looked like a big ol' mound of snow just sittin' there in the trees."

"But you're sure it was a car."

"I ain't dumb, Mrs. Rhodes," the boy said in an injured tone of voice. "I walk that trail all the time in the summer and I knew right away it weren't no boulder. I brushed the snow off, and sure enough, it was a real beaut. A '93 Jag, fire engine red!"

Bells started clanging in Caroline's head as she recalled the car Jim Morgan had sold to a doctor from St. Anne's. Now why would anyone park an expensive Jaguar in the middle of the woods? Especially in this weather.

"You said the killer was no madman, Mrs. Rhodes. Then why'd he do it?"

"Hmm? Oh, yes." Caroline pulled herself together. Elvira had lost interest in Jerry's story and was now showing signs of impatience. "We believe he was after a specific person on the psychiatric ward, Mrs. Harding. One of the patients, or perhaps Gail herself."

"What!" Elvira's face registered shock, then dismay. She buried her face in her hands and began to weep.

"Jerry, there should be a box of tissues on the desk." Caroline pointed across the lobby to the receptionist's area. "Why don't you go get it for your grandmother?"

The boy hurried off and Caroline placed an arm around Elvira's shoulders.

"Mrs. Harding, why was Gail so interested in James Belding?"

She waited while the woman composed herself. Jerry returned with the tissues and Elvira wiped her eyes, then reached for the boy's hand.

"This is my flesh and blood, my own grandson," she whispered. "But you've got to understand. Gail was like a granddaughter to me. I raised her when her mama died in the fire here at the dormitory. I never could understand my sister's attitude." Elvira took a deep breath. "Albina was Monica's mother, but she turned her back on the girl when that shifty minister showed up at the house with the record book. Monica tried her best to prove Peter Honeywell was her husband. She went all the way to Chicago to meet with that other woman and the Honeywell lawyers, but she got nowhere."

"Did Gail think James could help her uncover the truth?"

"I couldn't say," Elvira murmured. "I was surprised when his name showed up in the newspaper. I didn't know he was a patient here." She raised her head and looked Caroline square in the eye. "But Gail must have known. She was obsessed with proving Monica had married Peter. It wasn't the Honeywell name or the money she wanted. What mattered was Albina. Gail wanted to humble her grandma, make her pay for all those years of neglect." Elvira released Jerry's hand and took a deep breath. "I don't know why I'm tellin' you this, Mrs. Rhodes. You're a stranger here in Rhineburg, unfamiliar with our history."

"Actually, I was told about Gail's mom only this morning, Mrs. Harding. I hadn't realized before that anyone died in the dorm fire."

Elvira twisted a tissue in her gnarled hands. "My niece worked part-time at St. Anne's to pay her tuition. Everyone else went home for the holidays, but Monica stayed 'cause of her job. She was all alone here when it broke out. The police said she must have started down the fire escape and then lost her footing. They found her lying on the ground beneath the ladder."

'And the daughter followed in her mother's footsteps,' Caroline thought. 'Both in nursing and in death.'

"Was Gail searching for evidence of her mother's marriage here at St. Anne's?" she asked Elvira. "Is that why she enrolled in nursing school?"

The old woman nodded wearily. "I begged her to let it go, but Gail insisted Monica hid the marriage certificate where nobody but she could find it. It never turned up after Monica's death, you know, and I searched high and low at the house. Peter's letters were gone too. They must have been in her room at school."

"And Gail refused to believe they'd burned in the fire?"

"Like I said before, Gail was obsessed. She was on some kind of holy mission to clear her mama's name. Mind you, I believed what Monica told me, but I couldn't see how Gail would ever convince Albina of the truth. She'd only get hurt worse."

Jerry shifted from foot to foot and gazed longingly at the door. Caroline sympathized with the boy, but she needed more answers.

"Were you good friends with your cousin?" she asked him.

Jerry shrugged. "Sometimes she got on my nerves with all her talk about Aunt Albina. Gail could be pretty weird when it came to her grandma, but I liked her well enough."

"Did she ever confide in you?"

"I guess you could say so," the boy replied hesitantly. "She told me about that Belding fella and the funny things he said."

"What things?"

Caroline tried to restrain her excitement, but the boy sensed it in her voice. He glanced at his grandmother, suddenly wary of sharing a confidence with this stranger. She nodded encouragement to him.

"If you know something that will help this lady, you speak up,"

Elvira told the boy. "Maybe she's right about Gail bein' the one the bomb was meant for. Maybe them Honeywells were behind it all!"

Caroline held her breath. The boy's eyes darted back and forth between her and his grandmother. Obedience finally won out and he gave up with a sigh.

"If you say so, Gram. Still, Mrs. Rhodes might of been the one who ransacked Gail's room."

"I promise I had nothing to do with it, Jerry." Caroline spoke firmly. She had to assure the boy that she presented no threat to his family. "Michael Bruck wouldn't have let me come downstairs with you if he thought I was a dangerous person."

She'd pushed the right button. Evidently even Jerry trusted the three Archangels.

"OK," he said with a nod. "I don't see how it will help, but here goes. Gail and I had lunch together a few days before the explosion. She was talkin' about Aunt Albina like usual, but she was laughin' and sayin' as how she was gonna give her a real Christmas present this year. I told her to quit bein' stupid. Aunt Albina would take any present of hers and throw it right out the door! Gail thought that was pretty funny 'cause she laughed real hard and said, 'Not this one!'. Then she held up four fingers and waved 'em in my face." Jerry frowned at the memory. "I couldn't figure out what Gail was up to, so I just let her go on talkin'. She told me about James Belding and how he was always doin' this." He demonstrated, uncurling the fingers of his right hand one by one until only his thumb remained tucked in his palm. "It didn't make any sense to me, especially when Gail whispered 'Four to go', then started laughin' all over again."

Elvira grunted. "It doesn't make sense to me either. Sounds like Gail was joshin' you, Jerry."

"Maybe she was, Gram," the boy grumbled. "But you said I should tell Mrs. Rhodes about it, and I did."

"And I thank you, Jerry," Caroline said as she rose to her feet.

She wanted nothing more than to race upstairs and read Gail's diary, but she first had to get rid of these two. "I appreciate your candor, Mrs. Harding. You've been very open about Gail and Monica."

Elvira pulled herself up from the couch. "No reason to keep it a secret, is there? With both of 'em dead, none of it matters any more." She turned to her grandson. "Take me home, boy. There's too many bad memories here."

Jerry took his grandmother by the elbow and led her to the door. As he helped her into the truck a black sedan turned into the driveway.

"Oh, hell! He's here already!"

Caroline turned and fled upstairs, anxious to be gone before FBI Agent Tom Evans entered the lobby. If he'd doubted her innocence before, he'd be doubly suspicious once he heard she had a master key to the dorm. And Gail's diary, laying on the couch in her apartment, was proof positive she'd been inside the girl's room.

'The noose grows tighter around my neck!' she thought grimly as she took the steps two at a time.

Caroline cracked open the apartment door and peeked down the hallway. It was quiet as a tomb on the third floor. Apparently the FBI were still busy downstairs.

'Let it stay that way!' Caroline prayed as she slipped into the corridor, a briefcase dangling from her hand. She crossed to the laundry room, scraped frost off the little window there, and peered out at the driveway below. A state police car was now parked next to Evan's sedan, and a uniformed man lounged against its hood. Another officer was just walking into the dormitory.

"Damn! I'm trapped."

The tunnel to the hospital was inaccessible with police strolling about the lobby. She'd have to find another way out of the building. Refusing to panic, she forced herself to calm down and concentrate on the problem. There had to be... Caroline snapped her fingers.

"Why not try it? Evans will think I never even returned to my rooms."

Caroline hurried down the corridor to the student lounge. Once inside, she closed and locked the door, then tugged open the window facing the hospital. A fire escape ladder led from the window to the ground below. It took less than a minute for her to scramble down the rusty iron steps. The sidewalk encircling the dormitory was shoveled clean and Caroline left no traces as she made her way to a side door and entered St. Anne's. Five minutes later she exited through the Emergency Department and headed for the hospital parking garage.

The guard was nowhere in sight and Caroline pulled away from St. Anne's unobserved. She circled the Green at a leisurely pace, then picked up speed after turning onto the highway leading to Rhineburg. Once inside the town's limits, she slowed down again, reluctant to attract the attention of a 'radar ranger' with a quota to fill. It was best to keep well away from the police until she'd talked with Carl and, perhaps, a lawyer.

With that thought in mind, she pulled into the parking lot next to the German restaurant where she'd lunched with the Professor. It was probably only wishful thinking to imagine Carl was inside wolfing down a huge meal, but Caroline decided to look for him there anyway. As it turned out, she'd only just missed him.

"He left about five minutes ago," the waitress told her. "But he didn't say where he was going."

Caroline crossed to the telephone booth and called Carl's office. The machine took her message and she hung up, dialed again, and waited while the phone rang at Carl's home. Once more she reached only an answering machine. Frustrated, she gave up and went out to a booth. The waitress was by her side instantly.

"Can I get you something, miss?"

"Lemonade, please." Caroline had carried the briefcase into the restaurant and she placed it now on the seat of the booth. Unlocking it, she withdrew the letters she'd found in Gail's room, unfolded the first one, and smoothed it out on the table.

The paper looked old, its edges crinkled and tinged brown. She lifted it to her nose and sniffed. The musty odor of smoke still clung to the letter.

"Here's your drink, Mrs. Rhodes."

Caroline looked up expecting to see the waitress. Instead, a thin woman in a fur parka stood over her, an icy glass in one hand, a cigarette dangling from the other. The newcomer placed the glass on the table and slid into the seat opposite Caroline.

"I'm Elizabeth Morgan," she said as she shrugged off the coat. She extended a bony hand to Caroline. "I saw you the other day up at the house. You were grilling Alexsa about the bombing."

Caroline laughed. "I wouldn't call it grilling, Mrs. Morgan. We were just seeking advice."

"Call me Liz. Or Elizabeth if you prefer. There's really only one 'Mrs. Morgan' in this town and that's Jim's grandmother." The woman's voice held a hint of sarcasm but Caroline chose to ignore it.

"Then you'll have to call me Caroline. We'll cast formality to the wind and pretend we've known each other for years."

Liz blew a ring of smoke into the air and watched it disappear. When she looked back at Caroline, her eyes glittered mischievously.

"But we haven't, have we? We're nothing more than strangers in a very strange town." She held up a hand. "Now don't start prattling on about the rustic charm of Rhineburg. It's little more than a rural hellhole, and you know it."

Caroline shrugged. "It's certainly not Chicago. Still, I wouldn't call it 'strange'. I suppose it's typical of small towns everywhere."

Liz threw back her head and laughed scornfully. "Obviously you haven't been around long enough to appreciate the truly unique character of our village." She leaned across the table and the odor of whiskey floated past Caroline's nose. "Stick around, my friend, and you'll soon come to hate this place as much as I. The only people who truly belong are the wealthy and the old. The rest of us are looked down on as peons!"

"You're wealthy," Caroline reminded her.

Liz shook her head. "Jim is wealthy," she snapped. "I'm just a hanger-on, a poor girl from the wrong side of town who married well. Doesn't really count, you know." She leaned back and took another drag on her cigarette. "So tell me what you learned from Alexsa. Did the old girl provide you with all the right clues?"

"She told some fascinating stories," Caroline replied carefully. "But nothing she said actually helped us."

Liz raised her eyebrows. "Really? You mean you're no closer to a solution than before?"

"I wouldn't say that," Caroline retorted. "While Alexsa tried her best to lead us astray -- her comments about Thomas Adrian and May Eberle were truly inspired! -- the Professor and I are not exactly idiots. There are ways of checking out the facts."

"So tell me, who did it?" Liz asked casually. She ground out her cigarette in the ashtray, her eyes downcast as she feigned disinterest in Caroline's answer.

"Come on! You don't really expect me to answer that question, do you? Suffice it to say, you won't be surprised by the name."

Caroline waited to see the woman's reaction to the ruse, but Liz didn't rise to the bait. Instead, she continued to gaze downward, her face suddenly pale, her lips set in a grim line.

"Where'd you get that?" she whispered, pointing to Gail's letter lying open on the table. She reached for it but Caroline was quicker.

"It's just a note from an old friend," she said as she folded the paper and thrust it back into the briefcase.

"Liar!" Liz screamed. She slid out of the booth and nearly fell as she grabbed for the case. A waitress hurried over.

"Mrs. Morgan! Let me help you to your car."

"Let go of me!" Liz tore her arm free from the girl's grasp and whirled around to face Caroline. "Liar!" she hissed. "I know what you're up to, but it won't work! You can't frighten me, or Alexsa!" She straightened up with an effort and lifted her chin. "We're Morgans, you know. Our kind don't frighten easily."

"Please, Mrs. Morgan. Let me drive you home."

A broad shouldered fellow in a greasy apron approached the booth. He reached for Elizabeth's coat and placed it gently around her shoulders. She didn't resist him, and Caroline watched as he led her to the door, Elizabeth still mumbling to herself.

"I'm sorry about that," the young waitress said. "Sometimes she just doesn't know when to quit."

"It's all right," Caroline replied with a smile. She slid out of the booth and handed the girl a five dollar bill. "Keep the change. It's the least I can do to make amends for the ruckus."

The waitress protested but Caroline gathered her things and left the restaurant. She needed to be alone to think things over. Liz Morgan had abruptly emerged as another piece of the complicated puzzle, and where she fit in, Caroline didn't know. But Liz had certainly recognized Gail's letter, and that must mean something.

Caroline climbed into the Jeep and sat there considering her options. She couldn't drive back to the dorm; the police would surely be waiting for her. Martin's apartment was off limits too. No fool, Evans would guess she'd head in that direction. She had no idea where Carl lived, and his office was too near the hospital to risk a visit. The only other place she could think of was certainly secluded, but would she get lost trying to find it?

"God only knows!" she muttered, throwing the Jeep into drive. "But it's the last choice left to me."

With that cheery thought in mind Caroline pulled into traffic and headed out of Rhineburg.

The afternoon sunlight did nothing to improve the appearance of the Blue Cat Lounge. If anything, the exterior looked more decrepit than ever with its peeling paint and warped windows. The roof was an eyesore of multicolored shingles layered haphazardly bottom to top, and the wooden gutters were pockmarked by rot. Caroline viewed the building with a critical eye. To call it dilapidated was putting it mildly. Carl really ought to consider some repairs, she thought as she pulled open the door and walked inside.

The smell of beer and peanuts permeated the interior of the lounge. Although the room was empty, a glow emanated from the diamond shaped glass panel in the door leading to the kitchen. Caroline walked towards it hesitantly.

"Hello? Is anybody here?"

Her greeting was met with silence. She stepped around the bar and tapped on the door.

"Hello! Are you open for business?"

"Not for another half hour," came a voice from behind her.

Caroline spun around. "Who's there?" she cried out.

"My goodness. Aren't you the jumpy one."

A young man strode out of the shadows behind the stage, a mop in one hand and a bucket in the other. He set them down next to a table and grinned at her.

"Did I scare you?"

"I'm afraid so." Caroline blushed as she backed away from the bar. "I thought someone was in the kitchen. I didn't expect to see you over there."

The youth glanced over his shoulder. "I guess it's a bit dark in that corner. Sorry if I spooked you."

"Forget it," Caroline replied. "The past few days have been full of surprises for me. I guess I'm just on edge."

"Life can be that way sometimes," the young man replied. He glanced at his watch, then smiled at Caroline. "Like I said, we're not really open yet, but since it's the holidays, I'll make an exception. You look like you could use a drink."

Caroline thought of Elizabeth Morgan and quickly shook her head. "Nothing alcoholic. I'd love a cola, though."

"How about one of our world famous roast beef sandwiches to go along with it?"

"Well..."

"Now don't say no or I'll take it as an insult!" He grinned again. "By the way, my name is Shiloh."

"I'm Caroline Rhodes." Caroline slipped into a chair and sat watching the boy as he moved about behind the bar. "Would you mind if I just sat here awhile? I have some paperwork..."

"No problem," Shiloh answered. He walked over and placed a tray on the table. "Stay as long as you like. I've some work to do in the kitchen, but if you need anything, just holler." He flashed another smile and turned away.

Caroline hadn't realized how hungry she was. Or how tired. Leaning back in the chair, she closed her eyes and let the fatigue drain from her muscles before tackling the two inch sandwich. The beef was delicious and after two bites she concluded it deserved the designation of 'world famous'. Or at least, 'best in Rhineburg'.

She finished the meal quickly. After assuring herself that Shiloh was still safely tucked away in the kitchen she opened the briefcase and withdrew Gail's letters. She smoothed out the first one and scanned it rapidly. It appeared to be a typical love letter.

"Dearest," it began. "I don't think I can stand another minute of separation from you!" The body of the note contained a rather emotional protestation of devotion and concluded with the words, "All my love, Peter".

Caroline folded the paper and laid it aside. The second and third letters were similar in content and mood; the fourth, somberly intense.

"Father refuses to approve of our marriage. I'm tired of arguing with him, dearest. Perhaps we should just give up and make a new life for ourselves somewhere else."

Peter sounded even less hopeful in the fifth letter, but the sixth one indicated a plan had evolved between the two lovers.

"You're right when you say I simply can't break with my dad. It would kill him and, frankly, hurt me deeply. Better to do it your way. I'll meet you next weekend in Rhineburg and the Reverend can marry us then. Father may come around in time."

Caroline remembered her brother's words. Arthur Honeywell had wanted his son to marry into society. Monica's social status was nil, so she was an unsuitable match for Peter. The same could be said for Janice Belding, but then the letters weren't written to her.

Elizabeth Morgan's pale face invaded Caroline's thoughts. Why had the woman gone berserk in the restaurant? When she noticed Peter's letter, her cocky confidence had degenerated into antagonism. But it was a shocked sort of antagonism, the kind that occurs when someone is unpleasantly surprised and simply reacts without thinking. The episode disturbed Caroline. She suspected Liz recognized Peter's handwriting, which meant she'd seen the letter before, perhaps when she'd lived with Monica at St. Anne's. If that was true, Liz could have backed up her roommate's claim of marriage to the Honeywell heir. But neither Bill Morgan nor Elvira Harding had even hinted at such a possibility. Surely they would have mentioned it had it happened.

The letters didn't prove Peter had actually wed Monica Garvy. They indicated the young man's intentions, but without a legal marriage certificate, Monica didn't have a leg to stand on. And there was the rub. Reverend Belding had sworn Monica's certificate was fake. He had records to back his assertion that Janice, not Monica, was the actual Honeywell bride. Records could, of course, be falsified. The minister might have substituted his niece's name in the ledger, then registered Janice and Peter's supposed marriage with the state. If so, it was done at Janice's instigation; the Reverend had nothing to gain by working the scam alone. And if the switch was accomplished before Peter's death, it indicated an even greater crime in the works. Janice and Rev. Belding must have plotted Peter's demise. It was a profitless venture with Peter alive to refute his secretary's claims.

It made no sense to say the change occurred after Honeywell's death. Reverend Belding couldn't tamper with records already held by the state. Unless, that is, he'd never registered the marriage in the first place. But why not? The only answer again was that Janice planned to eliminate Peter and then pass herself off as his wife.

Either way you looked at it, Janice Belding and her uncle were after Honeywell Industries. They'd gotten it, too, despite the collective wisdom of the firm's lawyers and a circuit judge.

Caroline was totally frustrated by the time she started reading Gail's diary. She still didn't see where James Belding fit into the plot. And if he didn't fit, neither did the bombing. Maybe she was probing a crime other than the one she'd intended to investigate. Or maybe the puzzle was simply too complicated for an amateur like herself.

With her confidence ebbing by the minute, Caroline scanned the diary. There was nothing of note until an entry dated late in September.

"I managed to change the student schedule. It was in Halsey's desk -- can you imagine she leaves her office unlocked? -- and I penciled in my name for the first psych rotation. What luck that she picked St. Anne's for her brother!"

Caroline frowned. Evidently Gail was not above breaking into the nursing director's office and tampering with school records. The girl's actions spoke volumes about her integrity.

"This is impossible!" the next entry stated. "I finally get near to Belding and he's totally out of it! He doesn't speak at all! I can't believe I went through all this trouble just to be disappointed again."

Caroline flipped through the diary, skimming page after page of vitriolic comments aimed at James Belding, Janice Honeywell, and Albina Garvy. Gail's impatience grew more evident with each passing day as she made no headway with her chosen patient. Then, in an entry dated mid-November, the girl wrote something curious.

"That watchdog Grove is here again. He seems to be coming more often and staying longer. I have to be careful when he's around. I don't want to give myself away."

A little farther on Caroline noted a change in Gail's attitude.

"I think I'm getting through to Belding. He actually looks me in the eye when I talk to him. The big question remains, is there anything of value going on in his head? Of value to me, that is!"

Gail mentioned Tony Grove on the next page.

"He's back again--Honeywell's little spy! I know he's watching me. I have to avoid Belding when he's around. The good news is I got the nurses' aide job. Now I have an excuse for coming in late at night. I can snoop around the dorm while everyone's sleeping!"

A few days later Gail wrote: "Another night of adventure. One would think the maintenance men would occasionally check the lock on the sealed off wing, but their stupidity is my good fortune. As long as they don't realize it's broken, they won't install a new one. And our housemother is so dense! She never checks rooms after midnight!"

Caroline grimaced. Apparently both she and the maintenance department had fallen down on the job.

"I think I've found the right room. The window overlooks the spot where the two sidewalks meet, just like Mom described in her diary. The place is a mess, but I'll find where she hid it!"

'Hid what?' Caroline wondered. She turned the page, engrossed in the diary.

"Belding did something strange today. I repeated the names -- mom's, Peter's, and Janice Belding's -- the same as I do every day, and this time he reacted to them. He raised four fingers and whispered, 'Four to go'. I don't know what it means, but I aim to find out. Fortunately, no one saw him talk to me. Gardner would tell the doctors if she knew and then they'd be all over Belding. I'd never get near him again!"

'Poor James,' thought Caroline. Perhaps he'd be alive today if Gail hadn't been so self-centered. She read on.

"Success at last! I found the letters tucked behind the baseboard beneath the window. Mom must have been terrified of that bitch if she went to such lengths to conceal them. If I can only discover where she put the marriage certificate! Tomorrow, Albina. Maybe tomorrow!"

At least Caroline now knew why the letters reeked of smoke. They'd been hidden in Monica's burned out dorm room.

"Belding continues to behave strangely," a later entry noted. "I no longer have to mention the names to get a reaction from him. He only has to see me and he starts with the 'Four to go' business. I have to be very careful the other nurses don't notice. I'm afraid Grove may have seen him do it today. Old Tony was hanging around the rec room and he looked at me so oddly that it frightened me. But I think I finally know the meaning of Belding's message. I'm so close to the truth that I refuse to give up. And after all, what can Grove do to stop me?"

The last entry was dated five days before the explosion.

"This is driving me crazy! Just when I'm about to blow Albina out of the water, I've hit a dead end. I can't find the marriage certificate anywhere. I know that minister killed my mother. He must have stolen it from her before he set the fire."

Caroline sat back and stared at the ceiling. Could Gail's theory be correct? Was Rev. Ty Belding an arsonist besides being a con man? Why not? If he'd conspired with Janice to defraud the Honeywell family, he'd already lent his hand to Peter's murder. What difference would another death make to a man like that? Especially if it could be hidden under the guise of a fire?

Caroline finished reading Gail's last words.

"Grove's been here constantly this week and he's watching me like a hawk. I'm staying far away from Belding now that I know his words are a warning. Is Grove dangerous? I don't think so, but I'm sure he reports directly to Janice Honeywell. She wouldn't hesitate to come after me like she came after mom. I wish I could tell her I don't care about the money or the Honeywell name. It's Albina that matters. Only Albina!"

"So how was the sandwich?"

"Hmm? Oh, Shiloh. I didn't see you standing there." Caroline closed Gail's diary and smiled up at the boy. "You have a habit of catching me unawares."

"That's twice today, isn't it? Would you like a refill?" Shiloh pointed to her empty glass. Caroline nodded, grateful the boy seemed in no hurry to be rid of her. She needed more time to unravel the secret of Belding's message to Gail. Four to go. Was it really a warning?

"You've been to the Blue Cat before, haven't you?"

Caroline nodded. "Professor Atwater brought me here the night Andy Parker's band played. They were very good."

"Yeah," Shiloh replied. "They always pack the house."

"I'm surprised the fire department allows such a crowd in here. This building looks like it's ready to collapse."

Shiloh grinned broadly. "It's supposed to look that way. At least on the outside. Actually, the Professor sunk a lot of money into the place when he became a partner in the business. Behind the ramshackle exterior we have solid brick walls and a reinforced roof."

"Why in the world..."

"I know what you're going to say," Shiloh laughed. "Why would we rehab the inside and leave the outside looking like hell? Well, it goes like this. The Blue Cat is a refuge of sorts. Folks come here to relax, converse with their friends, and maybe hear some good music on the weekends. Pretty up the facade and we'd attract all those yuppie types who sail through Rhineburg on their way to somewhere else. They'd start pulling off the highway thinking, 'Now isn't this a quaint little place!'. Pretty soon they'd be taking pictures of the locals and congratulating themselves on finding 'Rustic America'!"

Caroline laughed despite herself. Ed and she had done the same thing themselves while on vacations. The temptation to experience rural living as you imagined it to be was strong among urban dwellers. City folks had been romanticizing the countryside ever since Thoreau popularized Walden Pond.

"I get your point: a little deception prevents a lot of trouble."

"Exactly! We prefer to keep the Cat a hometown secret."

Shiloh ambled off after pouring another cola for Caroline. She leaned back in her chair, watching the young man as he wiped down the bar preparatory to the start of business. The afternoon shadows were lengthening outside and patrons began to drift in for pre-dinner drinks. Caroline glanced at her watch. Four o'clock. Almost quitting time for Agent Evans.

Gathering up Gail's diary and letters, Caroline deposited them in the briefcase, then extracted a note pad and began to write. A half hour later she completed her task. Aside from a few missing details, she had the whole story of the bombing down on paper. Now all she needed to do was make several quick phone calls. The first was to the university security building.

"Hello, Michael? I'm glad I caught you in."

"Is that you, Mrs. Rhodes? I got to tell ya, Tom Evans is one angry man! He's on the warpath, searching all over for you."

"I figured he would be, but I had to clear up some unfinished business first. Michael, will you do me a favor?"

"Depends on what it is. You shouldn't have left the dorm, Mrs. Rhodes. It makes it look like you're hiding something."

"In a way I am. Or was." Caroline explained about the diary and letters. She gave Michael a concise summary of her deductions. "If we can clear up the loose ends, we can take the whole story to Evans and let him make the arrest. Will you help me now?"

"What do you want me to do?" Michael was all business now and Caroline sighed with relief. She could finally see a light at the end of the tunnel.

"I need a name." She told him what she knew about the person. "Perhaps someone at the high school remembers him."

"Don't worry," Michael assured her. "One of the counselors there is an old friend. He'll help me."

"My next request may prove more difficult to accomplish. Can you locate the records of a marriage? It may have taken place in Illinois, but it's more likely they were underage at the time. They probably crossed state lines."

"Tom Evans has better resources for ferreting out that sort of information, Mrs. Rhodes. Once you tell him your theory, he'll hunt down any records that exist."

"All right, Michael. We'll leave it to him. The last thing I need to know is the circumstances surrounding Rev. Ty Belding's death. Was it really an accident? Who found his body?"

"I'll talk to my dad. He was out hunting that day and arrived on the scene shortly after it happened. My brothers and I were in school, but I remember him discussing it at home."

"How soon can you get back to me?" Caroline asked.

"Not before tomorrow. Are you going back to your apartment?"

"Not if I can help it! I'd prefer to steer clear of the FBI until I have the answers to these questions. I'll call you again in the morning, OK? Say around ten o'clock."

Michael sighed. "I could be in big trouble for doing this, but all right. I won't tell Evans I've heard from you."

"Thanks, Michael. You're a real friend."

"Don't mention it. We Rhineburgers have to stick together."

Caroline smiled as she hung up the phone. She'd never been called a Rhineburger before; oddly enough, the designation bolstered her spirits. With renewed confidence in the ultimate success of her mission, she placed her second call.

"Mrs. Harding? This is Caroline Rhodes."

Elvira's voice was strained but polite. "What can I do for you, Mrs. Rhodes?"

"Earlier today you mentioned talking with Alexsa Morgan. You said she was asking you a lot of questions."

"What of it?" Elvira responded sharply. "Alexsa and I are old friends."

"I understand, Mrs. Harding." Caroline would have to tread cautiously; it wouldn't do to antagonize the woman. "Still, could you please tell me what she wanted?"

"I'm not sure it's any of your business!"

"It might help the investigation," Caroline replied. "You do want Gail's murderer caught, don't you?"

"Of course I do! But Alexsa..." Elvira hesitated, then suddenly gave in. "It's not like either one of us has somethin' to hide, Mrs. Rhodes. We were just discussin' that awful minister..."

"Rev. Ty Belding?"

"Yes, that was his name. He caused so much trouble for poor Monica with his lies. I was tellin' Alexsa he got his just desserts gettin' killed that way."

"He died in a hunting accident, right?"

"Sure did. They never found who done it either. I said it was a blessing, too, 'cause whoever shot him deserved a medal, not a jail cell!"

"Did Alexsa agree with you?"

"She said she was real glad I felt that way. Alexsa knows how my husband and I loved Monica. Charlie always wanted a little girl of his own, but the Lord gave us three sons instead. Monica was the closest thing we had to a daughter."

"Your husband was pretty upset then when she died."

"Upset ain't the word! Charlie was half out of his mind with grief. He blamed the fire on that preacher and he was angrier than a coon when the cops couldn't pin it on him. Charlie said it was set to stop Monica from claiming her rightful inheritance. He figured the Rev.

Belding was in cahoots with his niece."

"Jim Morgan shares that belief."

"Of course. And that's why he stood up for Charlie after the accident. It didn't look real good, my husband bein' the one who found the preacher's body."

Here was a new revelation!

"Your husband was out hunting that day?"

"It was deer season. Thank God, Charlie never got off a shot that day. The police checked his rifle and it was clean as a whistle."

"It must have come as a shock when he discovered the corpse. Did your husband happen to hear or see anyone else in the forest?"

"Now you sound just like Alexsa. She was curious about that too."

"Really?"

"Well, she figured Gail's death would stir up some unpleasant memories, and she was right. Doesn't seem to be a day that passes without one of us mentioning Monica. But Charlie won't discuss Rev. Belding, or the accident. He said all along he knew nothin' about it and he ain't gonna change his statement now."

"He's sure he didn't see another man that day. Someone who was a stranger to these parts."

"Charlie saw nobody. He was alone when he heard the shot and alone when he found the body. He was huntin' on private property, so he didn't expect to see anyone else."

Caroline had hoped for more information, but she'd have to be satisfied knowing Alexsa'd been stymied too. The old woman had learned nothing new from Elvira. Thanking Gail's aunt, she hung up the phone and dialed Carl's number. The answering machine was still turned on and in disgust she returned to her table. Shiloh was waiting for her.

"You don't look too happy. Is there anything I can do to help?" he asked.

"Not unless you know someone who attended Rhineburg High twenty years ago," Caroline replied flippantly. She didn't expect an answer from the young man, but he took her by surprise.

"My grandfather was the school's Principal back then."

Caroline stared open mouthed at the boy. "I can't believe this!" She gathered him up in a bear hug. "You're the answer to my prayers!"

"I don't know about that!" he replied in embarrassment as she finally released him. "Still, I appreciate the thought. Now tell me who you're looking for."

Caroline described the person she sought, giving Shiloh the approximate date of his graduation.

"Grandad will probably remember him," he said. "He's been following the progress of the investigation in the newspapers. He still can't believe someone would actually bomb St. Anne's."

Caroline waited patiently while Shiloh poured drinks for several customers before walking over to the telephone booth. He was gone several minutes and when he returned, he was smiling.

"My grandfather has a good memory. He gave me three names, any one of which could be your man."

He handed Caroline a list. She drew a blank on the first two names, but the third one practically leaped off the page at her.

"You tell your grandfather I owe him big time!" she exclaimed leaping to her feet. "I've got to get a hold of Professor Atwater. Could you tell me how to get to his house?"

"Sure, but he won't be there." Shiloh lifted Caroline's jacket off the back of her chair and held it while she closed and locked the briefcase. "Tonight's the Winter Festival."

"Winter Festival? Oh, right. Rhineburg's annual holiday bash. My daughter-in-law mentioned it just this morning." Caroline pushed her arms into the parka. "And you think the Professor's going to it?"

"Of course!" the boy replied with a grin. "They couldn't hold a Christmas parade without Santa Claus!"

It took a moment for the words to sink in before it dawned on Caroline what the young man meant. She began to chuckle as she pictured Carl perched atop a sled pulled by eight prancing reindeer.

"So that's what Jim Morgan meant when he said his father was buying the Professor a new suit."

"It's about time," Shiloh laughed. "Professor Atwater is the best darned Santa in the county, but his old outfit was getting mighty tight in the waist!"

Caroline zippered the parka and with one last hug left Shiloh and the Blue Cat Lounge. Preoccupied with thoughts of Carl and Christmas, she never noticed the red Jaguar when she pulled out of the lot and headed towards Rhineburg. It followed a safe distance behind her, its lights dim, its driver hidden by the darkness of the winter night.

Wilhelm Road sparkled with hundreds of Christmas lights. Strung from tree to tree, they formed a manmade Milky Way above Rhineburg's main thoroughfare. Normally Caroline would have reveled in the holiday decorations, but tonight her attention was focused on navigating the Jeep safely through a crush of pedestrian traffic. Apparently half the county had come together to celebrate the Winter Festival. People swarmed towards the town square, and parking was at such a premium that by the time Caroline found a spot, the festivities were already beginning.

Hoping to find Carl before the start of the parade she skirted the crowds on the sidewalk and jogged west down Wilhelm to City Hall. All about her were the sights and sounds of Christmas. Stores south of the square teemed with last minute shoppers. Some of the more clever merchants had set up tables outside their shops and were offering hot chocolate and cookies to passers-by. At the end of the block the local theater advertised Santa's arrival in foot high neon letters while green suited elves hawked fliers listing coming attractions.

Off in the square the activity centered around a large wooden gazebo that served as a bandstand inthe summer. On a platform inside stood an enormous gilt chair cushioned in red velvet. Garlands of balsam and holly encircled the support beams, and two life-sized toy soldiers guarded the entrance. The laminated figures saluted smartly in the glow of floodlights suspended from the gazebo's roof.

Caroline reached City Hall simultaneously with Mayor Schoen. Terrible Teddy, as she'd come to think of him, pushed through the mass of humanity gathered on the walk and climbed the half dozen steps to the Hall's entrance. There in the shadows of the town seal, he waved his arms for quiet.

"It's my great pleasure," he solemnly intoned, "to announce the official opening of Rhineburg's annual Winter Festival. The City Council and I, your elected servant..."

A mighty drum roll drowned out the Mayor's last words. All heads turned and the crowd let out a roar as from behind the building the high school marching band emerged. Trumpets blaring, they swung into a lively rendition of "Oh Tannenbaum".

Caroline dismissed any hopes she'd had of reaching Carl before his grand entrance in the parade. Instead, she squeezed into a space near the curb and joined the locals in cheering on the Rhineburg Marching Maniacs. Splendid in bright red uniforms with gold capes and gleaming black shakos, the band members dipped and swayed in exaggerated movements as they performed a series of choreographed dance steps down the center of the street. The spectators urged the band on with shouts and whistling, but they quickly circled the square and disappeared once more behind City Hall.

Puzzled by the brevity of the performance, Caroline was about to turn away when she glimpsed two familiar faces across the street.

"Martin! Nikki!" She waved frantically in an effort to attract their attention. Nikki saw her first and grabbed Marty's arm and pointed. The two of them dashed across the street.

"Hi, there! Where've you been hiding?" Martin gave Caroline

a peck on the cheek. "Professor Atwater's been trying to reach you."

"I'm sorry, Marty. It's been a rather busy day."

Nikki smiled. "Christmas shopping, I'll bet. So how'd you like the band? Aren't they fantastic?"

"They sure are, but the program was too short," Caroline complained. "Don't they know any other Christmas songs?"

"Just wait," laughed Marty. "The best is yet to come."

The words were hardly out of his mouth when the brassy wail of a trumpet split the night. Caroline swiveled around. She craned her neck to gaze over the heads of the people in front of her, but Wilhelm was empty. The music seemed to be coming from behind City Hall. It intensified to a fever pitch as the unseen performer raced up and down the scale, concluding finally on a piercingly high 'C'. The note died on the wind, and for the briefest of moments, all was quiet. Then suddenly a dozen snare drums shattered the silence. Their staccato tattoo rose to a crescendo of sound before three columns of majorettes high-stepped onto the street, flags and batons held at the ready. Behind them appeared the Marching Maniacs.

A collective roar went up from all sides. Each band member sported a snowy white beard and fur trimmed cap. They tore into "Santa Claus is Coming to Town" with a passion befitting their image.

"Look, mom!" Nikki cried. She pointed down the road. "Here comes the Professor!"

Caroline drew in her breath. Decked out in red harness dotted with fist-sized silver bells and led by the most unlikely trio of elves imaginable, eight genuine reindeer pranced right down the middle of Wilhelm Road. They pulled an emerald green sleigh emblazoned with the letters 'SC' in gold on both sides. It was decorated fore and aft with snow frosted garlands tied in place by scarlet ribbons, and a dusting of silver in the paint caused the sleigh to sparkle in the glow of the street lamps. Piled high on the back seat were brightly wrapped boxes of every shape and size, while perched up front, handling the reins as if he was born to it, rode Professor Carl Atwater, a.k.a., Santa Claus.

Dressed in crimson fur from head to toe, a black satin sash encircling his massive girth, Carl waved and 'ho, ho, ho'd' his way down Wilhelm Road. The crowd cheered wildly when the elves cleared a path into the square. They led the reindeer straight to the illuminated gazebo where Santa climbed down from the sleigh carrying a large canvas sack. He nodded his thanks to the elves and the reindeer, then carried the sack into the gazebo. A horde of children immediately surrounded him.

"That old ham!" Caroline chuckled. "He's thoroughly enjoying himself."

"You bet!" replied Martin. "My boss lives for this Christmas parade. Those 'ho, ho, ho's' come naturally to him."

Nikki laughed. "I like the new Santa suit. The Professor barely squeezed into last year's outfit."

"He does look better," Martin agreed. "But those elves are something else. I never thought I'd live to see the Archangels in tights! Kind of ruins their image, don't you think?"

The three of them watched Carl hand out gifts to a long line of Rhineburg children. After a while they drifted over to the steps of City Hall where the choir of St. Mark's Lutheran Church competed with their Catholic rivals from St. Mary's in a program of Christmas carols.

"Dueling choirs!" Martin joked.

Caroline enjoyed the singing, but her toes were almost frozen. She suggested they abandon the outdoors for a bit, and Martin and Nikki readily agreed. A north wind had sprung up, bringing with it the first flakes of yet another winter storm. The three revelers beat a hasty retreat to the Sugar Bowl Cafe where they ordered hot cider and watched the snow begin in earnest.

"There's a streak of practicality in these Rhineburgers," Caroline observed. Wilhelm was open to traffic again, and she noted how easily the pickup trucks and popular four wheel drives handled the snow encrusted road. "Look at the sturdy vehicles they own."

"And doesn't that one look out of place," commented Nikki. She pointed to a red Jaguar slipping into a parking spot across the street. "What's a little sports car doing out in this weather?"

Caroline checked out the auto. Her husband had been a car aficionado. It was a passion Ed shared with her brother Alan, and although her own interest was minimal, they'd taught her to recognize a gem when she saw one.

This particular vehicle fit that description. It was a late model Jag, dirtied by the weather but classy nonetheless. Ed would have given his eye teeth to own it. Caroline only wanted it to go away.

"Are you OK?" Nikki had seen her mother-in-law shiver.

"I'm fine, dear." Caroline couldn't tear her eyes away from the red car. She knew instinctively it was the Jaguar Jim Morgan had sold and Jerry had seen hidden in the woods. There could be only one reason for its presence in Rhineburg: the hunter was on the prowl.

"He's looking for somebody," Martin remarked. "Everyone in town is here tonight, so it's like searching for a needle in a haystack."

A man had climbed from the car and was now standing with his back to the restaurant. He surveyed the crowd in the square, then swung around and stared directly at the Sugar Bowl. Caroline's heart skipped a beat. Chances were slim he could pick her out in the cafe through all that falling snow. Still, the very thought of it was frightening. The man was an accomplished killer, adept at disposing of threats, and Caroline presented the most immediate threat to his safety. She'd seen him on the psych ward the day of the bombing, and as of tonight, she could put a name to his face. She was a liability he couldn't afford to ignore.

"He's lost," said Nikki. "Can't decide which way to go."

The man had stepped away from the Jaguar. Like a snake searching out its prey, his head swiveled left and right as he inspected the knots of people on the sidewalk. He started to cross the street, then changed his mind and turned instead towards the town square.

A prickle of fear ran through Caroline. She wasn't the only one who posed a problem for the owner of the Jag; Carl had made himself anathema by prying into the bomber's identity. The killer wouldn't neglect an opportunity to silence his second adversary.

She guessed the Professor was still passing out presents in the gazebo. Any minute now the man would approach him, and Carl, unaware he was facing a murderer, would simply look up and smile, his fate sealed by his own ignorance. Caroline refused to let it happen so easily. She must somehow warn him.

"Mother! What's wrong?"

"I forgot something in the Jeep," Caroline lied as she slid out of the booth. She grabbed her coat and made a dash for the door. "I'll be back in a minute!"

Now was not the time to confide in Martin. He'd try to stop her, or at least insist on coming along. Whichever way it went, they'd spend precious minutes arguing over a course of action, and time was something Caroline couldn't waste. It was imperative she reach Carl before he left the safety of the gazebo.

The weather was quickly deteriorating. The wind whipped out of the north with such fury that blizzard conditions now existed in Rhineburg. By the time Caroline crossed Wilhelm Road visibility had fallen to practically zero.

The floodlights illuminating the gazebo were her only guide as all around her people fled from the storm. What had begun as a night of merriment was ending on a sour note, the square emptying rapidly as families scurried to their cars. Caroline pushed her way through the departing crowds, the glow from the wooden structure a beacon pointing the way to Carl. She'd gone a few dozen steps when suddenly the snow lightened in intensity. The respite was brief, yet in that moment Caroline caught a fleeting glimpse of the Professor standing beside the laminated toy soldier at the entrance to the gazebo. He was alone and that fact cheered her. Either the killer had been swept up by the crowd or he was as blinded by the snow as she. Determined to reach Carl first, she hurried on.

In her haste, Caroline forgot there was ice lurking beneath the surface of the new snow. Her foot hit a slick spot on the path and she slid forward, crashing in a heap against a tree. She scrambled up, brushed the snow from her shoulders, and turned again towards her goal. One glance at the gazebo and her heart sank to her boots. Carl was no longer there. True to the tradition of Santa Claus, he had vanished into the winter night.

Snowflakes tumbled against Caroline's cheeks, melted on her eyelashes, and blurred her vision as she desperately searched the nearly deserted square. Carl should have stood out clearly in his red fur suit but the blizzard had changed everything. Colors had vanished beneath a blanket of white. Wet flakes clung to everyone and Caroline could barely distinguish men from women as the last of the festival goers trudged by in their snow shrouds.

'Think!' she told herself angrily. 'Where did he go?'

Forcing herself to concentrate, she turned in a tight circle and examined the routes leading out of the square. Her eyes came to rest on City Hall lying just west of the park. For the first time she noticed that all the lights were on in the building.

"Of course!" she cried out in relief. Carl wouldn't have driven into town in the Santa Claus suit. He must have changed clothes in Rhineburg, and City Hall was the logical place for him to do it. This is where the band had assembled, where they must have stored their instruments after the parade. The Mayor had stood on the City Hall steps to issue his proclamation, and the sleigh had emerged from behind the building. This was the headquarters of the Winter Festival and the most likely place for Carl to return to after his stint in the gazebo.

Caroline began to run. She abandoned the sidewalk and cut across the square, plowing through the ever-growing drifts of snow.

Her left ankle ached. She'd twisted it when she fell against the tree, but the cold and her own anxiety had numbed the original pain. The pressure on the stretched ligaments increased now as she tramped over the uneven ground. Each step became more difficult, still her fear for Carl's safety drove her on.

Caroline was halfway across the square when she stepped on a discarded mitten imbedded in the snow. The frozen glove slid beneath her boot and, off balance, she pitched sideways into a mound of snow, landing heavily on the injured ankle. Pain lanced through her foot.

'I've broken it,' she thought grimly, all the while praying it wasn't so. She pulled her left leg upward and touched the swollen ankle. A bone protruded against the inside of the leather boot where the fracture had sliced through the skin. Warm blood trickled down her foot.

"Damnation!"

Caroline knew she was in grave danger. Somewhere nearby a killer was stalking her. If he appeared, she'd never be able to escape on a broken ankle. To make matters worse, she was sinking deeper into the snow with every move she made. She'd been a fool to cut across the square. The snow on the path had been manageable, but out here in the open some of the drifts were waist high. The one she'd fallen into threatened to suffocate her. She had to get back on her feet. The question was, how to do it?

She lay perfectly still until the pain became more bearable, then wiped the wetness from her eyes and inspected her surroundings. All about her there was nothing but whiteness. Even the sky was white as the snow swirled aimlessly in the unrelenting wind. She thought of calling out for help, but the fear of being found by him prevented her from making a sound. Instead, she extended both arms and with slow, deliberate movements, she brushed angel wings in the snow. Each sweep flattened the drift a little more until it was packed down solidly on either side of her. She rolled to the right; the angel wing held.

Pulling her good leg underneath her, Caroline raised herself on one elbow, then pushed down with her hands until she was kneeling. She brought her right foot forward and planted it firmly on the ground. She had to somehow stand up and walk; crawling out of the drift was next to impossible.

"OK, here we go," she whispered. Willing her right leg to hold her, Caroline lurched upright. Pain shot from her ankle to her hip when she put weight on the injured foot. She grimaced in agony.

"I have to do this!" she gasped. Balancing precariously on her good foot, she clenched her teeth and hauled the injured leg forward. Cold sweat ran down her face. She managed another two steps, alternatingly hopping on one foot and dragging the other, before she tumbled back into the snow. By the time she got herself into a sitting position again, tears of pain and fear stained her face.

'I haven't a chance,' she thought with sudden clarity. 'I'll never get out of this snow alive.'

The notion so panicked her that Caroline neither saw nor heard the man approach. It wasn't until he squatted down a foot away that she even realized he was there.

She looked up into his cold eyes and her heart sank. Death no longer waited on the sidelines. It was staring straight at her.

"Well, well! What do we have here?"

The man walked in a tight circle around Caroline. She watched him without moving a muscle.

"Another accident, Mrs. Rhodes? How unfortunate!" He came to a stop directly in front of her. "But then, accidents do happen, especially in weather like this. Snow can be so deadly you know. An injured person, someone like yourself perhaps, could fall face down in a drift and simply smother." He leaned forward until his face was only inches away from Caroline's. "A terrible way to die, don't you agree?"

His breath hot against her frozen cheeks, Caroline shuddered. She was trapped but she struggled to remain calm.

"You'd never get away with it. An autopsy would show I was murdered."

The man straightened up and shook his head. A smile played on his lips as he replied, "I doubt it." He gazed around the empty square. "How convenient! We seem to be all alone."

Caroline drew her legs up and sank back on her arms. 'I refuse to die this way!' she fumed. How incredible to have survived the ordeal of Ed's death just to end up a corpse in the snow.

"Why'd you do it?"

The killer threw back his head and laughed.

"You've been watching too many movies, Mrs. Rhodes. You can't buy time that easily." He moved forward, his gloved hands reaching for her throat. "After all, time is a luxury I no longer have, thanks to...ahh!"

Stimulated by a rush of adrenalin, Caroline had pushed down on her bad foot and lashed out and up with the good one. The toe of her boot caught the man squarely between the legs. He doubled up in agony and she kicked again, this time hitting him in the chest. He grunted as the air shot out of his lungs, then he tumbled backward into the snow. Caroline scrambled to her knees, her ankle on fire with pain. She crawled out of the drift but the man recovered quickly and grabbed at her foot. She went sprawling to the ground.

Caroline was stunned by the fall. She shook the cobwebs from her brain and struggled to right herself. As she pushed against the soft snow, a gust of wind whipped ice crystals into her face. She raised a hand to shield her eyes and felt something sharp slash at her wrist.

Pain made her cry out. When she looked up she saw the man crouched over her. Sweat and melting snow ran down his face. His eyes glittered with hatred.

"Bitch!" he screamed. His hand flew up and Caroline spied the knife blade poised above her head. For a split second she glimpsed something else, something she vaguely remembered seeing earlier that evening. Long and thin, it twirled through the air, dancing in the wind as it rushed towards them. Then the knife was slicing downward. Instinctively Caroline rolled away from her attacker.

She heard a crack and a grunting sound before the man tumbled forward, the knife falling from his hand. His skull crashed into her ribs and knocked the wind from her lungs. Gasping for breath, she dragged herself from under his suddenly still body and crawled crab-like across the snow. Waves of nausea swept over her. She clawed at the drifts until several feet separated her from the man before collapsing to the ground in exhaustion.

Minutes passed. Caroline's heart finally slowed its frantic pace. She eased herself up on one elbow and looked over at the 'mad bomber' of Rhineburg.

Tony Grove lay sprawled in the snow, dead. His head twisted upward at an impossible angle and an expression of surprise transfixed his face. His open eyes stared blindly at the starless sky.

Off to the right Caroline's savior leaned against the drooping branch of a pine tree. He wore a lopsided smile and his right arm was cocked in a jaunty salute. Giddy with relief, Caroline waggled her fingers at the silent figure.

Then a gust of wind whispered her name. Intent on the vision of her rescuer, she paid no attention. The sound came again, this time louder and more insistent. It jolted Caroline out of her reverie and she sat up in the snow. 'It's not the storm,' she thought with sudden clarity. A human voice was calling to her. She opened her mouth to answer, but all that emerged was a strangled sob.

Suddenly, strong arms encircled her.

"Mother! Are you alright?" Martin's ashen face resembled the color of the trampled snow. His voice was tight with emotion as he hugged her to his chest. Then Carl was beside them. He took hold of Caroline's frozen hands and warmed them in his own huge paws. The Professor couldn't hide his concern when he saw the blood on her arm.

"She's hurt, Marty. We have to get her to the hospital."

"Let me help."

Michael Bruck pushed Carl aside. He locked wrists with Martin and together they lifted Caroline from the ground. She glanced over her shoulder as they carried her to a waiting police car.

"Nice going!" she whispered softly.

The toy soldier who'd guarded the gazebo could say nothing in return. He simply stood there at attention, his duty clearly done.

Six

December 31

"Happy New Year!" Caroline waved a fried chicken leg in the Professor's direction as he hung his coat in the closet. "Sorry we didn't wait for you, but the men were starving and the aroma from Nikki's kitchen simply overwhelmed them. As you can see, we ladies weren't much better at controlling our appetites!"

The three long haired redheads seated on the couch giggled in unison. Carl bowed to them before turning to Caroline.

"So you've finally met the Archangels' wives. A trio of beauties, aren't they?"

The triplets shared a blush.

"Oh, Professor!" exclaimed Faith. "You're embarrassing us!"

"Yes," agreed Hope. "You and your blarney!"

"There must be some Irish in you!" Charity insisted.

"Only on me mother's side," quipped the Professor.

The three giggled again.

"His mind is affected by hunger," Faith told her sisters. "Let's get him something to eat." She motioned the others to their feet and with broad grins aimed at Carl and Caroline, they moved off to the dining room.

"What a group!" Caroline shook her head. "Those three pairs of green eyes never stop twinkling."

"They're a jolly lot alright. And just what the Bruck boys need. A little Irish humor may temper their German sobriety." Carl collapsed on the couch. "So how was your Christmas?"

"Absolutely wonderful. Kerry and Krista drove in from Chicago on Christmas Eve. We had dinner here with Martin and Nikki, then the five of us sat up all night remembering past holidays. The kids really opened up about Ed, and by the time we left for church in the morning we were more or less talked out."

"You must have been bushed."

"Yes, I was," Caroline conceded. "But it was a pleasant sort of tiredness. You see, it turns out I wasn't the only one feeling guilty after Ed's death. The kids were carrying their own individual burdens, taking blame on themselves for what happened to me. 'If we hadn't gone back to school so soon!' 'If we hadn't gone back to Rhineburg so soon!' 'If we hadn't left you alone!'" Caroline shook her head. "It took awhile before I could get it through to the kids that my depression had nothing to do with them. But in the end, I think they believed me. We turned a corner somewhere between Christmas Eve and Christmas morning. We can talk freely again, without bitterness or remorse. And all of us are truly ready to get on with our lives."

"Sounds like that conversation was the best Christmas present you could ever give each other," said Carl. "I'm glad for you, Cari. So tell me, when did your daughters leave?"

"Yesterday. They had to get back to work and their boyfriends. And how about you? I wanted to call you on Christmas morning, but Martin said you'd gone out of town."

"I spent the holidays with old friends. It was nice, but it's good to be home. I sure didn't want to miss this New Year's Eve party!"

"Well, I'm glad you're back and you arrived when you did. The Bruck girls were bubbling over with absurd compliments. Talk about being snowed!"

"Have they sufficiently bolstered your ego?"

"Inflated is more like it. The Bruck women are suffering from an extreme case of hero worship."

Atwater chuckled. "Your prowess as a detective is a matter of record, Cari."

"Sheer luck, Professor. Sheer luck."

"I disagree, although Elizabeth Morgan appears to share your viewpoint."

"Oh?" Caroline shifted the pillow under her broken ankle. The cast was cumbersome and her foot kept slipping to the side of the footstool. "When did you talk to her?"

"Here, let me help you with that. I stopped by Alexsa's before coming here," Carl replied as he plumped the pillow. "She called me this afternoon, all apologetic about her conversation with Agent Evans. She really thought she was helping him, Cari."

"Right!" Caroline answered sarcastically. "She may be an old friend of yours, Carl, still Alexsa certainly made a mess of things for me. But let's forget her for the time being. I'm more interested in what the junior Mrs. Morgan had to say."

"Liz and Jim were at the house when I arrived. Jim asked a thousand questions about the night of the Winter Festival, but Liz seemed totally annoyed. She made several disparaging remarks."

"Like what?"

"For one thing, she called Jim a busybody. Said he sounded like an old woman gossiping over the backyard fence."

"The comparison must have riled Alexsa."

"Strangely enough, it didn't seem to bother her at all. In fact, Alexsa told her grandson to drop the subject. They'd been playing bridge and she appeared anxious to resume the game."

"She was probably embarrassed," Caroline remarked. "Didn't want to admit her theory had bombed."

"Did I hear the word 'bomb'?" Jane Gardner appeared in the doorway. She was carrying two plates of food and she handed one to Carl. "Faith told me to give you this. Michael waylaid her under the mistletoe." She settled down across from Caroline. "So, my friend, when do we get to hear all the gory details?"

"Not you too!"

"But of course! Do you expect me to believe everything I've

heard at the hospital? According to the grapevine, you're a combination of Miss Marple and Bruce Lee!"

Caroline laughed. "Don't I wish! I'm just fortunate to be alive, Jane. If it hadn't been for that wooden soldier..."

"I heard about that. Tell me, Caroline. Did it really come flying out of nowhere right when Grove was...well, you know what I mean."

"Was about to murder me? Yes, Jane, it actually happened that way. The soldier broke loose from its moorings by the gazebo entrance and the wind caught hold of it. I spotted it spinning towards us right before it smashed into Tony's neck."

"And I can testify to the fact that the toy soldier caused Grove's death."

Dr. Paul Wakely had entered the living room along with Martin, Nikki, and the Bruck contingent. He elaborated while the others dug into their food.

"It must have careened into him at a pretty good speed because his spinal cord was cleanly severed. Mr. Grove was dead before he hit the ground."

"According to the weather service, that storm packed gusts of fifty miles an hour," remarked Michael. "Those laminated decorations are pretty sturdy. Given the force of the wind, it's not surprising our toy soldier killed the man."

"What I'd like to know is how you figured it all out, Caroline. I would have never suspected Tony Grove."

"Yes you would have, Jane, if you'd known all the facts. Once I read Gail's diary and the letters Peter Honeywell wrote to her mother..."

"Wait a minute!" exclaimed Rafael. "How'd you get hold of them?"

Caroline explained about her search of the dead student's room. She was describing the ring in Gail's jewelry box when the doorbell rang and her son left to answer it.

"The letters 'MGH' puzzled me at first, but after..."

Her voice trailed off as Martin re-entered the living room with Jim Morgan in tow.

"Look who's joined the party! Make room on the couch, Mike."

"We were at my grandmother's house playing cards when Liz developed a migraine," Jim explained. "I drove her home but it seemed too early to call it a night. The Professor mentioned you'd all be here. I figured you wouldn't mind if I dropped in." He flashed a nervous smile. "You're talking about the bombing, aren't you?"

Caroline and the Professor exchanged glances. Jim's presence complicated matters considering his and Alexsa's role in the case.

"Mrs. Rhodes is a genius!" gushed Hope. "The way she figured it all out when the FBI were totally confused!"

"That's not quite true," Caroline remonstrated. "They'd have broken the case soon enough. Tony Grove was getting careless. Ransacking Gail Garvy's room was a huge mistake."

"He drew attention to the girl's part in the mystery," said Mike.

Caroline nodded.

"Carl and I realized the killer was after someone on the psych ward once the attempt was made on my life. I was working there that day and must have seen or heard something that threatened his identity. We began inquiring into the victims' past lives."

"That's why you went to see my grandmother."

"Yes, Jim, but Alexsa wasn't much help. She distracted us with stories of May Eberle and Thomas Adrian. She denied even knowing the Belding family."

"You make it sound like she purposely lied!"

Caroline ignored the Morgan heir.

"At first May and Thomas Adrian looked like possible targets of the bomber, but once Grove broke into Gail's room, it dawned on me that the diary and letters must hold incriminating evidence. Why else would someone search the room? The only other thing missing was the ring."

"You mentioned the ring before," Paul said. "Just what was its significance?"

"It was engraved with the letters 'MGH'," Caroline replied. "I assumed at first it was a family heirloom. Still, I was bothered by the newness of the ring. It wasn't worn like an antique should be. Then when we discovered the break-in, I noticed the jewelry box lying empty on the floor. The ring wasn't worth anything in itself, but the initials obviously were important to someone."

"I still don't get it," muttered Jane.

"Neither did I until I read the letters. You see, Gail's mother, Monica Garvy, was in love with Peter Honeywell of Honeywell Industries. Peter's father opposed their union so they married secretly here in Rhineburg. The missing ring was Monica's wedding band."

"MGH. Monica Garvy Honeywell!"

"That's right, Faith. Gail had her mother's ring, and she'd also found Peter's loveletters up in Monica's old dorm room. The only thing she didn't have was the marriage certificate."

"Back up, Caroline," warned Paul. "I've been reading the newspapers ever since Grove's death, but they didn't mention anything about Monica Garvy. Where did she fit in to all of this?"

"Honeywell Industries may have threatened to bring a lawsuit if the papers printed this, but the truth is, Grove planted the bomb to keep Gail from proving Janice Honeywell is the illegitimate heir to the Honeywell fortune."

"What!" Jane exclaimed. "You're saying all that money doesn't really belong to her?"

"Exactly," Carl replied. "Gail was about to blow her out of the water, so Janice conspired with Grove to plant the bomb."

"That's a rather drastic solution to the problem, Carl."

"Yes, Paul, but Gail came in contact with James Belding at St. Anne's. He was a threat to Janice also."

"Let me explain," said Caroline. "The story starts over twenty years ago when Peter Honeywell first came to Rhineburg to meet with Alexsa Stromberg Morgan. Alexsa was a major investor in Honeywell Industries and young Peter was in charge of keeping the stockholders happy. Monica Garvy spent a lot of her free time at the Morgan house since her aunt was Alexsa's housekeeper. She was attracted to Jim Morgan, but she fell for Peter after they met. They were probably introduced to each other by Alexsa, who never did approve of Jim dating the girl.

"The two started seeing each other and according to his letters, Peter eventually proposed marriage. Unfortunately, his father didn't approve of the match. Arthur Honeywell wanted his son to marry within his own social circle. They argued over it continuously until Peter decided to marry Monica without his father's knowledge. He arranged for Rev. Ty Belding to perform a quiet ceremony here in Rhineburg."

"And did they actually marry?" asked Jane.

"Of course they did!" exclaimed Jim angrily. "Monica wouldn't lie about a thing like that, regardless of what that damn preacher said!"

Caroline continued to ignore the uninvited guest. Her sympathy for Elizabeth was growing by the minute.

"Arthur Honeywell died suddenly of a heart attack. His son was away on business but he flew back to Chicago after hearing the news. Peter was driving home from the airport when he was killed in an auto accident. Father and son were buried together."

"How tragic for the family!" Hope said softly.

"Peter's mom died when he was a child and he had no siblings," Caroline told her. "Relatives appeared out of the woodwork, all of them claiming a piece of Honeywell Industries. The company would have been chopped into pieces except Janice Belding came forward with proof of inheritance."

"Was she related to that minister? The one who married Peter and Monica?" asked Paul.

"She was his niece," answered Atwater. "Ty, Janice, and James lived on a farm outside of Rhineburg. James entered the Army straight out of high school and when Janice graduated, she moved to Chicago."

"She took a job at Honeywell Industries," continued Caroline. "A capable young woman, she quickly assumed the role of Peter's private secretary. She accompanied him on trips, including the ones to Rhineburg. After Peter's death, Janice produced a marriage certificate signed by her uncle. She insisted she was young Honeywell's wife."

"But I thought Monica had married Peter!" Jane's eyes grew wide with astonishment. Caroline couldn't help laughing.

"Confusing, isn't it? Imagine how the lawyers reacted when Monica showed up with another marriage certificate signed by the same minister! Rev. Belding denied having performed the ceremony, insisting instead that Janice was Peter's legal wife. He had records to back his assertion, which he later showed to Monica's mother, Albina Garvy."

"That old bitch!" Jim swore. "She disowned her own daughter on the word of that shyster preacher!"

"Be that as it may, a court of law named Janice as Peter's legal heir and awarded her full control of Honeywell Industries. Monica later made a futile attempt to solicit financial support for Gail, whom she claimed was Peter's daughter."

"Honeywell was the father," Jim growled. "Monica told me that herself."

"She was unwilling to submit the baby to genetic testing, Jim," Caroline replied testily. "Do you really believe the Honeywell lawyers wouldn't demand proof of paternity?"

Morgan muttered something under his breath but Caroline didn't catch it. She hurried on, unwilling to be drawn into an argument.

"Monica dropped out of nursing school during her pregnancy. After Gail was born, Elvira Harding took on the baby-sitting chores so her niece could return to St. Anne's. Those of you who lived in Rhineburg at the time must remember the blaze that destroyed part of the school's dormitory. Monica was the sole casualty of the fire. She tried to escape down the fire ladder and fell to the ground where she died of a head injury. Carl and I believe Rev. Ty Belding set that fire."

"He was working for his niece?"

"Right, Paul. We think Janice knew Monica would never give up trying to prove her case. Maybe with a better lawyer handling it, she could have persuaded the court to change its ruling. Belding must have tampered with the records, altered them somehow to favor Janice. The FBI are examining the minister's old bank statements. Shortly after the fire, he started making regular payments into his account that exceeded his usual deposits. We believe Janice paid him to commit arson."

"Then Belding killed Monica!" Jim jumped up from the couch and began to pace the room. "Her name was mud in this town for years! People badmouthed her and Gail because they believed that son-of-a-bitch preacher!" He whirled around and glared at each of the others in turn. "Rhineburg owes Monica a public apology. I'll be damned if I don't see she gets it!"

Caroline recalled Bill Morgan's words when he'd told her about Jim's infatuation with Monica. 'Jim still thinks of her as some kind of martyr', he'd said. 'If he doesn't cut it out, Liz is going to walk out on him.'

Frigid fury engulfed Caroline as she watched Jim stalking about the room. No wonder Liz drank to excess. Her husband was a man obsessed with the ghost of his former lover. How could she possibly compete with the saint he'd created from his memories?

Alexsa's motivations became clear now. The matriarch of the Morgan clan had thrown Caroline a red herring in hopes she would concentrate on Thomas Adrian and May Eberle instead of the dead student nurse. Alexsa sensed the terrible destructiveness of Jim's emotions. She knew how fragile her grandson's marriage really was. Better Caroline stumble around in the dark than expose the truth and leave Liz to reap the consequences.

In a way, Caroline could no longer blame Alexsa for what she'd done. The old lioness was only protecting her cubs.

"Will the FBI prosecute Janice and Rev. Belding?" Paul asked.

"They're working on building a case against Mrs. Honeywell," said Michael. "But Ty Belding is long dead. He was killed in a hunting accident some time ago."

"Are you sure it was an accident?" inquired Jane.

Michael exchanged grins with Caroline. "You're beginning to sound like Mrs. Rhodes!" he told the nurse manager. "Much too suspicious for your own good! Actually, though, the FBI is asking the same question."

"I'm betting he was the first of Tony Grove's victims," Caroline stated. "The police considered the possibility that Belding was murdered, but they couldn't pin it on anyone from the area."

"My dad was involved in the investigation. Besides being chief of security at Bruck back then, he was a part time sheriff's deputy. He was one of the first officers on the scene."

"Why did they suspect murder, Mike?" Paul asked.

Michael shrugged. "The Reverend was dressed in an orange jumpsuit. It's hard to believe anyone could have mistaken him for a deer. He was shot in the back, but the bullet passed straight through his heart. That indicated someone had taken deliberate aim rather than he'd been hit by a stray bullet."

"Elvira Harding told me her husband was questioned," Caroline said. "He blamed Ty Belding for Monica's death."

"Harding found the preacher's body in the woods. My father checked Charlie's gun and it was clean. It hadn't been fired that day."

"Of course it hadn't!" Jim snorted. "Old Charlie couldn't hit the broad side of a barn! He's as poor with a gun as my wife, and only went hunting to get away with the boys."

"You're probably right," Mike conceded. "Still, he had a pretty good motive. Everybody knew he hated the man." He shook his head.

"It took a real marksman to nail Belding that way. Lots of folks around here handle guns during hunting season, but not everyone is an expert. Jim here could have done it. Alexsa was known as a sharpshooter in her younger days, and she taught her grandson a thing or two about rifles."

"I was at work and you know it!" Morgan retorted. "Both my father and I had an alibi. Anyway, Mrs. Rhodes just said this Tony Grove guy did it."

"That's what I suspect, Jim. It's possible Ty Belding demanded too much money from his niece. Perhaps he became a liability Janice could ill afford, so Grove murdered him."

"Caroline, when did Tony Grove come into the picture?"

"Actually, Jane, he was in it from the start. Tony Grove grew up in Rhineburg, only he was known as John Anthony Grovelli back then. My brother mentioned him while passing on some information to me, yet he didn't call him by name. It was Shiloh, a waiter at the Blue Cat Lounge, who discovered Grove's true identity. Tony was originally a friend of James Belding. They graduated from high school together, after which they joined the Army. They served in Viet Nam and went missing at the same time. James was captured and surfaced only recently, but Grovelli apparently escaped and took off for parts unknown."

"The Army listed him MIA," said Gabe Bruck. "We now know he was alive and running drugs out of Southeast Asia. The authorities were aware of him only as 'Dr. G.' When he suddenly dropped out of the trade, it was assumed he'd been eliminated by a rival. The truth is, he'd seen a magazine article about Honeywell Industries and its CEO, Janice Honeywell. It sent him packing straight home to Chicago."

"How'd you find out about the Asian connection?" asked Paul.

"Tom Evans filled us in," replied Rafe. "The FBI checked out Grove with the CIA. They were the ones who knew about his former activities overseas. As for the magazine, a copy was found in Grove's

Chicago apartment."

"But why did Tony come back to the U.S.?" asked a mystified Jane.

"Because Tony knew Janice when she had yet another name!" exclaimed Nikki. "Sorry, mom. I didn't mean to steal your thunder."

"That's OK," Caroline said with a smile. She turned to Jane. "Martin and Nikki have heard all this before. I'm surprised they're not bored with the story by now."

Paul waved off the interruption. "Go on, Caroline. You've got me on the edge of my seat."

"I agree!" said Jane. "Explain what Nikki just said."

"Between Belding and Honeywell, Janice wore the title of Mrs. John Anthony Grovelli, a.k.a., Mrs. Tony Grove."

Caroline's statement shocked her friends from St. Anne's; Paul and Jane wore twin looks of surprise.

"Janice wed Grovelli when the two of them were teenagers. She knew he was listed as MIA by the Army, and maybe she thought he'd died. But the truth is, she was still his wife when she inherited Peter's company. Tony's sudden appearance jeopardized her position as the Honeywell heir. Janice was not about to lose her fortune so she used it to buy her husband's silence. She's admitted to the FBI that she supplied him with a cushy job in the company. Tony did very little in the way of real work, but the position provided cover for the enormous salary Janice paid him."

"He was blackmailing her."

"In a way, Paul, that's an accurate assessment. Remember one thing though: Janice is no innocent victim. She manipulated the truth to get where she is today. And we believe she conspired with Grove to bomb the psychiatric ward."

"But how did you uncover the plot, Mrs. Rhodes?" Faith asked.

"Gail mention Tony Grove several times in her diary. I got to wondering what his ties were to Janice Honeywell since he seemed to be her right hand man. Once I discovered Grove and Grovelli were one and the same person, it all began to fall into place. I asked Michael to check the neighboring states for any records of a marriage between Janice Belding and John Anthony Grovelli, and bingo! There it was, in black and white, in Hazard County, Kentucky. The two of them were sixteen when they tied the knot."

"Unfortunately," Michael added, "I didn't learn this until after Grove attacked Mrs. Rhodes."

"The newspapers are saying very little about a motive for the killings. What's your theory, Caroline?"

"I believe the targets of the bomb were Gail Garvy and James Belding. You see, Jane, James may have recognized Tony as his sister's husband. I think Janice wanted him safely tucked away where he could do her no harm."

"She figured a hick town like Rhineburg was the perfect spot to hide him," Jane replied bitterly. "So she paid off Charles Paine with donations to St. Anne's, obligating him to do whatever she asked. No wonder Grove knew everything that was happening in the hospital!"

Caroline nodded. "Gail, on the other hand, was an unexpected problem. She enrolled in the school of nursing simply to gain access to the dormitory. Elvira said the girl was obsessed with revenging her mother. She wanted to shame Albina Garvy into admitting she was wrong about Monica. In order to do that, Gail had to locate Peter and Monica's marriage certificate. Elvira assumed it had been lost in the fire, but Gail was convinced her mother had hidden it somewhere in her room."

She told the others about Gail's midnight searches in the burned out part of the dorm. "She eventually found Peter's letters, but the certificate eluded her to the end. When Gail discovered James Belding had been admitted to the psych ward, she contrived to get herself assigned there. She started hounding the poor man, convinced he knew something about his sister's scam."

"Do you blame her?" demanded Jim. "That kid got a raw deal from her grandmother!"

"Pipe down," Mike said softly. "We all feel bad about Gail."

Jim glowered at the other man, then walked over to the window and stared out at the snow. Caroline nodded her thanks to Mike and continued the story.

"Gail mentioned the names of her mother and Peter, Janice, and Ty Belding over and over again to James. She kept watching for some reaction from him and one day he finally complied. James raised four fingers, one by one, and whispered the words 'four to go'."

"You told me about this before," Jane said. "But I'm still angry Gail never reported it. Belding was unresponsive to treatment. Any speech at all would have indicated an improvement in his condition."

"I realize that, Jane. But James seemed to confide only in Gail. I think he was trying to warn her off."

"What do you mean?" queried Faith.

"'Four to go' are the last words of a nursery rhyme. If you think about the rhyme, each line could refer to someone involved in this case. 'One for the money' would be Janice Honeywell. She sought to feather her nest by pretending she was married to Peter. 'Two for the show' probably alludes to Janice and Ty Belding. They worked together to put on a convincing act for the court. 'Three to get ready' might indicate Tony Grove had joined Janice and her uncle in the deception. I believe the last line, 'Four to go', pertains to those who had to be eliminated in order for Janice Honeywell's plan to succeed. Monica and Peter were already dead. The only threats left were James and Gail Garvy."

"If that's true, it's unfortunate Gail didn't heed James' warning. I told you she always backed off when Tony Grove visited the ward. She must have realized he was dangerous."

"He made her nervous, Jane," Caroline replied. "But Gail was unrelenting in her quest to clear her mother's name. It was the only thing that mattered to her. In a lot of ways, that girl needed psychiatric help as much as James Belding."

"Grove must have worried when he saw Gail hanging around James," Jane asserted.

"That's precisely why he murdered them. The bombing was a convenient way of disposing of both at the same time. Of course, I became a problem when I saw him leave the rec room." Caroline described the man she'd bumped into near the doorway. "I thought he was a patient trying to walk off the ward. I even followed him down the hall before going back to help with the refreshments."

"So you didn't recognize him!"

"No, Paul. I had no idea who Grove was until Jane pointed him out to me in the cafeteria. He looked familiar, but I couldn't place his face at the time. Later, of course, I figured it out."

"Tony was trained in explosives in the Army," Carl added. "He knew about the damaged Christmas tree because he was on the ward the day it was discovered. That tree provided him with the inspiration for his plan. He couldn't rig the bomb here, so he drove to Chicago for the parts, and he did so in a red Jaguar he bought from Jim Morgan."

"Grove was the rich doctor!"

"That's right, Jim. Tony didn't dare take his rental car; all that extra mileage would have shown on the odometer. And if he'd flown the company plane to Chicago, the police could have easily tracked his movements. Buying the Jag was a brilliant idea. Sure, it stood out in a crowd, but if you saw a sports car like that one tooling down the highway, would you stare at it or the driver?"

"I'd be too busy checking out the car to notice who was in it."

"Exactly!" said Caroline. "Tony counted on that kind of reaction, Paul. Once he arrived safely in Chicago, he knew just where to go to buy the ingredients for his bomb."

"Are explosives that easy to get in Chicago?" Faith asked in astonishment.

Mike slipped an arm around his wife's shoulders and gave her a hug. "Maybe not for you, honey, but you've got to remember one thing: our Mr. Grove was not exactly what you'd call an upstanding citizen. He'd been a drug runner for years, which meant he'd dealt with a lot of criminal types in the past. Making contact with the right people would be no problem for him."

"Michael's right," Caroline said. "The FBI are working on the Chicago connection even as we speak. But getting back to Tony, he rigged the tree and shipped it from Chicago, then hurried back to Rhineburg and hid his car up on the old logging trail near the bridge.

A couple of days after the bombing, Tony made his first real mistake. He began to worry someone might find the Jag, so he drove back to the woods to check on it. That's when Elvira's grandson, Jerry, saw him. Grove's behavior seemed so peculiar that after he left, Jerry decided to do a little investigating. He hiked up the trail and discovered the car buried under a snow drift."

"Jerry told you about it?"

"Right, Jane, but I didn't connect his story to the bombing until later that afternoon at the Blue Cat Lounge. I was talking with Shiloh, a young man who works there, and I mentioned how dilapidated the building looked from the outside. Shiloh said that was just a ruse to discourage tourists from dropping in. The structure is actually quite sturdy, but the locals would rather not share their favorite hangout with outsiders. The conversation got me to thinking about that pretty red Jaguar. Maybe it's purpose was to deceive people too."

"Grove's rental car was safe and sound in the hospital garage," Carl stated. "Everyone assumed that because the car was in town, so was Grove."

"But instead," Michael remarked, "Tony Grove was in Chicago building his bomb. What a deadly weapon! Those steel branches shot out like arrows when it was detonated. No one near the tree stood a chance of surviving."

A hush fell over the group as each person considered the havoc wrought by Tony Grove. Jane finally broke the silence with a question.

"Why did Grove kill Charles Paine?"

"Paine was tight with Janice Honeywell," Caroline replied. "He relied on her for hospital funding and was probably scared to death she'd back off once her brother died. I think he made an appointment with Grove to enlist his aide with Janice. Maybe he offered him a kickback. Whatever it was, Tony apparently misunderstood what Paine was hinting at, panicked, and killed him."

"It makes sense," Jane responded. "Our late administrator was a man used to getting his way. I could see him trying to bribe Grove."

"So many people dead and all because of greed." Nikki shook her head. "Not a happy way to start out the New Year, is it?"

"You forget Mr.Grove is safely six feet under,"Martin reminded her. "I'd say the world is better off without him!"

"And your mother is alive and well. Now that's something to be thankful for!" added Carl.

Caroline smiled at the Professor. Her physical condition was nothing compared to her mental state. She was feeling whole and alive again, and much of her progress was due to his friendship. She was the one who ought to give thanks.

"The past should be left in the past," she said. "Why don't we all make that our New Year's resolution?"

"Sounds good to me!" Martin sprung up and headed for the kitchen. "How about champagne everyone? It's almost midnight!"

Jim excused himself and left for home; no one seemed to mind his departure. The other guests were content to put aside all thoughts of murder and celebrate instead the beginning of happier times in Rhineburg. Carl led them in a toast.

"To life! May we all live it well!"

"Amen!" agreed Caroline with a smile.

SEVEN

January 1

Caroline picked up the remote control and switched channels on the TV set. The Rose Bowl Parade had just ended. It would be several hours before the game itself was played. Fortunately for football fans, of which Caroline was one, the Cotton Bowl was getting under way and the selection of teams this year was particularly good. She settled back on the couch to watch the kickoff.

Caroline was considered an oddity among her sex and she knew it. Football was supposedly a man's sport. Nevertheless, she regarded New Year's as the ultimate pigskin holiday, a day when she could revel in the game from noon until late evening. It was a shame no one else in her family shared her fanaticism. It meant she would spend hours alone in her apartment, but she really didn't mind it. Her ankle was still on the mend and although the sutures had been removed from her head and arm, her wrist continued to ache where Tony Grove's knife had pierced it. Alone, she could lounge to her heart's content, whereas if Martin and Nikki had joined her, she'd feel obligated to play hostess.

The phone rang just as the football was caught by a Colorado special teams' player. Caroline had half a mind to ignore it. The runner was surging up field, following his blockers through a swarming defensive line. He slipped tackles like a snake shedding skin while curling in and out of openings.

The clamor continued and Caroline covered the telephone with her hand. The runner was at the thirty, the thirty-five, the forty yard line. The opposition was crumbling before him.

But her caller would not be denied. Caroline snatched up the receiver on the fifth ring. The Colorado player was now at midfield and only the kicker was left blocking the end zone.

"Hello," she muttered distractedly, eyes glued to the TV.

"Cari? Is that you?"

The runner curved towards the side of the field. He evaded the kicker's flying tackle and scampered across the goal line

"Touchdown!" Caroline hollered as she threw both arms straight up over her head. The time honored gesture of victory sent the receiver clattering to the floor. It skittered across the rug and crashed against the leg of the coffee table.

"Oh my goodness!"

Caroline hobbled off the couch and grabbed up the phone.

"Carl! I'm so sorry! I was watching the Cotton Bowl and I got carried away."

"That's OK," the Professor answered tersely. "I apologize for bothering you, but..."

"It's no bother," she lied. Her eyes strayed back to the screen. The point-after attempt was up -- and good! The score was displayed, then the picture switched to an advertisement for beer. Caroline pushed the mute button on the remote control. "I was just relaxing on the couch, babying my ankle. What are you up to today?"

"Bill Morgan just called, Cari. Something's happened."

The hairs rose on Caroline's neck. She braced herself for the worst.

"What is it, Carl?"

"Jim's wife Elizabeth drove her car into the river this morning. The bridge was icy and apparently Liz was speeding when she approached it."

"She's dead, isn't she?" It really wasn't a question; Caroline already knew the answer.

"The river's running high with all this snow we've had. And the water's terribly cold."

Caroline carried the telephone over to the window. Down below her Bruck Green lay blanketed in white. The morning sun tickled the frozen landscape and a million icy diamonds reflected upward. It was too beautiful a day to die.

"Accidents can happen to anyone," she finally said. "Sometimes they're...unavoidable."

"Of course," Carl responded. A hint of formality cast a hollow ring to his words. "It's a tragedy for the entire Morgan family. Liz was a lovely young woman."

And a disturbed one, Caroline mused. But then, considering her life with Jim, who could blame her?

Eight

January 3

"So how'd you spend the morning?"

Carl placed his empty stein on the table and smiled at Caroline. At loose ends after Liz's funeral, he'd wandered back to her apartment and invited himself to lunch. They discussed the service over salami sandwiches and beer, Carl telling her how Jim had snubbed him at the cemetery and how greatly Alexsa had aged since the accident. He appeared depressed when he first showed up on her doorstep, but his mood improved with every sandwich he consumed. Now, having polished off his fourth one, he was almost his old self again. Caroline regretted spoiling his meal; still, he had a right to know about the letter.

"After you left for the funeral, I picked up my mail downstairs. Among other things, there was a note from Liz Morgan."

"What?" Carl appeared dumfounded. "When did she write it?"

"On New Year's Eve. Jim went home and told her everything we'd discussed at Martin's party. Liz wasn't thrilled with his reaction to the news about Monica. Apparently Jim's feelings for his old flame were rather transparent."

"Damn fool," Carl grumbled. "I suppose Liz blamed you for coming up with the truth.'

"Not really, but it seems my conclusions were a little off base," Caroline admitted ruefully.

Carl was taken aback. "What do you mean by that?"

Caroline stood up and crossed to the desk. Opening the top drawer, she withdrew an ivory envelope and handed it to Carl.

"Perhaps you'd better read this yourself."

Carl frowned, but he took the envelope and withdrew from it

three sheets of paper covered in spidery handwriting.

"This is too much!" he growled after reading the first couple of paragraphs. He tossed the letter on the table angrily. "You, Cari, are not responsible for Liz's suicide, regardless of what she says in this...this...piece of garbage! And let's stop beating around the bush. We know her death was no accident!"

"Of course we do, even if we've both been reluctant to admit it. But don't tell me you haven't felt just the slightest bit guilty since you heard what happened to Liz. I know I have! At least," she added, "I did until today."

Carl stroked his beard uncomfortably. "I've been wondering if things wouldn't have turned out differently had we'd only left it in the hands of the police. If Liz wanted to blame anyone for what happened, it should have been me." He faltered when he saw Caroline slowly shake her head.

"Forget the first part of the letter," she urged. "It's nothing more than the ranting of an angry woman. You have to read the rest of it." She pushed the pages towards him. "We were wrong about a lot of things, Carl. Liz held the answers to our questions, but she couldn't reveal them without destroying herself."

Carl hesitated, then curiosity got the best of him. He flipped the first page aside and concentrated on the second. Halfway through it, Caroline saw his face go deadly pale. He looked up and their eyes met.

"I don't believe it!" he declared. "This can't be true!"

"Liz didn't make it up," Caroline insisted. "It's the confession of a woman who could no longer live with herself.." She took the pages from his hand and started to read aloud.

"'Let me set you straight on a few details. Number one, Monica never married Peter Honeywell. I ought to know since I made the biggest mistake of my life by helping her steal the marriage certificate from Rev. Belding's office. I was there when she forged Peter's signature on it. I'll always regret that day.'"

"It's sheer vindictiveness, Cari. Jim hurt Liz. She wrote those words for revenge."

"Come on, Carl! You don't believe that! Listen to what Liz says: 'Money was all Monica cared about, and when Peter died so suddenly, she saw a chance to get rich quick. In exchange for my help, she promised to leave Jim alone. He was crazy about Monica, but I loved Jim and thought he would eventually love me too. All these years I've put up with that woman's ghost, but I can't fight her any longer. She's finally won.'"

Carl wasn't convinced. "If Monica's claim was a hoax, what about all those letters from Peter? How do you explain them?"

In answer, Caroline began to read again. "'That little bitch refused to let anyone stand in her way. When it came out that Janice Belding was Peter's wife, Monica drove to Chicago and broke into the woman's apartment. She searched for the marriage certificate, hoping to destroy it, but found only some letters written by Peter. She later tried to use them to back up her claim.'"

Caroline looked up. "She's talking about the letters I found in Gail's safety deposit box. I assumed they were written to Monica because, rather foolishly, I believed everything Elvira told me about her niece. Looking back, I realize they could have been sent to anyone. They all started with the words 'Dearest' or 'Darling'."

"That doesn't prove anything," Carl argued. "Monica may have told Liz about the letters years ago, then Liz saw them that day in the restaurant and made up all this nonsense."

"You're a stubborn man, Carl Atwater!" Caroline fumed. "But you're wrong! Remember how Monica died in that fire?"

"Of course. Ty Belding was behind that."

Caroline shook her head. "Another mistake on our part. Liz Morgan set it after she murdered Monica."

Carl's mouth sagged. He couldn't have been more surprised, or distressed. Caroline explained.

"Monica pretended Gail was Peter Honeywell's baby, but the company lawyers didn't buy it. They demanded blood tests to prove paternity. Carl, Monica refused to have Gail tested. She knew Peter wasn't the father and she told Liz that the night she died. Monica was seeing Jim again and Liz went to the dorm to try and persuade her to leave him alone."

"Bill Morgan said she came over once or twice after Gail was born, but Jim was dating Liz then." Carl frowned. He might be stubborn, but he wasn't a fool. "Tell me what happened."

"According to Liz, they quarreled, then Monica dropped her bombshell. She claimed Jim was Gail's father. She said if she couldn't have Peter Honeywell's fortune, she'd settle for the Morgan money instead."

"So Liz killed her?"

"Apparently she didn't mean to do it. Liz became so enraged she attacked Monica and the girl fell against an iron radiator. Liz says she panicked. She pushed Monica's body off the fire escape, then set the fire to cover the murder."

Carl traced a circle on the tablecloth with his knife. A moment passed, then he looked up and said, "Elvira mentioned that Monica went to see Janice after Gail's birth. I suppose that was when the lawyers asked for the blood tests." He shook his head grimly. "So did Liz show any remorse for what she did?"

"Not really," Caroline said. "The letter ended rather abruptly. Liz admitted starting the fire, then she simply signed her name to it."

Carl frowned. "That's very odd, don't you think?. If Liz was so distraught that she drove off and killed herself, you'd think you'd get an inkling of it in her note."

"I had the same thought, Carl. She wouldn't have mailed it to me if she hadn't intended suicide. God knows you can't make this kind of confession and then go on your merry way as if nothing's happened! Still, the letter seems so incomplete. It's like she lost interest in the story and just quit writing."

"Maybe that's exactly what happened," Carl suggested. Neither one of them believed it, but since there seemed no other answer, they let it go. After a moment, Caroline got up and put the letter back in the desk drawer.

"Now we have to decide what to do," she said as she walked to the frig. She got out two bottles of beer and opened them, giving one to Carl. "You realize we have a problem here."

Carl nodded. "We assumed Janice was in cahoots with Grove. Why? Because Belding and Gail Garvy could prove Janice never married Honeywell. Now we know she was Peter's wife, so actually, Gail was never a threat to her."

"Which brings into question the meaning of Belding's warning. Why did he repeat those words to Gail?" Caroline wracked her brains for an answer. She couldn't believe she was too far off the truth. Tony Grove had been dangerous!

"Well, it's possible he was communicating fear for his own life. He knew Grove had been married to Janice. That made him a walking time bomb as far as they were concerned."

It was Caroline's turn to be unconvinced. She'd pondered the problem all morning. "I don't know," she mused. "The man was in a psychiatric hospital, Carl. If he suddenly declared Grove was his sister's husband, you think anyone would have believed him?" She got up and paced the room. "I'm afraid I had it all wrong. If Janice was afraid he might talk, why bring James here? Why not just lock him up at home where nobody could get to him?"

Carl nodded. "We should have thought of this before we talked to Agent Evans. He's ready to arrest Janice for murder one!"

"And then there's another thing." Caroline sunk back into her chair. "Why did Alexsa lead us down the garden path with her innuendoes about Thomas Adrian and May Eberle? Why was she so reluctant to discuss Gail? To protect Jim and Elizabeth's marriage? And why did she lie about the Beldings? She claimed she'd never heard of them, but Michael Bruck told us everyone in town knew about the reverend's prayer meetings. Ty Belding was an important person in these parts."

"Alexsa is a very staunch Lutheran," Carl reminded her. "She probably never came in contact with the man."

Caroline was skeptical. "Alexsa is hiding something, Carl. She had business connections with Honeywell Industries -- my brother told me -- yet she can't remember Peter or Janice!"

"If you believe that, why don't you just ask her about it? She's bound to be home now. Let's go over there."

Caroline was taken aback. "I don't think this is the right time to question her. Alexsa's worn out. You said so yourself."

"Maybe she's just burdened with secrets." Carl shifted in his chair. He looked intently at Caroline. "I've known Alexsa for a long time. There's very little that gets past her and I'm wondering if she didn't know all along about Liz and Monica."

"You really think so?"

"It would explain her evasiveness. Alexsa would do anything to protect her family. And she's Elvira's confidant. If Elvira was worried about Gail, she'd have told Alexsa."

Caroline knew he was right. Carl helped her to clear the table, then they left the apartment. With the Professor driving, they reached the Morgan place in under ten minutes. Bill Morgan answered the door himself. He appeared glad to see them.

"I was hoping you'd stop by," he said. "My son's behavior this morning was unforgivable. I wanted to apologize for him."

The Professor waved it off. "He was under quite a bit of strain. Is he here now?"

"Naw! He's off driving around, trying to sort things out. You know he had a terrible argument with Liz the night before her accident." Bill led them into the living room and motioned to the sofa. "Would you like a drink?" he asked. When they said no, he poured himself one anyway, then settled back in a chair.

"He came home from your party and insisted on telling us the details of the bombing. He was so wound up over Monica! It's like an obsession with him!" He took a long pull on his drink before continuing. "I'm not the most romantic guy in the world, but even I know you don't rave about another woman in front of your wife. I didn't blame Liz for being upset with him."

"Is that when they had the argument?" Carl asked.

"No. Liz was one classy lady. She'd never fight in front of me and my mother. She went off to her room and Jim stayed here drinking. It was a good hour later when I woke up to the shouting. Frankly," Bill confided, "I don't believe in interfering in my son's life. I pulled the covers over my head and shut it all out."

Caroline grimaced. What a night it must have been!

"In the morning, Liz was gone. Jim looked like he hadn't slept any, but I figured it was his business so I let him be. I was watching football when the police called." He frowned as he swirled the whiskey in his glass. For an astute businessman, he was an utter failure at understanding his own family.

"I was surprised when Jim left the cemetery so quickly," the Professor commented. "I wanted to give him my condolences."

"He didn't leave," Bill retorted. "He took flowers over to Gail's and Monica's graves. I told you he's obsessed!"

Caroline glanced at Carl. He nodded sympathetically.

"Alexsa appeared very upset. Is she up to visitors now?"

Bill cocked his head to the side. "You're not a visitor, Carl. You're the closest thing to family we've got. I'm sure she'd want to see you." He got up and led them upstairs. "She's in her bedroom. If you wait in here, I'll go get her." He opened the door to a small library at the end of the corridor and went off to find his mother.

Carl sank down on the flowered sofa, but Caroline wandered

about examining the details of the room. It was decorated for a woman and she guessed it was Alexsa's private haunt. She probably came here to write letters and get away from her family.

"Good afternoon!"

Caroline spun around. Mrs. Morgan stood just inside the door. She was paler than usual and her voice quavered, but her eyes were sharp, her expression guarded. Carl rose to meet her and she motioned him back into his seat. She leaned heavily on her cane as she crossed over to where Caroline waited.

"Do you like my little hideaway?" She smiled tightly when Caroline nodded. "I thought so. You're a woman of good taste."

Caroline sensed a challenge in the words. She reminded herself that regardless of Alexsa's age, the old lady was still in control of her household. She was a force to be reckoned with.

"We came to extend our sympathy," Carl said.

"Really? How interesting!" Alexsa sank down on a straight backed chair behind the desk. "And why else have you come?"

'She knows,' Caroline thought. 'Somehow she knows about the letter. Well, why beat around the bush?'

"I received a letter from your grand-daughter-in-law today," she said. Alexsa tilted her head and waited. Caroline continued more strongly. "Liz wrote about Janice and Peter Honeywell. She also told me about Monica's death."

The old woman pursed her lips and stared at Caroline. "I must say I was surprised when no note was found here at home," she finally said. "Liz wasn't the kind to leave loose ends."

"You mean a suicide note," Carl murmured.

"They're calling it an accident, but we know better, don't we?" Alexsa smoothed the wrinkles from her skirt. It was a deliberate gesture and maddening to Caroline. It's a game of chess, she thought. Check and checkmate.

"What we told the FBI was incorrect," she remarked. "We can't change their minds now without showing them the letter."

"Why would you do that?" Alexsa looked puzzled. "What good will it do to harm this family any further?"

"It might save Janice Honeywell a lot of trouble!" Carl retorted. "The police think she's a co-conspirator to murder!"

Alexsa considered what he'd said. "She has many fine lawyers at her disposal. They won't allow her to be prosecuted."

You old lion! Caroline thought. You'll sacrifice anyone to shield the Morgans. "She'll be ruined nonetheless," she snapped. "You of all people must realize how important one's reputation is!"

"Oh, I do! That's precisely why I'm not going to risk ours!"

Caroline leaned over the desk and stared at Alexsa. "You'll have no choice if I give that letter to the FBI. I could also send a copy to Janice. Her 'fine lawyers' would have a field day with it!"

Alexsa's eyes narrowed. She glanced at Carl and saw he was in agreement. She hesitated less than a minute before saying,

"What is it you want of me?"

"The truth."

Alexsa's hands fluttered in annoyance. "How simple you make it sound! And what do I get in exchange for 'the truth'?"

"Partners in damage control." Caroline surprised Alexsa with that statement. "I admire you for trying to protect Liz, but I won't stand by and see an innocent woman prosecuted. If Janice was ignorant of Grove's plans, she shouldn't be hounded by the police or the press. Let's look at the facts, toss out what's irrelevant, and find some answers."

Alexsa remained silent as she weighed her options. Caroline figured none of them seemed attractive to her.

"Where shall I start?" she finally said.

"When did you first learn about Monica's murder?" Carl asked.

"The day Liz shot Ty Belding."

"What?" Carl almost leaped out of his seat. "Are you telling us Liz killed him too?"

"I thought you knew!" Alexsa whispered. Her face twisted in agony. "I thought she told you everything!"

Caroline pushed the letter into the old woman's hands. "You'd better read this. Evidently, Liz left some things out." She looked at Carl as Alexsa skimmed the letter. He was thinking the same thing as she: they were right when they'd guessed it was incomplete. Liz had ended it abruptly; the question was, why?

It was a subdued Alexsa who handed the letter back. The fight had gone out of her. "Everything Liz wrote happened just as she said. What you don't know is that Ty Belding saw her leave the dorm the night of the fire. He guessed she was the arsonist. After she married Jim, he began to blackmail her.

"Liz paid, but it was difficult to hide it from Jim. She became desperate. The last time he demanded money, he was going hunting and suggested they meet in the woods. She went, and she took Jim's rifle along. She shot Ty Belding in the back."

Alexsa sighed and shook her head. "I remember it like it was yesterday. I was standing at my bedroom window and I saw her on the path below. She was carrying the rifle. When I went downstairs, I found her cleaning it in the mud room. She was crying and she broke down and told me the whole story."

The matriarch of the Morgan family raised her head and glared at them. "Monica was an evil person! I knew it, yet I couldn't stop Jim from falling for her. She'd have ruined his life and Liz saved him from that. I was grateful to her. I couldn't let her suffer for what she'd done."

Carl frowned and huffed into his beard. Obviously he felt some empathy for his old friend who'd had a difficult choice to make: expose Liz, or become an accomplice to murder. But Caroline wasn't buying it.

"That's...quite a story," she murmured in admiration. Alexsa's gall had succeeded in luring Carl back to her side and Caroline was now on her own. "Let's go over what we know," she said crisply. "We can try to separate the facts from, shall we say, the fantasy."

She summarized the events of the past two weeks. Alexsa roused herself and listened intently. Carl also perked up. He added information until the picture was almost complete.

"What we don't know is why Tony Grove killed Belding and the others," Caroline stated.

"Since Tony Grove was still alive, Janice Belding's marriage to Peter Honeywell was invalid," Alexsa offered.

"You're right," Caroline admitted. "But Tony came home when he heard Janice was rich. He'd nothing to gain by exposing her bigamy. That would be like killing the fatted calf and then missing the feast!"

Alexsa chuckled at the comparison. She was acting more like her old self again and Caroline applauded her nerve.

"It's absurd to think that Janice felt threatened by her brother." She turned to Carl. "Like I said before: no one would believe James if he claimed Tony was his brother-in-law. He was a very disturbed man. According to Jane, he hadn't even spoken since his arrival." An idea flashed across her brain, but it was gone before she could grasp it.

"I agree," Carl said. "The man was lost in another world. I doubt he recognized his old buddy from twenty years ago."

"But would Mr. Grove have known that?" Alexsa asked quietly. "You made the mistake of thinking he had. Wouldn't it have been natural for Tony to assume the same thing?"

Caroline stared at Alexsa. They'd been dodging the truth all day and the old lady had finally pinned it down.

"But for a very different reason!" she exclaimed. "We've been looking at this from the wrong angle, Carl. Tony wasn't worried about being recognized as Janice Honeywell's husband. He was afraid James would remember him as Anthony Grovelli, his old pal from the Army!"

Carl was puzzled, but Alexsa nodded her head. She understood what the other woman was getting at.

"Desertion is a treasonable offense." Caroline explained. "Tony Grove deserted his Army unit in Viet Nam, then became a drug dealer in

Southeast Asia. If James had fingered him, Tony would have spent the rest of his natural life in prison!"

The light was dawning for Carl. "He'd never have told Janice about the drug trafficking. It was much too dangerous a secret."

"Exactly!" Caroline said triumphantly. "A secret worth killing for!" Everything was clicking into place; she was on a roll. "Now I'm convinced Janice wasn't involved in the bombing. Tony planned it himself to get rid of James. Gail's attention to James probably worried Grove, but his primary target was still Belding."

"But why a bomb? Why not just kill Belding alone?"

"It would have been so obvious," Alexsa told the Professor. She glanced at Caroline and the younger woman deferred to her.

"Grove wanted to muddy the waters. With so many victims, the police were forced to broaden their investigation. That took time and time was his ally. It allowed people to forget he was in the recreation room that day. Caroline only remembered when Jane pointed him out in the cafeteria. She put the face together with the voice she'd heard..."

"He was the one who called out for Belding to light the tree," Caroline interrupted.

"Of course. He had to make sure James was near the tree when it exploded."

"And because there were multiple victims, Janice was as much in the dark as the police," Caroline added. "The target could have been her brother or her company, one of the other patients, or the hospital itself. She had no reason to suspect Tony Grove."

"Good Lord!" Carl exclaimed. "If we can convince the FBI we finally have the right end to this story, they may drop their investigation of Janice Honeywell. That would let you off the hook, too, Alexsa. There'd be no need to pry into the past."

Alexsa smiled. "I still have a few friends in the government. A word in the right ear might cause the investigation to change directions. At least it's worth the try." She stood and picked up her cane. "It's been a very long day and I'm not as young as I used to be. You must forgive me."

Caroline took the hint. She nodded at Carl and the two of them accompanied Alexsa to the door. At the last moment, she asked to have a word alone with their hostess and Alexsa consented. When she came downstairs a few minutes later, Caroline was eager to leave.

"Alexsa mentioned something just now," she told the Professor. "She said it was unfortunate James Belding was captured only days before he was to ship out of Viet Nam. I suddenly remembered his obituary." She thought she'd kept the newspaper. "I must find it, Carl!"

It was dark when they returned to the dormitory and Caroline flipped on the lights as they entered the apartment. She tossed her coat on a chair, then rummaged through a pile of newspapers on the table.

"Got it! Look here, Carl!"

She opened the paper to the death notices. A boxed column at the top of the page bore the headline 'James Belding Laid to Rest'.

"'James Belding, brother of Janice Honeywell of Honeywell Industries, was buried yesterday at Roseland Cemetery after a private service. Mr. Belding was a former sergeant in the U.S. Army.'"

Caroline skimmed the article until she found the sentence she'd been looking for.

"'Sgt. Belding was presumed lost in a mission in Viet Nam four days before his scheduled return to the United States.'" She turned to the Professor and said excitedly, "Don't you see, Carl? James' words had nothing to do with Grove or his sister or anyone else in Rhineburg! He was simply talking to himself!"

Carl threw himself down on the sofa with a sigh. "You've lost me, Cari. This old brain of mine has absorbed way too much information today."

"Four to go, Carl! Four to go!" Caroline closed the newspaper and sat down across from him. "Gail thought it was some kind of cryptic message about her mother while Tony Grove feared James was whispering about him. We mistakenly assumed both were correct, but we should have been listening to Jane! James may have escaped Viet Nam, but emotionally, he was still a prisoner of the jungle."

She willed Carl to understand. "Think of the years he spent in captivity," she urged. "In the early days, when his mind was still clear, he must have gone over it a hundred times: 'Four days and I would have been out of here! Four days to go. Four to go.'"

Carl sat up straight. A grin split his face as he nodded slowly.

"I think you're right. With nothing else to hang onto, those three words became his personal mantra."

"And his only way to communicate! Jane said even the simplest tasks were too much for him. How stupid of me to think he could take a nursery rhyme and twist it into some complex omen!"

"Don't be so hard on yourself. We were both puzzled by the phrase and it was only natural to build on Gail's theory."

"I guess so," Caroline said grudgingly. She changed the subject. "I suppose we should get in touch with Tom Evans. Alexsa promised to call her friends in Washington tonight."

"Can't it wait 'til later? All this talk has made me hungry!"

The Professor rubbed his stomach and Caroline grinned. "You don't look particularly starved to me."

"I have to stay in training!" the Professor retorted. "Think what the children would say if they saw a skinny Santa next year!"

In the end, Caroline agreed to drive into Rhineburg for a steak. She insisted, though, that Carl give her a few minutes to change clothes.

"You look fine!" he said.

"But I feel frumpy," she countered, plucking at her sweater and jeans. "If we're going to celebrate, I'd like to get dressed up. Why don't you call and make a reservation for dinner?"

Leaving him with the choice of restaurants, Caroline went off to change clothes. She was more tired than she'd let on, and once inside her bedroom, she slumped wearily into a soft chair. The face-off with

Alexsa had exacted a heavy and unexpected toll. Unbeknown to Carl, she was now in league with the Morgan matriarch, an accomplice to yet another cover-up that must be kept secret even from the Professor. The curious partnership had formed after his departure from the library when Caroline had confronted the old woman with her lies.

"You have Carl convinced Liz shot Rev. Belding," she'd said. "But I'm not so gullible. I thought it odd the way the letter ended so abruptly. Now I know there was at least one more page to it."

Alexsa had stood there like a rock, apparently unmoved.

"Jim had an argument with Liz the night of her death. Bill told us he heard them shouting in her room. I think Jim found her writing that letter. He probably grabbed it, and when he read the part about the fire in the dorm, he just went crazy. He hit Liz, didn't he? It was another 'accident', just like twenty years ago when Liz hit Monica."

Alexsa turned away. "You have no proof," she said coldly.

"An autopsy would show Liz was dead before she hit water."

"There was no autopsy. Doctor Talens is a friend of the family and the pathologist for this county. He knows how dangerous that bridge is in winter. Others have gone off at the same spot."

Caroline smiled. "You have it all figured out, don't you? First you shielded Liz and now you'll shield your grandson." Alexsa refused to answer. She walked over to the desk and Caroline followed. "You knew about Monica and the blackmail long before Ty Belding's death."

Alexsa waved her hand in annoyance. "There's no need to be so dramatic. Make your point, Mrs. Rhodes, then get out of my house!"

"My point is that you're the one who shot Reverend Belding!"

Alexsa arched an eyebrow but said nothing.

"Liz didn't know how to handle a rifle. I found that out on New Year's Eve," Caroline said. "But the men at the party spoke favorably of your marksmanship. Seems you were quite good in your day."

"That was a long time ago," Alexsa asserted. "I haven't touched a gun in years."

"Yes, you have, Mrs. Morgan. You knew Ty Belding would bleed Liz dry before he was done. You're a strong woman and you make difficult decisions. You made a very difficult one the day you decided to kill that blackmailer." She paused to see the effect of her words on Alexsa. The old woman's face was expressionless. "You ran into Charlie Harding in the woods that day. He saw you carrying a gun and when he found Belding, he suspected you'd shot him. But Charlie hated the Reverend with a passion. He was more than willing to cover for you."

Alexsa folded her hands on the desk top and leaned forward.

"Charlie will never support your theory, Mrs. Rhodes."

"Are you sure of that, Alexsa? You called Elvira after Gail died and the two of you discussed Ty Belding's death. You were worried Charlie might spill the beans to the police." Caroline shook her head. "Liz understood what you did for her, but in her desire to make a clean breast of it, she included the details of Belding's murder in her letter to me. Jim mailed the cofession after he engineered Liz's plunge into the river. If the police didn't accept his wife's death as an accident, he expected me to come forward with proof it had been suicide.

"Still, he couldn't allow you to be arrested for murder. He loves you too much and he could forgive you where he couldn't forgive Liz. Ty Belding meant nothing to him; Monica did. He kept the last pages and signed Liz's name to what was left."

"A very clever story, Mrs. Rhodes," Alexsa said at last. "And what do you intend to do about it?"

"Nothing, for the moment."

Alexsa was visibly startled. Caroline pressed on.

"I don't believe Jim intended to kill his wife. He was furious and with good cause, but he made a stupid mistake by trying to hide the murder. Any good doctor would immediately see on autopsy that there wasn't any water in Liz's lungs. She couldn't drown because she was already dead when she hit the river."

In Caroline's mind it was senseless to punish Jim's daughters for what he'd done.

"The girls will only suffer if Jim is arrested. They'll always be known as 'those kids whose dad murdered their mom'. I see no justice in that, and I don't think Jim will ever harm anyone again."

Then Caroline listed her demands.

"Make those calls to your Washington friends today. Convince them they must listen to what Carl and I have to say. If you do that, and if you back us with all the power you wield in this state, I'll keep quiet about Liz's death. Not even Carl will hear what I've told you."

Alexsa bowed her head. After a moment she nodded.

"And there's one other thing," Caroline added. "I have a feeling Jim kept the remaining pages of the letter. If I were you, I'd destroy them."

Alexsa nodded again as Caroline turned to go. She didn't bother to say 'thank you', but in exchange for Caroline's silence she offered her the clue to James' Belding's last words. It was her own unique way of sealing the bargain.

Now, alone at last with her thoughts, Caroline took a long hard look at herself in the mirror. She'd changed since arriving in Rhineburg. The past was finally behind her and she was stronger because of it. Her immediate future was tied up in proving Janice Honeywell's innocence. After that, who could tell? Maybe she'd stay in Rhineburg, or maybe she'd move on. Whichever way it went, it would be her own decision, made not because she had to but because she wanted to. That was the beauty of life: one always had second chances.

"And I'm going to take mine!"

Caroline winked at her reflection, then turned away with a smile and began to change for dinner.

ABOUT THE AUTHOR

    Mary Welk is a lifelong resident of Chicago, Illinois, whose first published work appeared in a grade school newspaper when she was thirteen years old. A short story in three parts, only two episodes appeared in print before the paper folded, but the experience left her bitten by the writing bug. Ms. Welk turned her talents to song writing in the '60's, appearing as a guitarist with two folk music groups and performing her own music at various functions in the Chicago area. She has written two plays and over thirty songs, poems, and short stories, but *A Deadly Little Christmas* is her first full length novel.

    A Registered Nurse for thirty years, Ms. Welk graduated from St. Anne's Hospital School of Nursing in Chicago. During her career she has worked on a Surgical Telemetry Unit, in Home Health Care, and in a Department of Emergency Medicine with certification as a Mobile Intensive Care Nurse. Ms. Welk drew on her own experience in nursing when creating Caroline Rhodes, RN, the heroine of *A Deadly Little Christmas*.

To order additional copies of **A DEADLY LITTLE CHRISTMAS**, please complete the following information.

Ship to: (please print)

Name_____

Address_____

City, State, Zip_____

Day phone_____

___copies of **A Deadly Little Christmas** @ $10.00 each $_____

Postage and handling @ $2.97 per book $_____

Total amount enclosed $_____

*Make checks payable to **Kleworks Publishing Co.***

Send to: Kleworks Publishing Co.
6127 N. Ozark, Chicago, IL 60631

To order additional copies of **A DEADLY LITTLE CHRISTMAS**, please complete the following information.

Ship to: (please print)

Name_____

Address_____

City, State, Zip_____

Day phone_____

____copies of **A Deadly Little Christmas** @ $10.00 each $_____

Postage and handling @ $2.97 per book $_____

Total amount enclosed $_____

*Make checks payable to **Kleworks Publishing Co.***

Send to: Kleworks Publishing Co.
6127 N. Ozark, Chicago, IL 60631